Endeared

ALSO BY J.S. SCOTT

The Accidental Billionaires

Ensnared
Entangled
Enamored
Enchanted

The Sinclairs

The Billionaire's Christmas (A Sinclair Novella)
No Ordinary Billionaire
The Forbidden Billionaire
The Billionaire's Touch
The Billionaire's Voice
The Billionaire Takes All
The Billionaire's Secrets
Only a Millionaire

The Billionaire's Obsession

Mine for Tonight
Mine for Now
Mine Forever
Mine Completely
Heart of the Billionaire – Sam
Billionaire Undone – Travis
The Billionaire's Salvation – Max
The Billionaire's Game – Kade
Billionaire Unmasked – Jason
Billionaire Untamed – Tate

The Pleasure of His Punishment:
Individual Stories or Complete Boxed Set

The Changeling Encounters

Mate of the Werewolf
The Danger of Adopting a Werewolf
All I Want for Christmas Is a Werewolf
The Changeling Encounters – Complete Boxed Set

The Vampire Coalition

Ethan's Mate
Rory's Mate
Nathan's Mate
Liam's Mate
Daric's Mate
The Vampire Coalition – Complete Boxed Set

Endeared

THE

ACCIDENTAL

BILLIONAIRES

BOOK FIVE

J.S. SCOTT

Montlake

Published by Montlake, Seattle

www.apub.com

Amazon, the Amazon logo, and Montlake are trademarks of Amazon.com, Inc., or its affiliates.

ISBN-13: 9781542023061
ISBN-10: 1542023068

Cover photography and design by Laura Klynstra

Printed in the United States of America

Since this is the final Sinclair book, this one is for all of my Montlake crew. It's been an incredible journey from Maine to California, and from Grady all the way to Owen. I couldn't have asked for better people to share this adventure with me.

XXX Jan (J.S. Scott)

PROLOGUE

LAYLA

Over ten years ago . . .

"I'm really glad we could meet up," I told my best friend, Owen Sinclair, earnestly. "It seems like you've been avoiding me for the last few weeks."

I put my foot on the ground and pushed the playground swing I was sitting in to make it start moving again. Owen was gently swaying back and forth right next to me.

I wasn't sure how we'd gotten into the habit of meeting up at the local park after dark, but it had been our hideout for a couple of years now. There wasn't another soul around in this area after the sun went down in Citrus Beach, so it made sense. We definitely had our privacy here, so Owen and I talked about anything and everything while we mindlessly kept our swings in motion the entire time.

"I wasn't avoiding you, exactly," Owen said hesitantly. "I've just been busy."

I turned my head, but I couldn't really see his eyes. I could only make out his body and face in the moonlight.

I sighed as I gripped the metal chain on the swing. "I know. It's crazy. We're actually graduating in a few months, and you and Andie will be off to Boston for college."

My heart clenched at the thought of not seeing Owen and Andie every day. The three of us had been tightly bonded like we were super-glued together all through high school. I had other friends, but none of them could replace the two who were leaving Citrus Beach for college on the East Coast. Unfortunately, Boston wasn't in *my* plans.

"I wish you were coming, too," Owen answered in a grim tone.

I smiled. He sounded so grown up for a guy who was just finishing high school, but Owen had always been ultraresponsible, even at the beginning of our journey through high school.

Although I had to admit, he was a goofball sometimes. If things got too heavy, he'd be the first one to try to lighten the conversation or make me smile.

"I can't," I told him, my heart aching. I didn't have the funds to finance school out of state. Owen had gotten some large scholarships, which were well deserved, and he had family willing to help as much as they could. Andie had absolutely no shortage of funds, so she could well afford to go to school wherever she wanted.

I had . . . nobody.

Even if I got the scholarship I was hoping to be awarded, it would still make more sense for me to stay in California to lessen the financial burden.

"We can still talk," Owen commented. "Sometimes I wish I had stayed here for at least a bachelor's degree. It would probably be cheaper."

I snorted. "No, it wouldn't. You got good scholarships, and you need the prestige of graduating top of your class from a good school so you can get accepted to med school."

I knew Owen was worried about money. My situation had never been as dire as his was, but sometimes I wished I had his tight-knit family.

Owen released a long breath. "I guess I just feel guilty. My brothers and sisters have already done so much for me. Noah, Aiden, and Seth kept our whole family together. Noah took on the responsibility of raising us when he was barely older than I am. He should be free of that burden now, but he isn't. My sisters are still in college, and I'm just starting. I'll pay him back for all this once I'm a doctor, but that isn't going to help his financial squeeze over the next several years."

I didn't know Owen's brothers all that well. I wasn't as free to hang out at Owen's house as Andie was, but I knew Noah well enough to realize he wanted his younger brother to go to college. He'd be damn proud to see Owen become a physician. "He wants this for you," I said emphatically. "Your whole family is cheering you on. You know that."

"I know. I just wish I didn't feel so damn guilty about being the youngest and wanting to go to med school," he said, sounding frustrated.

"It will be okay, Owen," I said softly.

He chuckled. "What will I do without you to keep my spirits up, Layla?"

"You'll survive," I teased. "I think you're already practicing a life without me as your friend, since I hardly see you anymore."

I was joking, but in a way, I wasn't. I had to admit that it hurt that Owen had kind of been avoiding me lately.

He was busy, but there was something else going on. I just wasn't sure why he'd been backing away from me, even *before* he left for college.

"I'm not avoiding you, Layla. Not really. I just . . ." Owen stopped talking abruptly, like he'd thought better of saying what he'd planned to say.

"It's okay," I said hastily. It wasn't like he owed me an explanation. We were friends, not intimate boyfriend and girlfriend. As good friends, we'd never had expectations, and it wasn't fair for me to want more than he wanted to give. "We're both busy. I get it. There's so much going on right now with senior activities, graduation, and all that stuff."

Problem was, somewhere in the middle of our senior year, I'd realized that my feelings for Owen had shifted.

I'd started to want more than just friendship, even though I'd known *that* could never happen.

"I value every minute we spend together, Layla. If you don't believe anything else, believe that," he insisted. "You've *always* been there for me."

"You've been there for me, too," I said, and I meant it. I didn't share everything with Owen, because some things were just too embarrassing to tell, but he knew more about me than any other person on earth. There had never been a time when I really needed him that Owen hadn't been there to listen and help.

"Growing up sucks," he answered. "I thought I really wanted to be an adult, but leaving home and everybody I care about is so damn hard."

"And everyone I care about is leaving me," I commiserated. "I get it."

"Is everything okay with your mom right now?" Owen asked carefully.

I shrugged, even though he couldn't really see me. "As good as it's ever going to be," I said with a lightness I didn't feel. "I'll be fine."

I did a good job of hiding my situation at home, but I knew that Owen and Andie had always suspected things weren't good between my mother and me.

They have no idea what my life is really like . . .

"You always say that, and I don't think you're fine," Owen said, his tone concerned. "Is she even home right now?"

Thankfully, I hadn't seen my parent in over a week, which was why I was comfortable hanging out in the park. But she'd come back. She always did, eventually.

"She's gone," I admitted. "But I don't mind."

Having my mother out of the house was actually a relief for me. I didn't have to walk on eggshells, but I was always dreading the day that she'd return.

"You do mind, Layla," Owen argued. "Hell, you never see your father, so she's all you have."

"At least he pays his child support," I said brightly. "He's not a total deadbeat."

"I call bullshit. You need more than just a check," Owen grumbled. "When's the last time you saw him? A couple of years ago for dinner or something? You've basically raised yourself. Neither of your parents are ever around. I know they aren't, so don't try to tell me you're *fine*."

Actually, I hadn't seen my father since he'd walked out the door four years ago, but what girl wanted to broadcast the fact that her father hated her?

"I'm almost an adult now, Owen. My father travels the world for a living, so it's not his fault that he's never back in the States." I used that excuse a lot.

My father had left my mother right before I'd started high school, and he'd basically left me, too. I'd had to transfer from my private school to the public-school system. The only good thing that had happened during that time was meeting Owen and Andie, once I'd gotten out of the stuffy private school I'd been attending.

"If anything *was* wrong, you'd tell me, right?" Owen asked suspiciously.

I sighed. It wasn't the first time Owen had broached the topic of my home life, and I didn't want to discuss my mother now any more than I'd wanted to talk about her all the other times he'd asked.

Owen would never be able to relate to what it had been like growing up for me. The Sinclairs might be dirt poor, but they were tight, supportive, and loving.

"There's nothing to talk about, really," I assured him. "I'm all grown up now, and I'm doing okay."

I saw Owen get to his feet, so I rose from my swing, too.

"I better get home," Owen grumbled. "I have a ton of stuff to do for my college entrance."

I fell into step beside him as we silently headed for the exit to the park. We both lived in the same general area, but Owen always insisted on going a little out of his way to see *me* all the way home before he went on to his house.

I swallowed hard.

Owen had no way of knowing that when he looked after my safety, it was the only time I actually felt . . . valued. I might tease him about being a worrywart, but it honestly touched me that he cared about whether or not I got home okay.

He'd always been protective, like a big brother or something, and that meant a lot to me.

As usual, he veered toward my home without a second thought once we were out of the park.

"Thanks for all the times you've made sure I got home safe," I blurted out, feeling like it was important that he knew how much I appreciated him.

For once, I didn't even try to joke around with him about being overprotective.

"Are you kidding?" he asked. "I'd have to be an asshole if I didn't. Citrus Beach isn't San Diego, but you have no business walking around here on the streets after it's dark."

Didn't he know that most guys wouldn't even think about seeing a friend all the way home when it was out of their way?

"No other guys I know would do it," I told him.

"Then you know a lot of assholes," he said gruffly. "It would destroy me if something bad happened to you, Layla."

I felt something tumble low in my belly as I tried desperately not to take his words too seriously. Owen cared about *everyone*, which was something that made him entirely unique. I couldn't allow myself to think that I was a special female to him in some way.

He's leaving, and I'm staying here in California. We can never be anything except friends.

I had to stop wanting more from Owen. In fact, I hated that my feelings had changed at all.

I didn't want to crave intimacy with him, and didn't want to wish he'd kiss me just once so I could see how it felt to be closer to him.

Why can't I go back to feeling the way I used to when I'm with him?

Six months ago, it would have freaked me out if he'd tried to kiss me.

Now it was all I could think about.

"We're here," I said with feigned cheerfulness as we arrived at my condo building. "You can go home now."

He folded his arms in front of him and lifted a brow. "Not happening. You should know the routine."

My heart in my throat, I nodded. He'd wait here until I went up a couple flights of stairs and turned the light on inside the condo. Owen wouldn't leave until he could see that light in the window.

I started to turn toward the stairs. "Okay, okay. I'm going. Good night."

He reached out a hand and grabbed my upper arm. "Wait, Layla. Did you believe me when I said that I wasn't avoiding you?"

I turned and looked at him. Owen had gorgeous green eyes, but they were obscured by a heavy pair of glasses. Still, there was *something* in his expression that I'd never seen before.

I stepped closer to him. "You don't owe me an explanation, Owen. Really. We're just friends."

"I want you to understand—fuck! Forget it. You better go up. I guess I just wanted you to know that I care about how you feel." He reached out and brushed a stray lock of hair away from my cheek.

He was so close that I could feel his warm breath on my face.

Kiss me. Please just kiss me, Owen. Just once.

I closed my eyes as an intense bolt of longing shot through my body.

I opened them again when he stepped away.

What in the hell am I doing?

Unable to speak, I lifted my hand in a brief goodbye as I sprinted up the stairs.

I was panting as I opened the door of the condo and flipped on the light, my heart and my body still longing for something they could never have.

I vaulted to the window and watched as Owen's figure disappeared into the darkness.

I sighed as I lost sight of him, and made my way back to the door to pick up the mail that the mailman had dropped through the slot.

Picking up the mail from the floor was an ingrained habit. A simple task I did mindlessly nearly every day.

There was no way I could have known that one of those seemingly innocuous pieces of correspondence I picked up that night would change the course of my entire life.

CHAPTER 1

LAYLA

The present . . .

"Everything looks good, Layla," Dr. Owen Sinclair told me as he closed the last file on his desk and handed it to me. "You're probably the best nurse practitioner I've ever worked with, so I don't know why you even wanted me to look at these cases."

I had to stop myself from rolling my eyes at him. Like I really had a choice? Unfortunately, California was still one of about half the states in the country that required a nurse practitioner to work under the supervision of a doctor.

Okay, I didn't review *all* of my cases with Owen, but I liked to go through some of the more complicated ones to get his input. It just seemed like the right thing to do, even though I could barely stand to be in the same room with him.

"If I remember right, Dr. Sinclair, I did sign a practice agreement with you when you bought this clinic from Dr. Fortney a few months ago. Until the California laws change, I'm *required* to work under *your* supervision." My comment was a tiny bit sarcastic, but I couldn't help myself.

Honestly, working under the gray-haired, elderly Dr. Fortney, who had just recently retired, had never bothered me. He'd been my mentor during my first year of practice, and a partner of sorts near the end.

Maybe it rankled just a little that I now had to clear some things with *Owen*, who was fresh out of his residency and exactly the same age I was right now.

No, correction—he *was* actually a few months older than me.

No doubt, Owen's age and lack of experience practicing as a physician probably *wouldn't* have been a factor if we hadn't been friends in high school and the bastard hadn't been the person who turned my entire life upside down back then.

Owen had betrayed me.

And no matter how hard I tried, I couldn't forget that, even though I was now a completely different person than I'd been back then.

Owen lifted a brow. "Does that bother you, the fact that you have to work under me? It's not like I've ever breathed down your neck, Layla. I know you're perfectly capable of handling your own patients. I didn't demand to oversee your cases; *you* brought these files to *me*."

I squirmed in my chair just a little, because he was right. I had asked him to review the cases because it was what I'd done with Dr. Fortney. Old habits were hard to break.

I'd always thought it was better to have an extra set of eyes on some cases, and Dr. Fortney had felt the same way. We'd often gone over cases at the end of the day in this office, just like I was doing with Owen right now, and they hadn't all been *my* files we'd reviewed together. Some had been perplexing cases of Dr. Fortney's, too. The now-retired physician had been the one to teach me that sometimes it was wise to get a fresh perspective on a case from another practitioner.

The reason I'd continued to maintain that habit with Owen when he'd taken Dr. Fortney's place a few months ago escaped me at the moment. Maybe I just wanted the best for the people under my care, even if it meant consulting with an asshole to get that. "Sometimes I just appreciate a second opinion," I told him curtly.

Okay, that had sounded a *little* too defensive, but it was the truth. "My priority is to give the best treatment possible, so it helps to see if I may have overlooked something. Dr. Fortney and I reviewed a lot of cases together. It's just habit, I guess."

"I don't mind looking at them at all, and I'm all for sharing our expertise on any of the patients here at the clinic. However, you didn't really answer my question," he reminded me, his green-eyed gaze pinning me to the chair I was sitting in across from his desk.

Dammit! Why had Owen needed to become so damn attractive as a grown adult?

In high school, he'd been a nerdy guy with thick glasses and a brain way too big for his lean teenage body.

Now, a decade later, he looked good enough to be a male model, and I was strangely uncomfortable with those changes.

His intelligence had always been intimidating, so it definitely didn't help that his sharp brain was now encased inside a droolworthy, muscular body that delighted every one of my female hormones.

I took a deep breath. "No, it doesn't bother me," I confessed as I released the air from my lungs. "I respect your opinions and skills."

Truthfully, how could I *not?* He'd graduated from a top-rated medical school at the top of his class, in an accelerated program, for God's sake. He'd then completed his three-year family-medicine residency at one of the most respected teaching and research hospitals in the country.

There was no argument that he was impressively qualified, even if he was just starting his own practice.

I just don't like . . . him!

But did I *really* need to like the guy if I respected his professional competency?

No. No, I really don't need to like him personally at all to learn from him.

Even if he *was* technically my boss, I would have much preferred that we had an amicable relationship.

Owen Sinclair had been a close friend in high school until he'd burned me, but that had happened a decade ago. None of his behavior *now* led me to believe that he wasn't a very good physician. I'd seen him in action for a couple of months now, and even though I had my *personal* differences with Owen, I was in awe of the man *professionally*.

I just have to stay professional. I cannot let my personal feelings interfere with my work.

Okay, so *maybe* I'd had a bad case of puppy love for Owen by the end of our senior year in high school, but I'd gotten over *that* in a hurry. Once I'd realized he wasn't the guy I thought he was, that stupid teenage longing had disappeared in a heartbeat.

"We could discuss all this at dinner tonight," he said hopefully. "We both worked through lunch. Let's go get something to eat."

"No, thank you," I said snippily. "I have other plans."

It wasn't the first time Owen had suggested doing something outside of the clinic, but I wasn't about to go there with *him*.

I'd trusted him once, and he'd betrayed that trust. I had no desire to get chummy with him again as an adult.

We worked together, and I had to maintain a professional demeanor with Owen, but I *didn't* have to like or hang out with the guy.

Owen released a masculine sigh as he leaned back in his office chair.

His lab coat and scrubs were gone. He'd cleaned up in the clinic shower, and he'd put on a pair of dark jeans and a forest-green tee once office hours had ended, which was a really good, casual look on him.

I could almost see the old friend I'd once known, without the scrubs and the lab coat.

Not that I'd really been paying attention to how he looked, or what he did, but it was damn hard not to notice all kinds of things about him when we worked in the same space.

Oh, sweet Jesus, who was I fooling? It was difficult *not* to see a man like Owen, even if I didn't like him personally.

I'd have to be completely blind to be capable of completely ignoring him.

His jet-black hair was cropped, but there was just enough length to see that the mass of locks tended to curl if it wasn't cut short. His sharp green eyes, with thick, long eyelashes most women would kill to possess, were so compelling that they were almost mesmerizing.

Unfortunately, his powerful body was just as irresistible as his handsome face, and I couldn't help but stare as he reclined in his chair, that mouthwatering, masculine form on full display as he stretched like a lazy cat.

He's my boss, for God's sake. I have to stop looking at him like I would be more than happy to devour him for dinner. I need to remember that I can't stand the man—therefore, it shouldn't matter if he looks good enough to eat.

I shook myself and forced my eyes from his powerful, ripped body.

Owen lifted a brow. "Are you ever going to explain how we went from being the best of friends in high school to this cold, professional relationship, Layla? How did we go from sharing almost every secret we had with each other . . . to this?"

Maybe you shared some of your secrets, but you know nothing about mine!

I shook my head. "We're adults now, Dr. Sinclair, and I think you know exactly why I'm not interested in hanging out with you."

He popped his chair straight again and put his arms on his desk. "That's just it. I *don't* understand. You just stopped talking to me sometime near the end of our senior year. No explanation. Nothing. I never understood it. And then I was off to Boston for college, and we never resolved it."

I gritted my teeth. I didn't allow myself to think about my past relationship with Owen. It was the *only* way I could work with him without punching him in the face. "We both grew up," I informed him.

"So let's just drop it. It was high-school stuff, for God's sake. We've both come a long way since then."

I was never sure *exactly* when I'd stopped seeing Owen as just a really good friend in high school. At some point during senior year, that friendship had turned into a major crush that had left me swooning over the boy I'd once called a friend. The only good thing about that infatuation was that I'd never told Owen about it.

Thank God!

My silence had probably saved me from an even-greater humiliation back then, which had reinforced my belief that it was *always* better not to share any secrets at all.

"I want to know what upset you, Layla. I want to understand, because you were never the type to hold a grudge, even if I did do or say something I regretted," Owen said in the same solemn voice he'd had since high school.

I waited, almost expecting him to try to bring a little levity to the conversation with some kind of outrageous or humorous statement, just like he had when we were teenagers.

But he didn't.

He was deadly serious.

And I almost found myself mourning that lack of humor.

"I'm *not* holding a grudge," I said defensively, even though I knew I was still hurting over a stupid event from high school. "It was a decade ago, Owen. It just doesn't matter to me anymore. I see no reason to rehash the past."

My life had turned out well, and I felt like everything was exactly as it should be.

I liked my job.

I cared about my patients.

And if I spent time volunteering at the animal shelter giving a lot more love to four-legged creatures than I ever had to a human male, it was nobody's business.

I was happy exactly where I was, and I *didn't* wish my life was different.

The realization that I actually liked my life *had* helped me get over most of my resentment toward Owen.

Well, almost . . .

Maybe I didn't regret what had happened, but the whole resentment thing was hard to conquer.

It was some of Owen's old stubbornness as he insisted, "I'd still like to take you out for something to eat to try to change your mind about telling me what happened. We're going to see each other tomorrow outside of work at my place, anyway, so why not start tonight?"

"I'll be there tomorrow," I informed him. "I promised Andie I'd help set up for her reception."

His eyes lit up. "You're coming early for the setup?"

I nodded. "Why wouldn't I? She's my friend, too."

Andie had rounded out our close friendship trio in high school, and I'd stayed in touch with her even after she'd left Citrus Beach for college.

When Andie had returned to California a decade later, she'd fallen madly in love with Owen's older brother Noah.

I'd asked myself a million times why the man of Andie's dreams had needed to be so closely related to Owen, but she was so happy that it really didn't matter anymore. I could tolerate almost anything to see her as happy as she was with her husband.

Noah and Andie had eloped to wine country to get married, and now they were having a huge reception to placate the entire family, who hadn't been able to attend their wedding.

Unfortunately, I'd recently discovered that the large party was taking place at Owen's new waterfront home, a fact I hadn't been aware of *before* I'd offered to help Andie set up for the reception. I hadn't let that information sway me into backing out of the setup, though. The reception was all about Andie and Noah, and I refused to allow my personal feelings about Owen to spoil my happiness for them.

"I definitely don't mind that you're coming to my place early, Layla," Owen said gruffly. "You, me, and Andie were pretty close at one time. I've missed that."

I snorted. "Andie and I *always* stayed close friends."

He shrugged. "Andie and I have always been close, too, but that doesn't mean I didn't miss *you*. I told you things I never even told her."

"And she told *you* things she never told *me*," I said, unable to keep the sadness out of my voice.

I'd only found out recently that Andie had been diagnosed with a very aggressive type of cancer while she was studying journalism in Boston. She had, in fact, nearly lost her life while she was struggling through chemo and other types of painful treatment.

Yes, she was well *now*, and only had one more checkup in Boston before she never had to go back to be checked for her cancer again. Still, it bothered me that she'd never told me the truth.

Luckily, Owen had been there for her, since he'd been attending the same college for premed. Andie didn't have any real family she could count on, so I *was* grateful that he'd been there with her.

Owen grimaced. "If I hadn't been in Boston, I'm not sure Andie would have told *me* what was going on, either. You know how she is, Layla. She never wants to drag anyone down, so she isn't big on sharing the bad stuff."

"She wouldn't have dragged me down," I replied adamantly. "She's my friend. Maybe I could have helped her."

Reasonably, I probably wouldn't have been helpful to Andie, since my life had been in turmoil back then. I'd completely forgiven her for not telling me, since I'd kept a lot of things from her, too.

"She tried to kick me out of her life more than once," Owen shared. "I was just too stubborn to listen to her."

I bit back a smile, because I could see Andie doing something like that. She'd always been a lot bolder than I was about expressing her emotions. "Don't get me wrong, I'm glad you were there for her," I explained. "I just wish she would have told me, too."

The knowledge that I was straying away from clinic business for the first time with Owen didn't escape me, but I really *was* grateful that he'd taken care of Andie when she'd needed him in Boston. He deserved a couple of kinder words for that.

"There were times I wanted to call you and tell you," he confided. "But I knew that Andie didn't want anyone else to know, so I had to respect that."

I nodded. I actually admired the fact that he'd kept Andie's confidence. "I'm glad she's well now."

"Me too," he said grimly. "There were way too many times that I wasn't sure she'd make it."

I softened just a little as I still heard a bit of fear in his tone.

Sometimes, I'd actually wondered if something more than friendship had developed between Andie and Owen during the years they were together in Boston. Andie had never talked about any guy except for Owen. Now I understood *why* he was the only person she'd mentioned, since she'd been ill at the time, and Owen had been the *only* person who had been by her side in the hospital.

Watching Andie with Noah, and seeing firsthand how much she adored her new husband, put any question about Andie and Owen being an item to rest. But I could tell from the concern in Owen's voice how much he cared about Andie, even if it wasn't and never had been a romantic relationship.

"It must have been difficult for you," I murmured. "Andie said you were doing a heavy load in college to get through all the premed stuff in two years, and that you were holding down a job, too. I can't imagine dealing with the stress of Andie being sick on top of all that."

"It wasn't a big deal," he scoffed. "I just did what any other friend would do."

No, not *everyone* would have found a way to juggle that many balls in the air, but Owen could be just as stubborn as Andie.

I stood, afraid I was getting way more personal with Owen than I wanted to be. "I better go. Thanks for looking over those cases, Dr. Sinclair."

"Owen," he corrected as he folded his arms across his muscular chest. "Are you late for whatever plans you have that are keeping you from having dinner with me?"

I gathered up the files on his desk. "Yes."

I froze as he grasped one of my wrists and asked huskily, "What are you doing that's so important, Layla? It's Friday. Do you have a date?"

I actually did have a date . . . with a middle-aged bulldog I adored, and many other four-legged creatures who needed some attention.

Our eyes met, and I couldn't look away. "If I do, that's my business," I said sharply, tugging to get my arm back.

I wasn't about to ask permission from Owen to go on a damn date.

He had no idea that my love life was nearly nonexistent, but even if it wasn't, it was absolutely none of his concern what I did with my free time.

He let go of my wrist. "I'm not going to stop trying, Layla. I hate the way things are between us right now. Maybe whatever happened *was* a decade ago, but we were tight. Whatever is bothering you, I want to make it right. I tried like hell to get you to talk to me back then, but I had to leave for college, so I had to let it go. But I'm not going anywhere now."

He *had* nagged me to talk to him after he'd screwed me, and a few times, I'd *almost* broken down and told him off. But in the end, I'd kept my silence, just like I always did.

Like he can actually change our past now? Not possible.

"And I'll keep saying no to you," I answered as I picked up the last file and put it in the pile I was holding. "We're colleagues, Dr. Sinclair. That's all we'll ever be. I love Citrus Beach, and I want to be here with the patients I've established at this clinic. If I *didn't* want to stay, I could easily go somewhere else. Please don't pressure me out of this office."

I was single, and I was free to travel to another location, or maybe to a different state, where I could open my own independent practice.

I'd definitely considered all my options when I heard that Owen was buying Dr. Fortney's clinic, but I'd stayed because this was where I wanted to be.

I'd told myself that I could handle working with Owen, and I *was* perfectly capable of doing that—when he wasn't trying to persuade me to get personal with him.

"Don't go because of me," he said hoarsely. "I don't want that. I just want things to be . . . different."

I swallowed hard and moved toward the door to escape as I said, "I've learned the hard way that you can't always get what you want."

I didn't say another word as I opened the door, exited, and closed it quietly behind me.

CHAPTER 2

Layla

Dark: So what you're saying is that you can't stand your boss, but you still have to go to this party, or your best friend will be disappointed.

I nodded like Dark could actually see me, even though we were conversing via text in a dating app.

He'd summed up my situation pretty accurately. I wasn't looking forward to going to Owen's house at all.

Me: Exactly. But it's just one evening. I'll get through it. It's just not how I'd like to be spending a Saturday evening.

I glanced at the clock and let out a sigh as I rose from my kitchen table. Although I would have enjoyed talking with Dark for a while longer, I *had* to get to Owen's place to help set up.

Me: Time to jump back into the real world.

Dark was a fun distraction, but he wasn't exactly . . . real. He was just a guy I'd met while helping Andie's husband test his new dating app, Not-Just-A-Hookup. I'd started conversations with several people over the last few weeks in an honest effort to assess the app for Noah, but Dark was the only person who hadn't creeped me out or sent up a ton of red flags.

Dark's full handle was *Dark Humor*, so his name had gotten shortened to Dark.

My app moniker was *California Dreaming*, and he called me Dreamer.

Other than that, we knew next to nothing about each other, but we'd always found something to talk about.

The two of us pretty much checked in with each other daily. It was a nice, nonthreatening kind of communication, and a fun escape.

Dark: I don't get why you're helping your boss. I thought you didn't like him. He annoys the hell out of you, remember?

I let out a tortured groan. It wasn't like I *wanted* to be near Owen any more than I had to be.

Me: I offered to help before I knew the reception was being held at my boss's place. Honestly, I like my friend's husband, and almost all of his family.

I could hardly tell him that my friend's husband was the developer of the app we were chatting on, and I was only using it to help Noah out. Dark and I didn't share information like that. We kept personal details, like names and places, to a minimum.

Dark: Do you always put your own personal feelings aside to help a friend?

I thought about his question for a moment.

Me: Not always, but this one is special to me. She's been through
a lot, and she deserves all the happiness she can get.

I was thrilled that Andie was finally starting to live her life after
cancer with a man she loved, even if that man just happened to be
Owen's eldest brother.

Who could have predicted that one unexpected trip to Cancún
with Noah would have turned into a lifetime commitment for
Andie? The relationship had developed quickly, and it had taken
some time for my friend to let go of her fears, but Noah had dog-
gedly pursued her until Andie couldn't and didn't want to say no to
him anymore.

Noah had promptly taken her to wine country to get married so
they could both avoid the hoopla of a big wedding.

Not that I could really blame her for wanting to avoid *that*. The
Sinclair family could be a little overwhelming, and that was *without* the
East Coast branch of the family who were all flying in for the reception.

Dark: What did this guy do to you, Dreamer? You don't seem like
the kind of woman who hates somebody that easily.

I frowned at my phone. Did I really want to spill my guts about
something that had happened in high school? To a guy I'd never even
met face-to-face?

Nope. I definitely *didn't* want to try to explain. Sometimes even I
didn't understand why I couldn't let go of something that had happened
a decade ago.

Me: I don't exactly hate him. It was high school stuff. Nothing
that important. But it taught me not to trust him. We were

friends for years, but he was never really the guy I thought he was.

Dark: Maybe you two should talk about it. Maybe it's possible that you could get past all the old stuff.

I knew he was trying to help, and his desire to be a friend was one of the things I liked about Dark. In fact, I wasn't sure he actually cared about romance, even though he was on a dating app.

Me: I'll think about it.

I'd tried very hard to drop my animosity toward Owen. After all, the hurt had been inflicted years ago, and I wouldn't change the way my life had turned out. I'd probably forgiven Owen a long time ago, but I could never quite forget.

Dark: Would you rather I just beat the crap out of him for hurting you?

I laughed. Dark always seemed to be so willing to jump in and protect me from anything that might hurt me. Sure, I knew he was all talk, but it was kind of sweet.

Me: I can take care of myself, and I'm not exactly in high school anymore. I don't ask my friends to beat up people I don't like, but thanks for the offer. I think I'll just find a way to suffer through the afternoon and evening.

I looked at the clock again and added to my text.

Me: I have to get going. I'll be late if I don't get moving.

Owen's new home was on the other side of town, right on the water. My apartment was as far from the ocean as a person could get and still live within the city limits of Citrus Beach.

> Dark: I say make the bastard wait. You're helping him out. Every moment you spend talking to me is one less that you have to spend with him.

I smiled.

> Me: I offered to help set up, so that would be a little rude, don't you think?

Honestly, I *might have* dragged my feet getting to Owen's place if it wasn't for Andie.

She was pretty stressed about the whole meet-the-entire-Sinclair-family thing, and Andie rarely got anxious about anything.

> Dark: You agreed to help a friend before you had all the facts. Does your friend even know that you're uncomfortable with her new brother-in-law?

> Me: No. I can't exactly talk to her about disliking someone in her husband's family. It's something I'll have to deal with myself.

Andie might *suspect* that things weren't all that friendly between Owen and me, but I'd never told her about what had happened in high school, because I was afraid it might affect her friendship with Owen.

Now, the last thing I wanted to do was jeopardize her happiness in any way, and Owen was not only a close friend, but part of her family as well since she'd married Noah.

Dark: You don't have to do everything alone, Dreamer. Talk to me if you need someone to listen.

Me: Isn't that what I've been doing?

Really, I hadn't given him many details, but I'd told him the basic situation without revealing too much about myself.

Dark: Just know if you really want to talk, I'm here. I don't think this is just an uncomfortable situation for you. I think it's more than that. Let me know if there's anything I can do to help. My offer to hurt him is still on the table.

I laughed. I couldn't help myself. He didn't have the name Dark Humor for nothing.

Me: You're so twisted.

Dark: But you like me anyway.

I knew that was his sign-off statement. He always ended our conversations with some kind of cocky pronouncement.

I backed out of the app and put my phone in my purse.

Arrogant or not, I *did* like Dark. I was convinced that his occasional brashness was some sort of bravado to cover the fact that he actually had a kind heart. We'd had too many insightful conversations for me to buy into his smartass comments as being part of his true personality.

"It isn't like it really matters who he is, or what his real personality is like," I said out loud as I scooped up my keys and my purse. "It's a beta test for an app. It's not like I'm looking for love on a real dating program."

I'd only agreed to work with the app to help Noah.

It wasn't that I didn't want to find a good guy someday, but I kind of wanted to bump into Mr. Right *in person*. So far, that particular event had eluded me, but I wasn't ready to put my faith into a guy I'd never met face-to-face. Sure, dating sites and apps worked out just fine for some women, but not for me. I'd tried meeting someone nice online once, right after I'd finished nursing school. I'd ended up getting catfished, which had been more than enough to put me off cyberdating for the rest of my life.

I'd been hesitant to even get involved in the beta testing for Not-Just-A-Hookup because of my previous bad experience, but I'd blown off any misgivings I'd had to help Noah out. He'd made Andie so happy, and it wasn't like I had to take the dating-app thing seriously.

So far, I'd done my best to give the program a fair shot. I *was* still talking to Dark, even though I'd dumped all of my other conversations.

I slipped my feet into a casual pair of sandals by the door. I'd dressed pretty laid-back. The party was going to be big but relaxed, so I'd settled on a halter-type sundress that was colorful without being gaudy. Really, it was about the only thing I had other than jeans and shorts.

I spent a lot of my spare time in an animal shelter, and it wasn't like Brutus, the English bulldog I adored, or any of the animals I loved, gave a damn what I looked like.

I grimaced as I locked up my apartment, wondering how many women would be drooling over Owen at the reception.

I was probably the only single woman in Citrus Beach who would actually turn down the chance to have dinner with him.

Yeah, Owen *was* seen as the most eligible bachelor in the area, even if I didn't completely agree with that analysis.

He was a doctor, but there were plenty of single physicians in Southern California.

He was young and incredibly attractive. But hot guys in Southern California were a dime a dozen.

Okay, so maybe, if one were to put all of those things together, he was a doctor, young, *and* attractive, so that gave him *several* desirable qualities.

However, did that really mean that the entire single female population of Citrus Beach had to act like fools over him?

I rolled my eyes as I thought about how many of his female patients looked far from deathly ill when they walked into the clinic. In fact, their blatantly flirtatious behavior actually made *me* nauseous.

To give him credit, Owen *had* handled those situations well. He'd certainly done nothing to encourage them.

The unfortunate truth was, even with all of his desirable bachelor qualities, I knew it was the whole billionaire thing that was motivating every one of those women.

Owen had gone from a very poor, struggling medical resident to a billionaire literally overnight. He'd come into a large inheritance he definitely hadn't expected, and it was dollar signs those females saw when they looked at him.

The sad part was . . . those women didn't even *know* him. The only thing they knew about Owen was his staggering net worth.

They didn't know that he could be incredibly protective of the people he cared about.

They didn't know that he was a little shy about speaking to a big audience, even though his IQ was off the charts and he had a lot of knowledge to share.

They didn't know that Owen was like a walking, talking encyclopedia, and that he retained a lot more information than most people did about things he'd read or heard.

They didn't know that he had a habit of saying outrageous things at what seemed like the worst possible times, or that the tendency came from his desire to ease other people's pain.

They didn't know about the guilt he carried because he was the youngest and he thought his older brothers had needed to sacrifice way too much for him.

Nobody had a clue that he could be the sweetest guy on the planet without even knowing his actions were pretty exceptional.

Stop! That's what I thought before he screwed me over. I don't think about him that way anymore. I haven't for a long time.

I put on a pair of shades to shield my eyes from the sun as I strolled to my vehicle, unwilling to admit, even to myself, that I *hated* the fact that all those women just wanted Owen for his *money*.

Even sadder, he *had* to know their attention was motivated by the billions of dollars at his disposal. It wasn't that he *wouldn't* have been pursued at all now because he was scorching hot, and he had a good career as a physician. Owen would be very good boyfriend or marriage material at this point in his life. But I highly doubted those things alone would have produced the frenzy of women hot on his trail right now.

It's all about the money.

No woman had *really* seen Owen's value *before* he'd come into a fortune.

Well, no female had . . . except me.

CHAPTER 3

OWEN

"Is Layla there yet? I'm stuck in traffic. I'm going to be late. I should have just let them deliver the damn cake." Andie sounded uncharacteristically frustrated. She hadn't even said hello when I'd answered my cell phone.

"Well, hello to you, too," I said with a smirk as I plopped my ass into a recliner in my living room. "Calm down, Andie. This is supposed to be a casual, fun party. And no, Layla isn't here yet, but I did manage to get through medical school and my residency all by myself. I think I can handle this reception if she doesn't show up early."

"Easy for you to say," she grumbled. "Most of the people attending are *already* your family."

"Your family, too, now," I reminded her. "And it's not like I really know my half brothers and cousins from the East Coast, either."

Although most of my siblings were well acquainted with the Maine Sinclairs now, I'd never been around to see them on their frequent visits to Citrus Beach. I'd spoken to Evan quite a bit on the phone, since he'd been the one dispersing the funds that had changed all of our lives. But other than that, I'd only connected with my newfound family from Maine a couple of times in person. We might share DNA, but they were pretty much still strangers to me.

"But they're still your blood. What if they don't like me, Owen?"

I frowned. Andie wasn't a woman with huge insecurities, so it was a little disconcerting to hear how worked up she was over this whole wedding-reception thing. "Absolutely *nothing* will happen, Andie. Noah will still love you, and he won't give a damn what anybody else thinks, family or not."

Jesus! Didn't she know that Noah would happily throttle any person who said a bad word about his new wife?

She released a large breath. "You're right. I'm being ridiculous. I guess I've gotten myself all worked up from sitting in traffic. God, I hate San Diego traffic. Where in the hell are all these people going on a Saturday?"

I hesitated to remind her that it *was* still summer, and most people were out and about in nice weather. "Why didn't you just do something local?"

She sighed. "Noah and I went to a bakery here, and we fell in love with their fresh lemon-berry cake. It's a vanilla-bean cake infused with almond syrup and filled with zesty lemon curd and white-chocolate mousse. Then it's topped with seasonal berries. We both loved it. I wanted to surprise Noah by getting him this cake for our reception."

I grinned. My best friend had gone from a carefree food critic to a woman who was head over heels in love. I still wasn't used to her being so happily married. Yeah, I *was* accustomed to her waxing poetic about food, but she'd never given a damn about whether that food made someone else happy or not. "Sounds pretty damn good to me, too. Is there anything you won't do to make your husband happy?"

"Nothing," she said adamantly. "Noah deserves a little pampering after everything he's done for me."

Truthfully, I thought the two of them were perfect for each other, since Noah busted his ass to make sure his wife was deliriously happy, too. "Take your time, Andie. I have everything under control. The caterers have already been here to drop off food, and they'll be back to run the barbecuing. There isn't a ton of stuff to do."

I'd discovered that one of the benefits of being a billionaire was that I could pay *somebody else* to do all of the things I used to have to do myself. I couldn't say that I was completely adapted to having the kind of funds I'd inherited, but after being dirt poor my entire life, it wasn't exactly a hardship to roll with it.

I'd worked with an interior decorator to help me get my new waterfront home together. Granted, my brother Aiden *had* needed to remind me that I could afford to hire one, but I was completely on board once I realized how inept I was at doing anything remotely artistic.

Andie snorted. "Of course there are things to do, but maybe I didn't need to tell Layla to get there so early. She should be there in a few minutes, and I'm still sitting in traffic."

"It's okay," I assured Andie. "I think Layla and I need to talk. This might be the only way I can meet up with her outside of work. I offered to take her to dinner a couple of times, but she turned me down flat."

"You two still aren't getting along?" Andie questioned. "I don't understand. The three of us used to be such good friends in high school. I know you and Layla didn't really keep in touch, but I feel like I picked up my friendship with her like we'd never really been across the country from each other."

"I don't get it, either," I confessed. "She and I *couldn't* stay in touch because she wasn't talking to me when I left for college. I don't know what I did to piss her off so damn badly."

"I don't know, either. I've tried to ask her, in a subtle kind of way, but she's not biting. She doesn't want to talk about you, so I haven't pushed. Is this hurting your professional careers?"

"Not really," I told Andie. "We both do our jobs, and it's obvious to me that Layla cares a lot about her patients. It just bothers me . . . personally."

Best friend or not, I wasn't about to tell Andie that my dick didn't care if Layla hated me. It got hard every single time the woman was within my sight.

"Do you want to be friends with her again, Owen?" Andie asked hesitantly.

Well, not exactly. How in the hell was I supposed to explain that what I had with Layla in high school wasn't going to work for me anymore?

Hell, it hadn't even really worked in high school, either.

Yeah, we'd been really good friends, but during our senior year, my feelings had changed. My abundant teenage hormones had suddenly noticed her, and nothing had been the same after that.

I'd just never *done* anything about that crush. I hadn't wanted to lose Layla completely by telling her about it, so I'd kept my mouth shut.

Now, as an adult male, my dick was a million times more insistent about making my relationship with her more . . . carnal.

"Yeah. I guess I do," I said noncommittally. Andie was like a sister to me, so talking to her about the way I lusted after Layla just seemed . . . wrong.

"It would be great if you two could spend some time together outside of work," Andie said enthusiastically. "Most of our other old friends have scattered, and you really should get out more. You've earned your leisure time, but you don't seem happy that you actually have some of it now that your residency is over."

"I have no idea how to spend my free time," I scoffed. "I don't know what to do with myself. My siblings are all married, so it's not like I can just go hang out with them like they're single."

Truthfully, my new life was a little like stepping into an episode of *The Twilight Zone*. I'd spent an entire decade doing nothing except working and studying medicine. The rest of the world had moved on while I'd been studying to be a doctor, and now that I was ready to join it, everything had changed.

Every one of my siblings was just as filthy rich as I was, but they'd had a little more time to digest their newfound wealth. I'd been so busy just trying to get through my residency that I hadn't had time to think about it. Nothing had really changed for me while I was finishing my residency, even though I'd had a pretty hefty bank balance for a while now.

"Of course you can hang out with them," Andie scolded. "Every one of them is elated because you're back in California and done with school."

I wanted to explain to Andie how surreal my life seemed now, but I wasn't sure how to do it. "I know that. But things are definitely different. It's me. It's not them. I guess I'll get used to all of the changes eventually, but I'm not there yet."

"I'm sure it's weird," Andie said thoughtfully. "I mean, you've gone from a struggling resident in Boston to a billionaire doctor in Southern California. Your siblings are all married now, and you weren't around to see all those changes as they happened. Their new homes, and their new lives. It will take you a while to catch up. But try to enjoy the freedom you have now, Owen."

"It's not that I don't like it," I explained. "I'm glad that I'm done with school and back home in California. I'm happy that I'm finally a physician with my own practice. And I sure as hell don't mind that I'm *not* a new doctor drowning in student debt. I'm just not sure what to do with all the extra time and money I have now. I've caught up on my sleep, and I've done all of the pleasure reading I wished I could have done while I was in school. What else is there to do?"

I'd been a fantasy-series junkie in high school, but I hadn't had the time to read that kind of stuff once I'd gotten to college. I'd made up for that once I'd gotten back to California. I'd plowed through several long fantasy series, reading books back-to-back until I was caught up.

"Maybe you could try dating," Andie suggested dryly.

"Now that I'm extremely wealthy, I doubt that any woman will be interested in me. Just my money," I told her. "I've had a bunch of women ask *me* out, but I'm not even tempted. I'd like a woman who wants to get to know me, not my bank account. I knew some of those women in high school, and they definitely weren't interested when I was a penniless guy in secondhand clothing."

It wasn't like any of the women after me now had suddenly woken up to what a great guy I was or something.

It was *all* about the money.

"I get that," Andie sympathized. "But there has to be somebody out there who *will* care about you. You're such an incredible guy, with or without billions of dollars."

I wasn't exactly an experienced dater. I'd had some hookups during college and medical school, but that's all they'd been. Most had been one-nighters with women who were students as busy as I was, and who didn't have time for a relationship, either.

"The only woman who really cared about me ended up married to my older brother," I joked.

She chuckled. "And she *still* cares about you, even though she's married. I want you to be happy."

"I'm happy enough," I assured her.

Since I didn't really want to explain that my dick only saw one female right now, and that woman apparently hated me, I really needed to get off this whole topic about me and dating.

"I hope you can work everything out with Layla," Andie said softly. "It would be nice if you two could be friends again."

I wanted to tell her that it would be even nicer if Layla and I could become a hell of a lot more than friends, but I didn't.

Luckily, I was saved from thinking up some kind of neutral response by my chiming doorbell. "I think she's here," I informed Andie. "Don't worry, and just get here whenever you can. Don't drive crazy."

"Okay. I'll let you go. Hopefully, this freeway will stop looking like a parking lot soon," she answered, her voice a little less stressed.

Andie and I said a hasty goodbye, and I headed for the door, determined to resolve any issues Layla had with me *today*, since it might be my only chance.

Our relationship had been strained since the very first day I'd started work at the clinic.

Obviously, my attraction to Layla *didn't* go both ways. She'd looked horrified every time I'd suggested grabbing dinner together. I could only imagine how she'd react if she knew I wanted to get her naked.

So yeah, the fact that she didn't want me the same way I wanted her *did* bother me more than I wanted to admit, but it wasn't just lust that drew me to Layla.

Hell, the two of us had a history together that had started long before I'd become infatuated with her during senior year, and that meant something to me.

I *didn't* want her to hate me, and I *did* want to fix whatever had happened in the past.

At some point, I might even get over my hellacious physical attraction to her if we could just hang out as friends again, right?

I opened the door, fully prepared to approach Layla about the possibility of clearing up our past and being friends again.

My resolve lasted all of a couple of seconds.

Once I saw her standing on my doorstep, her curvy body encased in the sexiest damn sundress I'd ever seen, I was speechless as my eyes greedily consumed every inch of creamy skin the garment revealed.

Holy shit! Why in the hell did she have to wear that sexy dress!

I wanted to pull her into the house and nail her hot and hard against the first available surface I could find.

Every thought of being her friend again flew out of my brain, exiting like it had been a ludicrous idea in the first place.

I'd gone from *hopeful* to *fucked* in less than five seconds, and I had no idea what to do with that lightning-fast reaction.

"Owen, is everything okay?" Layla asked hesitantly as she removed her sunglasses.

Damn. She was *finally* calling me Owen, and my body was reacting to the small intimacy like it was the sweetest kind of endearment.

I need to get a grip. Layla is staring at me like I've lost my mind.

"Yep. Good. Fine," I muttered. *Damn.* Ten years of higher education, and *that* was the only response I could think of giving her?

Apparently, my intellect had completely left the building when I'd heard my name on her gorgeous lips.

I shook my head, thoroughly disgusted with myself.

I opened the door wider, and then watched as temptation sashayed right on into my house.

CHAPTER 4

LAYLA

"Well, I guess that about covers everything," I said to Owen in an overly bright voice that I wasn't feeling as I stepped back inside his home.

I'd spent a lot of time outside arranging, and then rearranging, the tablecloths, napkins, and all of the decorations I'd put up. Honestly, there hadn't been all that much to keep me occupied, since Owen had hired a caterer for the food. The tables had already been set up for the barbecue, so I'd killed as much time as possible fussing with basically . . . nothing. All so I could avoid spending too much time alone with Owen.

I was having a really hard time finding anything to say to him. I could handle being in a professional atmosphere with him, but it was awkward being outside the office and in his home.

What does he know about my life?

What do I know about what his life is like now?

It was sad that two friends who'd never run out of things to say to each other could be so uncomfortable in each other's presence now.

"Do you need anything else?" he asked as he poured himself some coffee.

I walked up to the kitchen island as I said, "You still drink a lot of coffee?"

Owen had studied like a madman in high school, and he'd held down a job at a local auto store, too. It had seemed like he was always slugging down coffee during his senior year. If Noah had allowed it, Owen probably would have worked every available moment he had, since he'd been saving for college. But his eldest brother had put restrictions on how many hours he'd let his little brother work in high school.

Owen turned to face me with a mischievous grin. "How do you think I made it through medical school and my residency? No lectures about how I'm a doctor and I know how bad it is for me, if you don't mind."

It was the first time I'd actually seen Owen smile like that since he'd returned to Citrus Beach, and the sight *almost* melted my heart.

I shrugged as I picked up a Diet Coke he'd given me earlier. "I won't say a word if you promise not to comment on my addiction to Diet Coke. A person has to have a vice or two, even if they know it's bad for them."

Owen moved until he was right across from me, resting one hip against the island. "Agreed. Something is going to get all of us someday. I'd rather enjoy my life than worry about every single thing that could end it."

I swallowed a mouthful of soda with more force than was necessary. I didn't like how uneasy I felt with him this close to me, even if there was the barrier of the granite island between us. "Same here. I mean, I try to be as healthy as possible, but I'm not giving up pizza, hamburgers, and Diet Coke completely. Life would suck if I did."

"Speaking of pizza," he drawled. "Is that incredible family-owned pizza joint on Baker Street still open?"

I nodded. "Russo's. Yeah, it's still going strong, and hasn't changed a bit. They still have the best pizza in the area. You haven't been there yet?"

"I haven't," he confirmed. "Citrus Beach has changed, and I wasn't sure it was still there. There are so many new restaurants in this city."

I sat down on one of the stools along the island. "I guess since I've been around to see those changes, it doesn't seem like Citrus Beach has grown that much," I answered. "It doesn't seem all that different to me. Most of the places we went to as teenagers are still operating. You haven't taken time to explore?"

It wasn't like he'd just gotten back to California yesterday. I knew I sure as hell would have sought out some of the best restaurants in town if I'd been gone for a decade.

"I'll get there eventually," Owen answered. "I guess I'm still not used to having the time and the money to go out to eat. I still feel a little lost. I spent a whole decade of my life pretty isolated. Now that I'm finally exactly where I want to be, everything has changed. The world has moved on while my life outside of school has been on hold."

Okay. Maybe Owen and I weren't friends anymore, and I'd probably never let go of my resentment toward him, but I could relate to what he was feeling. "I get it," I told him. "I felt the same way once I finished graduate school. I spent years in college, and I worked as a registered nurse once I was able to take my boards, so there was nothing except work and school for me, either. When I was finally done, I realized all of my friends had moved on without me. Most of them had gotten married and had a kid or two by the time I was finished."

I could still remember how sad I'd been that I had nothing in common with most of my old friends once I'd finished college. They'd built a whole new network of friends who were married with kids, and I didn't fit in with any of them anymore.

"So you finished your bachelor's, became a registered nurse, and then went on to grad school?" he asked, sounding genuinely curious.

"Yes . . . and no," I started to explain. "Like you, I tested out of general classes and took classes in high school to knock out some of my prerequisites. I got through the rest of them in a year, and then went into the nursing program for my associate's. After that I took my boards and started working as an RN. I wanted a job that would pay me decently so I could afford to pursue my bachelor's and then my master's."

His compelling green eyes studied me as he rested his elbows on the island. "What happened to all of those dreams you had about becoming a veterinarian? I thought that's what you wanted."

"I did," I said in a clipped tone, unable to keep the irritation out of my voice. "I think you know what happened, Owen. Can we just cut this whole pretense?"

Why had he needed to go *there* just when we were managing to have a civil conversation?

God, was he really going to keep acting like he had no idea why I didn't like him?

"No, I really don't know," he said, his gaze never leaving my face. "We need to talk about whatever happened. It's been over ten years, Layla. We've been adults for a while now. If I did something to hurt you, I want to fix it. I hardly saw you during the last few months of high school, and then I was gone to Massachusetts to get my shit together before I had to start college. I hate the way we parted, and I hated not being able to talk to you while I was gone. I missed you, and I never did understand why you ended up hating me."

My heart ached as I remembered how much I'd missed him, too. It had been really painful for those first few years. Eventually, I'd convinced myself that his betrayal didn't hurt me anymore, but I'd been lying to myself.

I'd learned to live with what Owen had done.

But I'd buried the hurt rather than resolving it.

"You're right. We *are* adults. Do we really need to discuss something that happened a decade ago?" I asked tersely.

I didn't want to pull the scab off old wounds. Not now. Owen and I had to work together.

"Yeah," he said huskily. "I think we do. What does this have to do with your education and your desire to be a vet?"

Like a cork from a champagne bottle, I exploded. "I *couldn't* go to college the conventional way. I needed the Manheim Scholarship to do a bachelor's program, Owen. I got several smaller scholarships I applied for, but I needed something bigger to help me get my bachelor's so I could apply for vet school. I'm sure that you probably wanted that scholarship, too, but you got more than one major scholarship, and you had more financial aid available than I did. I never saw my father, but he paid a ton of money for child support, money that covered all of my expenses since my mother didn't have a job. I think that was the agreement with my mother so he could claim me as his dependent. I had to claim that on my FAFSA, so my financial aid was minimal, even though I knew my father would never cover another dime of my expenses once I turned eighteen. There was no way he would help me with college, but I couldn't get much financial aid, either. I knew I'd be screwed without that hand up that the Manheim would have given me to get through a bachelor's with whatever low-paying jobs I could get while I was completing that degree. I just *didn't* know that my entire opportunity to even be considered for it would be undermined because *you* lied to me."

I'd stood up during my rambling explanation, and I had to rest my hand on the counter and force myself to breathe.

Having been thrown back to the moment when I'd discovered that Owen, a guy I'd trusted more than anybody else in life, had screwed me over, my buried emotions had come flying to the surface with a vengeance.

The anger.

The pain.

And the tumultuous sense of betrayal.

Maybe I should have said all those things years ago, but I hadn't because I'd avoided confrontation as much as possible back then. To some extent, maybe I still did.

Owen moved until he could wrap his hand around my shaky fingers. "Hey, calm down, Layla. I never lied to you. Ever. I swear. I never have and I never would. What the hell happened? Shit! Don't cry."

I lifted my chin and looked him directly in the eyes. The warmth and concern I saw there almost soothed my emotions. *Almost*, but not quite. I tugged to get my hand back, but he had a firm grasp on it. "Please cut the bullshit, Owen. If I'd known that you'd applied for the scholarship, too, I never would have asked for a peer recommendation from you in the first place. But you were graduating as the valedictorian of our class, and you were so respected scholastically that I wanted your letter of recommendation. I didn't know that you never sent it until the scholarship board informed me that they didn't receive one of my peer recommendations, so I'd become ineligible. I understood *everything* once the announcement came out that *you* were the recipient."

Owen finally let go of my hand and straightened up. The warmth in his eyes cooled as he asked, "So you just assumed I was the one who *didn't* send in the recommendation? Why would you think that, Layla? If I hadn't wanted to write one, I would have just told you. We were friends, dammit! I wrote the most honest reference possible. I told the board that you were deserving, truthful, hardworking, and so gifted that you should be the one to get the scholarship. Yeah, I applied, just like I put in an application for anything and everything that could help take the load off myself and my family, but I didn't expect to get it. The Manheim tends to lean more toward students who plan on pursuing veterinary programs, since the founder was a vet. But I put my application in anyway since it's open to anyone pursuing a bachelor's in the sciences. And I put my application in right *before* you asked me for a letter of recommendation. If I'd known that you were applying before I sent in my application, I wouldn't have sent in my info in the first place."

I saw what looked like genuine pain in the depths of his eyes, and I had to jerk my gaze away from his face.

How was it possible that he really did send that letter?

Was this just another diversion so he didn't have to admit that he'd screwed me over?

Did I believe him?

Really, it wasn't possible that he was telling the truth. "Who else would have done that?" I asked coolly. "Andie wrote hers and sent it. She even showed me a copy."

"I didn't think that Andie knew why you were pissed off at me," Owen said stiffly.

"She didn't. I didn't tell her that I didn't get that scholarship because you didn't send your recommendation in."

Owen clenched his free hand into a fist. "I did send it," he rasped. "If I remember right, the scholarship committee required three peer recommendations. It was an unusual process because they asked for them to be sent after you applied, with the name of the student applying and their application number. You, Layla Marie Caine, were applicant number 997-543-145."

I wasn't surprised that he could pull that number and my full name out of his head. I nodded sharply. "Too bad you never put that on my recommendation letter."

I jumped when his fist connected with the granite. "I sent the damn thing," he said, sounding agitated. "Who was your third reference?"

"Bea Stanley," I said flatly. "You know, class president, cheerleader, very popular, very friendly, teacher's pet even though she wasn't anywhere near the top of the class. *Everybody* loved her. She was never late for a single class. Ever. The woman was perfect. It's not like *she'd* screw up."

"But you think it's possible that I did? Did you ask her if she sent it?" Owen questioned sharply, the muscle in his jaw twitching.

I rolled my eyes. "Of course I didn't ask *her*. She said she'd send it the next day, and she always did everything right."

"So it was easier to believe that I'd screw you over than to ask her? What the fuck, Layla? I know you hung out with her sometimes, but you and I were close friends. Didn't I deserve the benefit of the doubt, too?"

A single tear dropped onto my cheek, and I swiped it away ruthlessly. The last thing I wanted was for Owen to see me cry. "I thought so, until I found out *you* won the scholarship, and *I'd* become ineligible. It made sense that you'd been the one who *didn't* send it. Especially since you'd been pretty distant toward me for a couple of weeks before I got the letter telling me I was disqualified. I got the news that you'd received the scholarship a couple of days later. I assumed you were trying to push me away because you knew that I'd find out."

"That's not why I was backing off," he answered curtly. "What happened to Bea?"

"She's one of those friends who moved on with her life while I was in school. She married the captain of the football team and has a couple of kids now. She's in San Diego," I said. "We tried to hook up for coffee or lunch a couple of times, but something always came up with her husband or her kids, so we never ended up meeting in person."

"Do you have her number?" he asked gruffly.

"In my phone," I replied.

"Call her," he demanded.

I shot him a startled look. "Now? Andie will be here any minute."

"This party isn't starting for another hour. Call her. You owe me that, Layla. You just accused me of lying and intentionally stealing that scholarship from you," he said grimly.

"You did lie to me," I shot back at him as I opened the small crossbody purse I'd left on the island. "I just don't understand why you won't own it. Maybe then I could completely get over it. It's not like I don't know that you needed every scholarship you could get."

"Maybe because I *didn't* do it. Whether you believe it or not, I *wanted* you to get that scholarship once I'd found out that you'd applied. I was aware of just how badly you wanted to be a vet. Hell, I was blown away when Andie mentioned that you were going to nursing school instead. What I don't get is why you'd ever believe that I could crush your dreams like that intentionally and still be able to live with myself, Layla. You never shared all that much about your family life, but I knew enough to know that it wasn't good. Why in the hell didn't you tell me you couldn't get much financial aid, or that your chances of becoming a vet were heavily dependent on that scholarship?"

I rarely discussed my home life with anyone back then. I'd been ashamed of what I had, compared to the way Owen's brothers and sisters always supported and encouraged him.

Maybe I'd been embarrassed to tell him too much about my life.

Owen had never had two pennies to rub together, but he'd had so much . . . more.

I took a deep breath. "There was nothing I could do about it, so I didn't talk about my home life, and there wasn't much I could do about my college situation, either," I said defensively. "I was hopeful about getting the Manheim to help get me through a bachelor's program since I did a lot of volunteer work for the animal shelter and a couple of other animal-welfare organizations."

Actually, it had been the director of the shelter who'd made me believe I could become the recipient of the Manheim. She'd known one of the committee members for the scholarship, and she'd shared that I was at the top of the list when I'd first applied.

My dreams of going directly into a bachelor's and then to vet school had been flying high.

Which had made the crash-and-burn part pretty damn painful when I'd found out that all of the required recommendations hadn't been received before the deadline.

"You never told me about your financial worries about the future," he commented.

I snorted. "You never told me much about yours, either."

"I was a hell of a lot more open than you were," he contradicted as he nodded to the phone I'd pulled from my bag. "Call her."

Did I really owe it to Owen to get a confirmation from Bea that she'd sent my recommendation for the scholarship? It wasn't like all the evidence didn't point toward him.

If I don't owe it to him, maybe I owe it to myself.

I'd never even considered the possibility that it could have been Bea who didn't send in the required letter.

Everything had pointed toward Owen, and I'd been blinded by the pain of his perceived betrayal.

I need to just do it. Even though I know it was Owen, I'm a grown-up now. I have to rule out every possibility.

Now that I was discussing all of this with Owen face-to-face, maybe there was a small, niggling doubt in the back of my mind.

Yes, it still made sense that he'd been the one to crush my adolescent dreams.

But it was really difficult to completely ignore the devastated expression on his face.

I turned my back on Owen, found Bea's number in my phone, and waited for her to pick up.

CHAPTER 5

OWEN

"Oh, God. I'm so sorry, Owen." Layla dropped her phone on the counter and plopped onto one of the stools at the island.

I was so pissed off at her that I didn't *want* to feel any empathy as I watched the crushed, completely remorseful expression on Layla's face, but damned if I didn't want to comfort her. Even after she'd accused me of being a liar.

I hadn't heard the whole five-minute call she'd had with Bea, but what I did hear had been enough for me to know that Layla's former friend had confessed to not sending in her recommendation.

Layla shook her head as she related the truth. "She was sick, and her grandmother passed away, and she forgot. Bea swears she felt so guilty that she couldn't tell me. I don't know what else to say. All these years, I was so sure you did it, but it never was you. I'm so sorry, Owen. I should have never jumped to conclusions like that. Everything just seemed to fall into place for me once I found out you'd gotten the scholarship."

I had to give Layla credit: the woman owned up to her mistakes. Not that it was any excuse for her calling me a liar, but I had probably contributed to her conclusions by avoiding her before I'd won that damn scholarship. "Do you want to know why I backed off our relationship near the end of senior year?" I asked. My voice was colder than I'd meant it to be, since I was still stinging from her accusations.

My gut ached as she looked at me earnestly with tear-filled eyes and then nodded hesitantly.

Those beautiful baby blues had always done something to me, and I didn't like seeing them this damn solemn.

"Somewhere in the middle of our senior year, I stopped seeing you as just my friend. I developed a massive crush on you, Layla, and every damn time I saw you, my teenage-boy hormones took control." I stopped, cleared my throat, and then continued. "I pretty much wanted to nail you every moment of every day. It got . . . uncomfortable. I thought about asking you out on a real date, but I thought that would just make things worse since I had no idea how to date, and let's face it, I was a dork in high school, and you were beautiful. What chance did a guy like me have with a girl like you? Besides, I was leaving for college in Boston, and you were planning on staying in California for school. Looking back, I should have just talked to you about how I felt, but I was too embarrassed to bring up the topic. So I just backed off."

"D-did you think I'd say no if you did ask me out?" she stammered with a stunned look on her gorgeous face.

"Of course I did. I was a nerd, and you, well, *you* were *you*."

She shook her head, the amazed expression still on her face. "I was never one of the really popular girls like Bea."

"Didn't matter," I informed her. "In fact, I kind of admired the fact that you could float around to different crowds but never made a firm commitment to being one of any of them. You could kick ass in a math competition, and then go do some sexy pom-pom routine with the marching band. I'm not sure which one of those made my dick harder, but there was *nothing* I didn't like about you, Layla."

Her tears started to flow faster, and she sounded choked up as she answered, "I cared about you, too, Owen, and I'm sorry I messed everything up. I want to make it up to you, but I don't know how. I don't know what I would have said if you'd asked me out, because I didn't really date, either. I didn't even kiss a guy until after high school. Maybe I did have friends in every crowd, but you and Andie were always my best friends. I could be myself when I was with you."

The anger I'd felt earlier began to melt away. Layla looked so destroyed that I couldn't beat her up over making a mistake. Hell, we'd been kids back then, stupid teenagers who did and thought ridiculous things.

Sure, it had wounded me that Layla had thought I was capable of being devious enough to make sure she didn't get a scholarship she'd needed, but really, neither one of us had been thinking like an adult. "So you didn't go to be a vet because you didn't get the Manheim?"

I hated the fact that I'd achieved my dream but Layla hadn't.

She brushed another tear from her cheek. "There was really no guarantee that I was going to get that scholarship anyway," she said. "I had a backup plan to go to nursing school, and I'm not sorry for the way everything worked out. I love what I do at the clinic, Owen, and I think I like spoiling the animals at the shelter more than I'd enjoy operating on them. Now that I'm older and wiser, I think fate pushed me in the right direction, even though I didn't think so at the time. I can't imagine doing anything else."

"Are you still volunteering at the shelter?"

She nodded. "As much as I possibly can."

It was believable that Layla was happy doing women's health at the clinic. I'd seen her in action. Her patients adored her, and she happily gave a lot of herself to the people under her care. "I'm glad you're happy, Layla. I've thought about you a lot over the years."

"I've thought about you, too," she answered softly.

"Probably none of those thoughts were pleasant," I said dryly.

She sniffled a little louder. "Not all of them were bad," she argued. "And I'm so glad you were there for Andie. I wish she would have told me. It must have been difficult to be her main emotional support when you were in school and working, too."

I shrugged. I'd managed, even though it hadn't been easy. "The hardest part was watching her suffer. She went through hell, and I think it would have been hard on you to watch that, too."

"But I would have done anything I could to help her."

I nodded. "If it helps, I did encourage her to call you so she had your support, too, but she refused. She said she thought you were going through some stuff yourself."

"She's so stubborn," Layla said, not sounding the least bit disgruntled. "I know how she can be. She never wants to bring anybody down. I'm so glad she's happy with Noah now."

"More like deliriously happy, and it's weird having one of my best friends married to my brother, but I'm glad, too. He needed her as much as she needed him."

"I don't know Noah all that well, but I think you're right. Andie said he was a serious workaholic."

"He was," I agreed. "But he's lightened up significantly."

There was a pause before Layla asked, "So what can I do to make all this up to you, Owen? I feel horrible about what happened. I mean, I'm not asking to be your friend again or anything, but I don't want hard feelings between the two of us anymore."

I held up a hand with my palm facing her. "Please don't say you're sorry one more time. And for fuck's sake, don't start crying again. It's over, Layla. All I really wanted was to put things right between us. Yeah, it hurt that you'd think I was capable of being such a dick, but we were teenagers. Except for that mistake, you were always a good friend to me."

Layla had always encouraged me to reach for my dreams, and she'd been there during some rough times. I could easily give her a break. "Maybe the next time I ask you to go get some dinner, you could say yes," I suggested.

She smiled. "Maybe I will, since you haven't been to Russo's yet."

It wasn't that I didn't want her to trust me again like a best friend, but I couldn't exactly see her as a buddy when all I wanted to do was get her naked.

One step at a time.

At the moment, I could enjoy the fact that she didn't hate me anymore.

"I think you should probably be mad at me, but I'm glad you aren't," Layla said in a hushed voice. "And I still want to make all this up to you somehow."

The sound of regret in her tone was more than I could handle. I walked around the island and held out my arms. "Come here."

I'd wanted to be closer to her for so long that I was willing to play the "friend" card to get her into my arms.

She jumped up from her stool and ran toward me, throwing herself into my arms as I wrapped her into a bear hug.

I knew I'd fucked up almost immediately.

But I didn't give a damn.

I buried my face into her hair and inhaled her seductive scent.

I savored the way she wrapped her arms around my neck without hesitation and plastered her body against mine.

She let out a contented sigh. "I should have known that you'd never do something horrible like that to me. I wish I would have just talked to you."

Really, I didn't give a damn about what had happened in high school anymore. All I cared about was *now*. I stroked a hand over her hair. "Forget about it, Layla."

I didn't want her to keep torturing herself over a stupid mistake.

She'd drive herself crazy if her conscience was as powerful as it used to be. Layla had always owned the things she did wrong, and then she'd beat herself up over those errors endlessly.

"It's really hard to forgive myself for just tossing our friendship aside like that," she murmured.

I tightened my arms around her, trying to tell her without words that I fucking forgave her for that.

Stroking a hand down her back, I said, "If you say one more word about what happened in high school, I *will* get angry."

She pulled back from me and tilted her head a little to meet my gaze. "No you won't. You've always been quick to forgive other people, but you're hard on yourself."

"You only see that because you're the same way," I informed her as I pushed a strand of her glorious blonde hair out of her face.

Having Layla this close to me was torture because my dick was so damn hard, but I must love torment, because I couldn't let go of her, either.

That's why I knew I was fucked.

Her scent, the feel of her soft curves, and her warm, silky skin—all of them were addicting.

"Layla," I said hoarsely, not even knowing what I wanted to say.

My eyes were focused on her plump lips, and the fond look in her eyes that made me suppress a groan of frustration.

I wanted to see the same hungry expression on her face that I already knew was evident on mine.

I wanted her as a man, not a teenage boy.

But she obviously didn't see me any differently than she had a decade ago.

Somehow, I needed to figure out a way to make her want me as much as I wanted her.

I lowered my head slowly, knowing I had to kiss those succulent lips of hers before I lost my mind.

I'd only moved a fraction when the doorbell rang.

Fuck!

"It must be Andie," Layla said, her voice breathless as she slowly backed away.

Maybe later, I'd be thankful that I was saved by the goddamn doorbell.

But right now, I was wishing that Andie had gotten stuck in traffic for just a few more minutes.

The only positive thing at the moment was the slightly dazed look in Layla's eyes, because it told me she wasn't *completely* immune to the chemistry between the two of us.

As I made my way to the door to let Andie in, all I could think about was how I'd missed the opportunity to kiss Layla.

Again.

It had happened once before, the last time I'd had a friendly conversation with her in high school. We'd gone to the park, and when I'd seen her home safely, it had taken everything I had to let her go. I'd wanted to kiss her then, but I'd managed to back off right before I made a total fool of myself.

This time, I hadn't planned to stop, but maybe it was a good thing that Andie had arrived before I could screw things up by moving way too fast.

There wouldn't be a third *attempt*.

I'd waited over a decade for another opportunity to kiss the only woman I'd ever really cared about.

The whole damn world could go to hell until I got exactly what I wanted next time.

CHAPTER 6

LAYLA

"I want to come and see you in the clinic when I get back from my extended honeymoon," Andie said to me casually as we sat in side-by-side loungers on the beach.

The party was winding down, so we'd stepped away from the crowd for a few minutes to relax and chat.

We hadn't gone far. We were still just outside the makeshift dance floor in the sand, but far enough away so we could hear each other speak.

The reception had gotten a little bit crazy—in a fun kind of way. The dancing-on-the-beach part hadn't been planned, but once everyone had indulged in a few adult beverages at the bar, quite a few guests were more than willing to participate in Andie's spontaneous salsa lessons. Including me. We'd danced until we'd nearly dropped before we'd sought out a quiet place to chat.

I eyed her suspiciously. "Why? Is something wrong?"

Maybe I knew that her cancer wasn't at all likely to pop back up, but I was instantly anxious anyway, just because I knew she'd been through so much.

She shook her head. "Nothing is wrong. But I think I'm finally ready to find out if I have any chance of having a child someday. It's quite possible that all of the treatment I had during my cancer made me infertile. If it did, I want to know."

My heart ached for Andie. All of her suffering should have been over, but apparently it wasn't. She was still pondering what damage the chemo and radiation had done to her body. "Do you want to have a child?" I asked gently.

She hesitated before answering. "Several months ago, I would have said *no*. But now that I've found Noah, I guess I want to know if that option is on the table in the future . . . or not."

I cocked my head as I looked at her, feeling slightly confused. "So Noah wants to have a child?"

"I don't know," she answered. "We haven't really discussed it much, but if it's absolutely impossible, he should know, right? Noah kind of swept me off my feet, but it's something I should have thought about before I married him. I should have asked. What if he ends up wanting to have kids, and I can't?"

"Oh, Andie," I said softly. "Haven't you seen the way Noah looks at you? You're everything to him. If he's never asked, he obviously doesn't give a damn whether you have kids or not. I think the man just wants . . . you. Maybe a child would be a bonus someday if you both want it, but you're not stressing over this, are you?"

She flopped back into her lounger with a sigh. "I think I am. Sometimes everything just feels so good with Noah that it's almost too good to be true. I never thought I'd get this kind of happily ever after. At one time, I didn't think I was even going to live long enough to fall in love. Now that it's happened, it's almost terrifying. Even this party scared the hell out of me, because I was meeting all of his family from Maine for the first time, and every one of them is filthy rich. There's even a celebrity or two thrown into that mix."

"And look how good that turned out," I reminded her. "I met his East Coast relatives. They're all really nice. I have to admit that meeting Xander Sinclair was a little surreal. I had a mega crush on the guy at one time, and I've always loved his music. But he surprised me. He seems so grounded and normal for a guy who was such a huge rock star."

"I know," she said with a groan. "They all hugged me and welcomed me to the family like they really meant it."

I rolled my eyes as I leaned back in my lounger. "They *did* mean it, Andie. You're an amazing woman. They're lucky to have you in their family."

I had no idea when Andie had become so unsure of herself. She generally had balls of steel, and wouldn't be intimidated by someone with money since she wasn't exactly poor herself.

My guess was that it wasn't the *family* that really unsettled her. It was the thought of losing Noah for any reason, because she loved him so damn much.

"I guess I'm setting myself up to deal with disappointment in case something happens," she confessed, confirming my suspicions. "Nothing this good has ever happened to me, Layla. And I never imagined having a guy like Noah for a husband. He'd do just about anything to make me happy, and nobody has ever cared about me that much."

I felt my eyes well up with tears as I considered her situation. Honestly, she was a lot like me, and came from a background of neglect. Andie's parents had never given a damn about her, and she didn't really have any other close family. She was also an only child who had grown up lonely. "You're long overdue for somebody who *does* love you that way," I told her. "Don't sabotage the relationship because you're afraid, Andie. You'll get used to it. It's just so . . . new. But have you noticed that every single Sinclair male looks at his wife the same way Noah looks at you? Yeah, they're intense, but I certainly can't fault any of them for being desperately in love with the women they married."

Andie snorted. "I'm starting to think it's a Sinclair thing. Once they fall in love, they're pretty much doomed. They *have* to make sure the women they love are safe, loved, and happy, or they won't be content, either."

"You'll never convince me that it's a bad trait for them to have," I responded.

What woman *didn't* want a guy to really give a damn about her happiness?

"It's not," she admitted. "You're right. I'm just not used to it. But I want Noah to be happy, too. It goes both ways. I guess that's why I'm worried that he might want to have kids someday, and that I might not be physically capable of giving him that. Plus, I've kind of changed my mind about having children myself. I'm not quite ready for that yet, but I might be in the future if Noah wants it, too."

As a friend, I wanted to tell Andie that everything would be fine.

But as a medical practitioner, I knew that her worries weren't completely irrational.

There was a chance she could be infertile, especially considering how aggressively they'd needed to fight her cancer.

"Let it go for now," I advised. "Enjoy your very long honeymoon, and we'll deal with that issue when you get back. Is there any chance you can get Boston to send me your medical records?" It would help if I knew exactly how much and what kinds of chemo and radiation she'd been through.

"I definitely can," she confirmed. "I'm just not sure you're going to love going through all those files."

"I can handle it," I assured her as I smiled. "I think you should talk to Noah while you're away. I'm sure he can convince you that he's not going to be disappointed if you can't have a child someday."

"I think you're probably right, Layla. He did spend all of his adult life raising his siblings."

"What do *you* want?" I asked.

"Him. I just want Noah. I think I'd be okay either way."

"I think he would, too, so I think you should talk about it."

She took a deep breath and exhaled. "I will. I know I sound a little crazy—"

"You're not crazy," I interrupted. "You *should* know if it's an option, but I don't want you to feel like the answer to that question is going to change your relationship with Noah. It won't."

"How did you get so damn wise?" she asked.

I laughed. "Women's health is my specialty."

"Yeah, so speaking of your work, is everything okay between you and Owen? I know you don't really want to talk about what happened between the two of you, but I think you should give the man a break, Layla. I think he's a little hurt and confused. Put him out of his misery and talk to him. Whatever happened, he's still a good man. Not many people would stick by a friend like he stayed with me. Yeah, he's a pain in the ass like most men can be sometimes, but Owen has a huge heart. I think that's what makes him such a good doctor, but it's also his Achilles' heel. Seeing so much human suffering ate him up sometimes. He just can't distance himself enough all the time, so there were some cases that ate him alive."

What Andie was saying made sense to me . . . now. Owen had worked in a big-city hospital, and he'd seen so much sadness, so many tragic deaths. My voice was shaky with regret as I told her, "I did something bad to him, Andie. I misjudged him, and I hate myself for that. I just found out that he wasn't the person who I thought had screwed me over, but I blamed him for it for so long. He *is* the guy I always thought he was, but I just didn't realize it until today."

She was right. Owen *was* a good man, and I'd hurt him by accusing him of being a liar and a person who would be nasty enough to kill my chances of having a shot at that scholarship—intentionally.

It didn't matter how obvious it had seemed to me at the time, I should have confronted him, given him an opportunity to explain. I *had* owed him that because we'd been friends for so long.

"Hey," Andie said gently. "Owen isn't the type to hold a grudge. Grovel a little bit and he'll get over it. We had plenty of arguments while I was in Boston, but he never held any of my mistakes against me."

Maybe Andie had said some things she regretted to Owen, but she had an excuse. She'd been extremely sick, and fighting cancer.

"He says he's already over it," I explained. "But how can he be after I've been such a bitch to him over something that never happened?"

"Because he cares," Andie answered softly. "Owen is the kind of guy who believes life is too short to hold something against someone once they apologize for it. He doesn't take it personally. It's one of the things I adore about the man."

"I still feel guilty," I muttered.

"Cut him a break and he'll be happy. Honestly, I think he could use a friend. I'll be gone, and he's in a weird period of his life right now. Owen has spent his whole adult life studying to be a doctor, and then suddenly, he's been dropped into a whole new life. I don't think he has any idea what to do with *this* life of not studying, not going to school, *and* being filthy rich on top of all that."

"Yeah, we talked about that a little," I shared.

"I think you can probably relate," Andie mused. "Be there for him, Layla, because I can't be. He needs somebody right now, and I feel like shit about leaving him when he was always there for me. Owen has never asked me for anything. He's always been a giver."

"What can I do?" I asked her eagerly.

I wanted to do whatever I could to help Owen, if he'd let me.

"He'll never really admit that he needs someone, or that he can't handle everything himself," she warned. "But if you get to know him again, you'll see how his mind works. The man is freaking brilliant, but I don't think he was prepared for how much his life would change once he was actually done with school. He was too busy just trying to get through each day."

"Do you think coming back to Citrus Beach was a little bit weird for him? I think he feels like so much has changed here," I said thoughtfully, remembering what little Owen had said to me earlier.

"It has changed. For *him* and for *me*. You probably haven't noticed because it's grown a little at a time, and you never really left. But it's grown a lot. There are so many new businesses and new housing tracts that were built after Owen and I left. It's kind of embarrassing, but I actually got a little lost a couple of times looking for places I thought I knew so well. All of the previous landmarks that led me to those places were gone, or hidden by new builds." Andie chuckled as she mocked her own ability to find her way around Citrus Beach again.

"Maybe that's why he's never been to Russo's," I mumbled. "But he must have GPS."

"Oh, God, no!" Andie exclaimed. "It took me forever to finally admit that I needed my GPS to find some places. This is my hometown. I felt like I should remember, but I finally gave up and pulled out my GPS to find Russo's. When I did, I found out they'd moved. They had a fire in the old building. The owner told me that they used that opportunity to expand and rebuild right down the street. They sold their old site. I think it's a fast-food joint now."

"Oh, God," I groaned. "That was over seven years ago."

"I've been gone for over a decade, so it was all new to me."

It had to be new for *Owen*, too, but it had been so long ago for me that I'd actually forgotten that they moved down the street a little. "Owen asked about Russo's and if they were still on Baker Street. I told him they were, because they're still there. But I didn't think to tell him that they weren't in the exact same location."

I was almost certain now that Owen had been asking because he'd tried to go there and hadn't seen the pizza restaurant.

He can pull a nine-digit number out of his head after only seeing it a couple of times over a decade ago, but he's too damn stubborn to turn on his GPS?

I smiled. Yep. That kind of sounded like Owen.

Andie sighed. "Like I said, it's new if you've been gone for ten years. Maybe you should just take him there and feed him. The guy could use a few good meals. I think he lived on hot dogs and ramen noodles in Boston, and he only had those when he had time to eat."

"And coffee," I added.

"Yes," Andie agreed. "He didn't sleep much, so coffee was a staple for him."

Andie was silent for a moment before she added in a hushed voice, "Don't look now, but I think you've drawn Jaxton Montgomery's attention. He's been staring at you for the last five minutes. I kind of think he's getting ready to make his move."

CHAPTER 7

LAYLA

I forced myself not to look back toward the reception guests. "I don't think I've met him. Obviously he's not a Sinclair like most of the people here, but his name does sound familiar."

"It should," Andie answered, her voice much more upbeat than it had been a few minutes ago. "Reporters are always chasing Jax and his brothers all over San Diego, and they get a lot of media attention. I think the press is really hot on Jax's and Cooper's tails right now because the oldest Montgomery brother, Hudson, is taken now. But Jax and Cooper are definitely still single and available."

"How in the world do you know so much about the guy? And why is he here?"

I was definitely familiar with the family name. Montgomery Mining was a worldwide giant. But I had no idea why anybody in that family would be here in Citrus Beach.

I doubted that the Sinclairs floated around in the world of the ultrarich. Granted, they *were* billionaires, but that had only happened recently.

"I've met them all," Andie informed me. "They're Riley's brothers. They show up at some of the family barbecues. Even though they're disgustingly wealthy, they're all surprisingly friendly. Seth claims he was never sure if they were going to kill him or welcome him into the family at first."

Seth was another one of Owen's older brothers.

As I remembered that Riley's maiden name *was* Montgomery before she married Seth, the mystery started to fall into place. Riley was actually a patient of mine, so I knew her on a professional level, but we didn't exactly hang out together.

"So they *are* actually family . . . by marriage," I said thoughtfully.

Andie laughed. "Yeah, and family isn't all about blood for them. Once the Montgomery brothers decided that the Sinclairs were family, Seth said he couldn't get rid of them. They were pretty protective of Riley until they were sure that Seth was good enough for her."

I chuckled. "That must have been a little intimidating for him."

"I don't think he really cared," Andie replied. "He was too obsessed with Riley to give a damn."

"I've never met any of them, and I didn't see them earlier," I told Andie, certain that if I'd seen the brothers, I would have recalled meeting *them.*

"I think they came in after most of the dancing was over. But I did notice that Jax can't seem to take his eyes off you right now," Andie said teasingly.

"He's probably looking at you, not me," I argued. "He doesn't know me, and it is kind of dark over here."

"It's light enough," she disagreed. "Slowly start turning your head toward the crowd, and then tell me he isn't staring directly at you."

As she suggested, I moved slowly, adjusting my field of vision little by little. Once I was actually looking at the guests, I froze as my gaze locked on the most intense set of gray eyes I'd ever seen.

Jaxton Montgomery was breathtakingly handsome, but there was something so raw about his blatant, fixed stare that I was more fascinated with his personality than his looks.

The guy was definitely bold. He didn't seem to give a damn that he was staring, nor did he look away in embarrassment.

"Holy! Shit!" I whispered as I broke eye contact with him and looked at Andie.

"Told ya," she said smugly. "Here he comes. I think it's time for me to make my exit. He's a nice guy, Layla. All of the Montgomery brothers are a little edgy on the surface, but you'll like him."

"Oh, my God. Andie, don't you dare take off on me," I said in a threatening if-you-leave-I'm-going-to-kill-you voice.

She wasn't intimidated at all as she stood and greeted the newcomer. "Hey, Jax. It's good to see you again."

I watched as Jax gave Andie a brief hug. "It's a pleasure to see you, too, Andie. Congratulations on the new marriage. Noah is a lucky guy."

I watched and listened as Andie made small talk with Jax. It was evident that the man could be completely charming when he wanted to be. Obviously, he'd grown up in a very privileged world, and he clearly knew how to mingle in a party.

"I don't think I've met your friend," Jax said casually as he turned to look at me.

His eyes were no longer intense. He smiled, and his piercing stare from earlier morphed into a much friendlier expression.

Andie smiled and said obligingly, "Jax Montgomery, meet one of my best friends, Layla Caine. Layla is a nurse practitioner. She and Owen work together at the clinic now." She took a deep breath before she added, "I better go find my new husband. He probably thinks I deserted him."

I shot Andie a dirty look as she waved, right before she hightailed it toward the guests.

Traitor!

It wasn't that I didn't like meeting new people, but it would have been a lot less awkward if she'd stayed for a while.

Jax sat down on the end of the lounger that Andie had vacated.

I put the back of my seat up and curled my legs up beside me, so I could finally see his entire face.

Like every other guest, he'd dressed casually in a pair of jeans and a nice collared shirt.

On the surface, he seemed relaxed, but I felt like there was a predator right beneath that thin layer of amiability, ready to spring the second it became necessary.

"I met Owen just a few minutes ago," Jax said in a laid-back tone. "He seems like a pretty nice guy. What's it like to work with him?"

"I've actually known him for a long time. We were friends in high school," I explained. "It's good to have him back in California, and I love what I do. Honestly, we haven't really been working together all that long. He just bought the clinic a few months ago."

Jax smiled at me, and really, I should have been swooning. The guy was absolutely gorgeous. His brown hair had some stunning auburn highlights, and I would probably call his face beautiful because his bone structure was perfect, but he was much too rugged to actually be a "pretty boy."

His low baritone was enough to make a woman shiver in anticipation.

Problem was, I just wasn't *that woman*.

I had no doubt that Jax was probably pursued relentlessly.

He was a billionaire.

He was gorgeous, tall, and muscular.

But for some reason, he didn't do a thing for me.

Nada.

Nothing.

Not even a twinge of attraction.

Andie's matchmaking attempts were a complete fail.

I *did* start to *like* Jax as we began talking and got to know each other. He seemed interested in what I had to say, and he kept me entertained with stories about what it was like to circulate in the world of the superwealthy.

"I think it would drive me absolutely crazy to have to spend time with a bunch of uptight people I didn't like," I told him.

He shrugged. "It's not all bad. I think you just have to put the whole thing into perspective. I treat it like a game, and I never forget that those people live in a bubble. Sometimes, in my business, it's necessary to play in their sandbox and make friends, but I actually avoid it when I can."

I tilted my head as I looked at him. "Don't you live in that same bubble?"

He chuckled. "Jesus! I hope not."

"What makes you so different? You grew up rich and privileged, right?"

"I did," he admitted. "But I was also a Navy SEAL until I had to give it up to go back to San Diego to help manage Montgomery Mining with my brothers. I broke out of that bubble pretty early, and now that I'm back, I can't take that superficial world all that seriously. I saw a lot of the uglier side of life, and once I saw it, I could never forget that life isn't easy for most people."

"I'm sorry," I said softly. "I had no idea you were in the military."

He grinned. "So you just thought I've always been a useless rich guy?"

I smiled back at him. "Pretty much. I'm starting to think I make way too many assumptions, and it gets me into trouble sometimes."

What I'd done to Owen immediately came to mind, and I knew I needed to work on my tendency to jump to conclusions.

But really, it was a little hard to imagine a wealthy, handsome billionaire like Jax leaping to the call of Uncle Sam.

Jax shook his head slowly. "I don't blame you for thinking I was a spoiled rich kid. But kids with money don't always have an idyllic childhood. Let's just say everything my parents did revolved around money, and neither of them were nice people. I guess I wanted to get away from all that, and do something more honorable than writing a check."

God, I admired him for that. Most rich guys would probably shudder in horror at the thought of roughing it in the military without all the luxuries they were used to having. "Are your parents still alive?" I asked curiously.

"My father is dead, and my mother is dead to me," Jax answered grimly. "We aren't on speaking terms. I can't go into details, but I recently found out that she did some things to Riley that I can never forgive."

I could relate to shitty childhoods, and having parents who let their kids be casualties instead of caring about their welfare. "I'm sorry."

"Don't be," he insisted. "You didn't do it." In a lighter tone, he said, "It sounds like Xander Sinclair decided to break out his guitar and do a couple of his ballads. Do you want to dance? I want to talk to you about something, but I can easily do that while we're dancing."

I shook my head. "I'm a terrible dancer. I know you missed the whole salsa-dancing thing that happened before you got here, but I was a total disaster."

Since I'd spent most of my adult life in school, I'd completely missed the years where most of my friends were clubbing and partying. Not that a lot of my college classmates hadn't indulged in the club scene, but I'd always held down some kind of job while I was going to school, so I'd never had time to join them.

Jax stood and held out his hand. "I'm a pretty good teacher."

"Not happening. Don't touch her," a familiar voice said from behind me. "Layla promised all of the rest of her dances tonight to me."

I knew exactly who that edgy baritone belonged to, but I whipped my head around anyway. "Owen?"

I was startled by the look on his face. It was an expression I'd never seen before, one of pure, unmitigated anger.

Jax held his hands up. "Hey, dude. Calm down. I didn't know you two were actually an item."

I quickly said, "We aren't—"

Owen interrupted with "We are. So I'd appreciate it if you'd just back the hell off."

I opened my mouth to say something, but the words never had a chance to exit my mouth. Owen grabbed my hand, pulled me to my feet, and dragged me away from Jax before I could say another word.

CHAPTER 8

Layla

"What in the world was *that* all about?" I sputtered as Owen kept right on walking until we were far away from the other party guests. "Stop," I insisted. "We've already walked at least half a mile from the reception."

"Not far enough," he grumbled, but he did slow his pace a little.

I yanked on his arm. "I said *stop*, Owen. I'm not even wearing shoes, and I can't see where I'm walking."

I'd taken off my sandals before I'd gotten into the lounger, so I was at the mercy of any sharp objects in the sand at the moment.

He came to a halt immediately. "Shit! I'm sorry. Are you okay? I didn't even notice that you didn't have shoes on."

I pulled my hand loose from his, and propped both of them on my hips. "I will be okay after you tell me what the hell just happened."

Owen pulled his phone from his pocket and turned on his flashlight app. "Let's head back. I'll keep the light in front of you so you can see where you're stepping."

"I'm not moving until you tell me exactly why you were so rude to Jaxton Montgomery," I said stubbornly.

I heard him audibly exhale before he said, "Layla, you can't honestly be thinking about dating him, right? Jax Montgomery is a player. He's been pictured with more women than anybody can really count. He's the worst of all the Montgomery brothers. A guy like that will chew you up and spit you out without a single ounce of remorse. He's not right for you."

My temper flared. "Since when is that *your* decision to make?"

Not that I was interested in Jax, but it was really none of Owen's business who I decided to date.

"I didn't want you to make a big mistake," he rumbled as he reached out, took my hand off my hip, and enfolded it into his own again. "The guy is trouble."

I let out an exasperated breath as I started to walk with him back toward his house. "And you know all this just by meeting him once at the party tonight?"

"When I saw him talking to you, I was hanging out with Aiden, Seth, and Noah. All three of them agreed that Montgomery goes through women like they're disposable. Did you know that Jax is called 'the one-date wonder' because he never does a second date with any female? It's not that my brothers don't like him, but they all said that he's a womanizer," Owen grumbled as he steered me around some rocks in the sand.

"Don't you think it's a little unfair to judge somebody by other people's opinions?" I asked.

"Not when the information is coming from my older brothers," he replied mulishly. "I trust them."

I released a soft sigh. One of the things I'd always loved about Owen was his protectiveness, but dragging me away from Jax was pushing it a little too far. "You haven't been around for over a decade, Owen, and I've managed well enough without your intervention."

"Yeah, well, I'm going to be around from now on. Get used to it," he said gruffly.

My heart skipped a beat, and I tried not to let his words get to me too much. Maybe he *would* be around for a while, but he'd eventually find new friends in Citrus Beach, and probably a woman he was romantically interested in, too.

Even though he'd confessed to being interested in me in high school, I hadn't told him that I'd felt exactly the same way back then. We were different people now, and we weren't kids with a teenage infatuation.

Then why does my heart still ache to be close to him?

When I'd hugged him before Andie had arrived, I was almost certain that Owen had been ready to kiss me. But I'd come to my senses right after Andie had entered the house, and Owen had given her the same welcoming bear hug he'd given me.

The man wasn't afraid to show his affection for his friends, and I'd realized that Owen was just being . . . Owen.

Did I really think that he still harbored some kind of interest in me as a female after ten years of not seeing each other?

Ridiculous!

Owen wasn't the boy I used to know.

He was now a billionaire, all grown up and gorgeous, and the physician he'd always wanted to be.

Women were falling at his feet, for God's sake.

As we neared his house, he broke the silence between us. "Let's sit for a minute, Layla. I'm not ready to go back. I want to ask you something."

I was puzzled as he plopped onto the sand just outside the bright lights of his patio, but I let him pull me down with him.

He let go of my hand to switch off his phone light, and I smoothed the cotton material of my sundress, so it covered me to the knees.

"What do you want to ask me?" I questioned curiously.

It felt almost surreal to be sitting side by side with Owen again. Like we were back in the city park as teenagers.

Yet it was different, too.

Owen and I were pretty much strangers to each other now. We'd lived completely separate lives as adults.

He was quiet for a minute before he answered me. "Maybe I've changed my mind about asking, since I'd have to spill my guts about all the things I can't do or haven't done in my life."

"Tell me," I urged. "I want to help."

The sea was extremely calm tonight, and the gentle lapping sound of the waves hitting the shore lulled me into a more peaceful state of mind.

I'd do whatever I could to help Owen. All he had to do was ask.

He released a masculine sigh. "I was telling you earlier about how I feel out of place now that I'm done with school. I feel like I don't belong in this new world of no studying, no classes, and only working office hours most of the time. I started making a list of the things I don't know how to do or have never done, and it's pretty damn long."

He sounded so uncertain as he admitted how inept he felt, and it made my heart ache. "I think it's pretty normal," I explained. "I told you that I felt the same way. Sometimes I still do. It takes a while to adjust."

Owen was just starting to come back into the real world, after putting his personal life on hold for years to get through med school and his residency.

"Sometimes I'm not sure that I even belong in my own family anymore," he shared. "I mean, I've always been tight with my siblings, but I was never really there for any of them. While they were struggling with relationships, problems, and handling this inheritance, I basically ignored the money. When we all get together, sometimes they talk about stuff that means nothing to me. I wasn't around to share any of those experiences with them. Good or bad."

For a guy who valued family, it had to be hard to realize how much he'd missed. But it wasn't his fault. "You'll catch up with everything that happened eventually," I assured him gently. "You've lived a separate life in another state, but everything will fall into place."

"It's not just that," he rumbled. "Jesus, Layla, I don't even know how to dance. I wasn't a partier in college. I didn't date, either. I've never been drunk off my ass, and I didn't do anything just because I *wanted* to do it. I was grinding every minute of the day just to keep up with my studies, and to keep eating. I didn't have time for anything frivolous or nonessential. Hell, I barely slept."

Owen really hadn't dated anyone? Ever?

I had no idea why that was so hard to believe when I hadn't done much dating myself. "Do you want to do all those things you put on that list?"

"Yes, and no," he answered thoughtfully. "I could do without the getting-drunk-off-my-ass part. It usually doesn't turn out all that well the morning after, but I would like to catch up with my family, and do things a normal guy my age would be doing now. If you're serious about being willing to do anything to make up for your misguided assumptions about me, there is something you could do for me."

"All you have to do is ask," I said emphatically.

"If I'm going to date like a normal guy, I need practice. I'd like to practice with *you*. Be my love interest, Layla. Once I get comfortable with that kind of relationship, I'd really like to be friends again."

I opened my mouth to tell him I absolutely could *not* be his temporary girlfriend test mannequin, and then closed it again.

I *did* owe him for all the horrible things I'd said, and for the way I'd treated him. Was he really asking me for all that much in return?

He'd so readily forgiven me that maybe I needed to figure out what he wanted before I turned him down flat.

"What exactly does this arrangement require?" I asked carefully.

"Dating. Romance. Fun. New experiences," he explained. "Helping me find my way around this damn city again, and figuring out what I want to do when I'm not working. You said you felt this way when you got out of school, so you probably know what I need, right?"

"I'm . . ." I coughed hard before I continued. "To be completely honest, I'm not exactly an experienced dater, either, Owen, so I'm not sure how much I can help you with that. By the time I was finished with school, my mother was sick with liver disease. She died eight months ago. I was pretty much in the same position as you were."

And still am . . .

"Fine," he said agreeably. "Then we'll learn together. I'd actually feel more comfortable with somebody who wasn't all that experienced. Less chance of me feeling like an idiot if I do something wrong." He hesitated before he added, "I'm sorry about your mother, Layla. I didn't know."

Nobody knew because I hadn't talked much about my mother's illness, or her death. The only person at her funeral had been me. The woman hadn't exactly inspired love or warmth of any kind while she'd been alive.

"Thanks," I said softly. "I just wanted you to understand that my life has pretty much sucked so far, too, except for having a career I love, and my volunteer work at the shelter."

"Then let's learn all this stuff together," he suggested.

"You can't just force romance, Owen," I said, exasperated.

"It wouldn't be forced for me. I care about you, Layla. Always have."

The big problem was, it wouldn't be a complete facade for me, either. I'd cared about Owen, *even* after he'd presumably burned me. Maybe I'd had to get a lot of information secondhand from Andie, but I'd paid attention when she'd talked about Owen and how things were going for him in med school and his residency.

All these years, I'd probably been more hurt than angry. I'd just buried my more tender emotions underneath a furious exterior. And now that I knew that Owen had never betrayed me, I was realizing that my fondness for him had never really completely gone away.

He still got to me, and I knew I could end up falling hard for an adult Owen who wanted nothing more than some kind of teacher or . . . grown-up playmate.

But I didn't want to say *no*, either.

Because I did care about him, I wanted to spend time with him, see how he'd changed and how he'd stayed the same. For some reason, I craved that after not seeing his face or hearing his voice for over a decade.

And if hanging out with him meant sharing a kiss or two, it wouldn't exactly be a hardship. Much as I tried desperately not to be, I *was* ungodly attracted to him.

Okay, maybe we *needed* to talk about the whole kissing thing.

We'd *have* to stick to a timeline, because I'd need an end to remind myself that it was all a limited-time deal.

"Two months?" I questioned. "Is that the time limit?"

"Unless you dump me before that if I act like an asshole," he said playfully.

I rolled my eyes. God, some things *never* changed.

Obviously, Owen could still pop in goofball one-liners when we were *supposed* to be having a serious conversation. But I wasn't going to complain about that. I'd actually missed those silly comments. A lot.

"No sex," I insisted. "I can't do *that* in a make-believe romance."

Oh, hell yes, I'd probably end up *wanting* it because I *was* attracted to Owen, but we needed to set down some rules right now.

"Not a problem," he agreed readily. "As long as you don't tell me that you won't *kiss me*, I'm flexible."

I swallowed hard. *That* was going to be my next request, but was a kiss or two really that big of an issue?

"Okay," I said reluctantly, wondering if there was anything we hadn't discussed but should. "Then I guess we have a deal."

"Are you still a virgin, Layla?" Owen asked. "You don't have to answer that question if you don't want to, I'm just being a curious friend."

"No," I had no problem admitting. "You?"

"Nope. I've never actually dated, but I did get laid," he said candidly.

His honest reply had made me *want* to share my past with him, but I wasn't ready for that. I might *never* be ready to share that part of my life with anyone.

"Now that we've got all of that settled, what are we doing first?" I asked, trying to lighten the atmosphere.

"You tell me," he suggested. "I want you to enjoy this, Layla. It seems that I have more money than I know what to do with, so nothing is off-limits. Let's do some of the things we couldn't do when we were poor teenagers. Just do one thing for me," he requested.

"What thing?" I queried.

"Stay the hell away from Jax Montgomery, at least for the next two months. I guess once this is over, you're going to end up doing whatever you want to do, but I can't try to romance you while you're drooling over some other guy," he said tersely.

I snorted. "Owen, I was *never* drooling, and I don't think he's interested in me, either. We had a friendly conversation, but I'm just not attracted to him that way."

"If that's true, you're probably one of the few single women in the world who feels that way," Owen said dryly as he stood and held out his hand.

I shrugged once he'd pulled me to my feet. "I doubt that. I mean, he is good looking, insanely rich, and very smooth. But there was zero romantic chemistry between us. I would have to argue with you about him being trouble, though. He was pretty nice to me."

"Probably because he knew it was the only way to get you to drop your panties," he said, sounding disgruntled.

I rolled my eyes as we slowly made our way back to the guests on the beach and the patio. "You said you have a list of things you've never done, and of things you feel inept at doing. Can you show it to me?"

"I'll give you a copy," he agreed, sounding a little bit reluctant. "It's kind of a long list."

Later that night, Owen did give me a copy before I left his house. My heart nearly broke as I looked it over, and I suddenly couldn't wait to get started.

CHAPTER 9

OWEN

"There's no way that this place was here when we were kids," I told Layla right after I'd taken a slug of my coffee and savored the mocha flavor before I swallowed it.

It was Sunday, and the mall was busy, but once we'd ducked into the specialty coffee shop, it was a little less noisy.

She shook her head as she swallowed a mouthful of whatever concoction she'd just ordered. "It wasn't here. It was built about two years after you left. There are a lot of high-end places here, so I don't shop here much. But if you've never stopped at a specialty coffee place, this is the place to experience it first. We have the usual chains like Starbucks, but this place is special. They care about serving the best coffees on the planet."

Layla had plucked this excursion off my never-have-I-ever list I'd given her. I'd known it the minute I'd seen the sign across the entrance to the coffee place.

"I'm surprised you didn't pick the Coffee Shack. It's been in town for as long as I can remember," I mused.

She held up her hand. "Don't get me wrong. The Coffee Shack is amazing, too, and I go there a lot, but it's nice to splurge once in a while. They're pretty expensive here, but they have some really exotic coffees."

"I think I can afford it," I teased. "And it is damn good coffee."

Honestly, it was the best coffee I'd ever had. Then again, it wasn't all that hard to top the cheapest generic brand I could find in the grocery store.

During med school, it had been more about quantity than quality.

Layla and I had gotten a small table in the corner of the shop where we could sit and enjoy the extra-large coffees we'd ordered.

I'd been relieved that she'd traded her sexy sundress for a pair of jeans and a colorful tank top when she'd swung by my house earlier. But I'd eventually discovered that it didn't really matter what she was wearing. I was pretty sure I'd want to nail her, regardless of her attire.

There was something about this woman that always took my breath away.

"Is this really a first for you?" she asked, her beautiful blue eyes studying my face.

"Yep," I said honestly. "I could never justify the money it would cost to buy my coffee at an expensive coffee place. In Boston, I could buy a whole can at the grocery store for the price of a large coffee in some of those places. I made coffee at home and carried around a very large, insulated cup when I left my apartment. Once I got to the hospital, almost every department had a pot brewing somewhere."

She nodded. "I was pretty tight when I was in school, too. But once I started working as a nurse practitioner, I decided I could splurge occasionally."

"I'm definitely willing to renegotiate your salary, Layla. Fortney didn't pay you all that well." Hell, I'd give the woman whatever she wanted. She deserved it.

She sent me a sweet smile that made my dick so hard that it was almost uncomfortable as she said, "I was fresh out of school when we negotiated that contract. I was a new grad, so he was pretty generous considering I had no experience. Even now, I'm kind of a newbie. I've only been at the clinic for two years, and my salary is fine. I'm still paying off student loans, and I'd like to eventually buy my own place, but I'm not complaining. It's nice to have a little money for the extras now."

Layla had never been a complainer, no matter her circumstances. "We'll be reviewing the contract soon," I warned her. "You aren't fresh out of school anymore."

Hell, I'd just bought a beachfront home that had cost millions, and Layla was still saddled with student loans.

She swallowed a sip of coffee before she insisted, "I'm fine, Owen."

"I can knock out those student loans in a matter of minutes, Layla. Let me help you," I insisted.

"Absolutely not," she scolded. "Owen, I knew I was going to have to pay back my student loans, and it isn't crushing me. They're my responsibility."

"My money grows enormously every damn day, thanks to the investments Evan helped me make." I hesitated a second before I said, "Which brings me to a question I've been wanting to ask you."

"Ask," she encouraged.

"How would you feel about working in a free clinic? I've thought a lot about the change in my circumstances, and I sure as hell don't *need* any income I generate as a physician. Obviously, I'll keep the contracts I have for insured patients, but I'd like to expand and offer care on a sliding scale for the uninsured. And free for patients who really can't afford it."

I watched her face as her eyes grew wide and then got that glassy sheen that meant that tears were imminent. I'd grown up with twin sisters. I *knew* that look.

Fuck!

"You'll still get a generous salary, Layla, and benefits," I added quickly.

She took a sip of her coffee and blinked several times like she was trying to keep the tears from falling. "Owen, I think that would be amazing. I'm not worried about my salary. I was just thinking about how many people we could help. Maybe we could offer free mammograms and Pap smears for women who can't afford them. So many uninsured females put them off for so long because there isn't enough money in their budget to feed their kids and take proactive measures for their health. You'd save lives, Owen. I know you would."

Hell, if I'd known she'd look at me the way she was now, I would have started to reorganize the clinic before the ink was dry after closing.

The woman was looking at me like I was her hero, all because I suggested revamping the clinic to help people who had no insurance and no money for basic healthcare.

It wasn't like I was sacrificing anything. I could afford it.

"We'd have to add staff," I warned her. "And probably expand. We could definitely do preventive medicine for women and families."

I'd been thinking about exactly how to change things up now that my financial circumstances had improved. Drastically.

Her face lit up. "Maybe we could try to find grants, or do fundraisers. You shouldn't have to foot the entire bill for the clinic yourself."

I shrugged. "It wouldn't matter if I did. I'd never miss the money. But I had a long talk with Evan while he was here, and he had some good ideas. One thing I can say about the Sinclairs is that they're all pretty generous with charities, so they know a lot about fundraising and helping those entities support themselves as much as possible."

"I'd feel good about working at a clinic that could help people who really needed it," she said, her face still lit up like a Christmas tree.

"Me too," I agreed. I'd gone into medicine because I'd wanted to help people, and I was glad as hell that I could offer way more than I ever thought possible when I'd first started med school. "But it's your clinic, too. I wanted to know how you'd feel before I started planning."

She rolled her eyes. "It's *your* clinic, Owen. I just work there."

I shook my head. Maybe she didn't have ownership in the clinic, but she *was* the heart of it. It had only taken me a single day of working with her to figure that out. "It wouldn't be the same if you weren't behind me on this, Layla."

"I'm one thousand percent behind you," she said excitedly.

I hadn't really expected her to reject the idea entirely, but I was a little surprised that she wholeheartedly supported it. It was going to be a lot of work, and it would mean there were going to be a lot of changes, but that didn't seem to concern her at all.

She really hasn't changed much. Layla still has a damn good heart.

I grinned at her like an idiot. "We'll talk about the details when we're at the office. I'm supposed to be wooing you right now."

She held up her cup. "You bought me a coffee. I think I'm already falling for you."

She batted her eyelashes at me flirtatiously, and I laughed at her goofy expression, even though I was so fucking hard that I was wincing underneath that humor.

I have two months to get her to trust me, and to make her want all of this to be real.

I knew achieving that goal was a long shot, but I'd been pretty damn desperate once I'd seen Jax Montgomery eyeing Layla like he wanted to fuck her.

I knew *that look*.

Hell, I probably had the same expression on my face every damn time I looked at her.

Whether Layla knew it or not, Jax probably *had* been making a move on her. Guys recognized that kind of shit from other men, and he'd definitely had more than a casual interest in her.

Everything I'd told her about me was true, except . . . I didn't need a teacher or somebody to practice on. Not really. I just needed . . . *her*. Period. I wanted to spend time with Layla outside of the clinic, and if cashing in my favor coupon with her was going to get me that time, I'd been willing to do it.

I had zero interest in all the women who were suddenly eager to date me because I was a billionaire.

What I really wanted was the woman who had accepted me as I was when I was poor.

Maybe there wasn't much of a chance that Layla would decide she wanted to be more than friends. She'd made it pretty clear that we were like strangers now. Unfortunately, I just didn't feel the same way.

I downed the last of my coffee before I asked, "So what's the next first?"

She shook her head firmly. "Your turn. You decide. Did you enjoy your coffee date?"

"I did," I said huskily.

The only way I could have enjoyed it more was if we'd had hot and heavy sex at my house before we left.

There were so many things I wanted to do with Layla. Unfortunately, the naked activities were out, but there were a lot of other things to choose from on that list.

"We're already here at the mall. I say we go shopping," I suggested.

"That wasn't on your list," she said, sounding confused.

"It wasn't, but we can be spontaneous, right? I actually forced Andie into taking me somewhere in Boston right after my inheritance came through so I could get new clothes. And I did shop for a new house. But I'm sure there are still some things I could use."

She looked disappointed as she replied, "I wish I could, but I'm due at the shelter today. I'm sorry. Cages don't get cleaned and the beasts won't get fed if I don't go."

"Okay, so I've never cleaned dog cages or fed dogs, so that would be another first for me, even if it isn't on the list. You'll just have to show me what to do." I'd go clean toilets with her if that was what she needed to do. Whatever it took to spend more time with her.

"You'd really do that?" she asked doubtfully. "You're a doctor and a billionaire, for God's sake. You don't need to be cleaning dog cages at the shelter."

"You don't *need* to do it, either, Layla, and I'll be perfectly happy if I'm doing it with you," I argued. "Do you know how many dirty jobs I had to do as an intern?"

She smirked. "Probably the same things I had to do as a nursing student."

I got up and held out my hand. "Let's get started. If we finish early enough, maybe you could help me find Russo's. I've been craving their pizza since I got back home."

She laughed as she took my hand without hesitation, and I pulled her to her feet.

I felt like I'd been kicked in the gut when she graced me with a full-faced smile that was reflected in her beautiful eyes.

It was weird, but when I was with Layla, I didn't feel even the slightest bit lost or out of place anymore.

CHAPTER 10

LAYLA

"Why don't you have a dog of your own?" Owen asked as he reached for another piece of pizza.

Russo's had been really busy, so we'd decided on takeout instead of eating in.

Owen must have been hungry, because he'd ordered a couple of Russo's enormous family-sized pizzas, way more than the two of us could ever get through in a single sitting. Plus bread sticks. Plus dessert. Our bounty was spread out on his kitchen island. We'd pulled up a couple of stools and dug in as soon as we'd gotten home.

I *had* finished at the shelter pretty early. Owen had helped me a lot, so we'd even had time to play with the dogs and cats before we left.

I sighed. "My landlord doesn't allow animals in the apartments. If I could, I'd probably have more than one."

"So find a new place," he suggested.

I pushed back from the island because I couldn't possibly eat one more piece of pizza. "Easier said than done," I explained as I picked up my Diet Coke and watched Owen continue to demolish his food.

"Most apartments don't allow dogs, and I'm hoping my next home will actually be *mine*."

"You really want to adopt Brutus, don't you?" he asked in a more serious tone.

Brutus was a middle-aged English bulldog. One of his ears was forever damaged from past abuse, and he'd been at the shelter for months because he wasn't exactly pretty. But the intrepid animal had turned out to be so loving once I'd gained his trust. His favorite place to rest his head was on my thigh. "How do you know that?" I questioned him.

"Come on, Layla. It's pretty obvious you two adore each other. He's probably the ugliest dog in town, but I don't think you care."

"He's adorable," I said admonishingly. "It's pretty amazing that he would give his trust to anybody after the horrible life he's had so far. But he does, and it's kind of humbling."

"What are you going to do once he's adopted?" Owen questioned.

I took a sip of my soda before I answered, "I'll probably want to stalk the new owner to make sure he's well loved. It would be selfish of me to want him to stay there just because I'll miss him, but I hope that he goes to a home where they'll take good care of him. He's such a good boy."

"You'd be heartbroken if he goes. Admit it," Owen challenged me.

"I would," I agreed. "But I don't want him to live the rest of his life in the shelter."

"Then let me buy you a damn house. You could be close to him every day."

I nearly choked on my Diet Coke. "Owen, you can't just walk around offering to buy everybody a home."

"I'm not asking *everybody*," he corrected. "I offered one to you. Andie's house is going up for sale. Although, I am *definitely* convinced now that it's cursed. Everyone who has owned that place ended up married to a billionaire. First Jade, then Riley, and now Andie."

"I can't afford a house on the beach."

"It's not exactly a mansion."

"Owen, I couldn't afford a one-room shack in this part of town," I said.

"You don't have to afford it if I pay for it. Brutus would love it. If you could get him to stay awake long enough, he'd love to play on the beach."

Owen's willingness to help me after not seeing me for a decade, and then having me call him a liar and sleazy cheat, was beyond remarkable. It touched me that he was so damn worried about my welfare, especially when he didn't need to be.

"I'll get a place someday, but it will probably be in our old neighborhood."

He turned his head and scowled at me. "That area sucks."

"You didn't think so when we lived there as kids."

"It's gone downhill since then, but it wasn't the greatest area even when we were younger. Please tell me you don't still live there," he said in a concerned tone.

I avoided answering him directly. "Not everyone can afford a house on the beach. Owen, we don't exactly have slums here in Citrus Beach."

He let out a groan. "So you *do* live there," he guessed.

Dammit! The man could still tell when I was hiding something.

"It's not so bad. My apartment building is nice. And I don't want to pay an astronomical rent, because I'm saving for my own home." My decision not to upgrade my residence once I'd become a nurse practitioner made perfect sense. I wanted a new home where I could have pets of my own, and keeping my place with a modest rent was going to get me there faster.

"You wouldn't have to save anymore if you'd just let me buy you a place," he argued stubbornly. "Dammit! It's not like I can help my family with this sudden wealth. They're all as loaded as I am. So why can't I help the other people I care about?"

I melted as I looked at the frustrated expression on his face. How many people would immediately want to reach out and help their friends if they became an instant billionaire?

Furthermore, how many would make a free clinic their first concern?

Owen was a giver. He always had been. It was obviously driving him crazy because all he wanted to do was use that money to help other people, but nobody in his family needed anything.

I reached out and put a gentle hand on his arm. "You'll figure all of this out eventually, Owen. Give it some time. I know you didn't plan on becoming a billionaire, and even though it's confusing, it's a good thing, right? Your plan for starting a free and low-cost clinic is amazing, and knowing you, that isn't the only way you're going to make a difference in the future. You're doing enough right now. Enjoy the fact that you're filthy rich. In fact, you should wallow in it. You deserve it."

"I don't feel like I do," he answered as he pushed back from the food, too.

Obviously, he'd finally had enough pizza.

He was quiet for a moment before he added, "My whole life changed in one day, Layla. Before the money, I wasn't even thinking of coming back to Citrus Beach right away. Even though my family helped as much as they could, and I was awarded scholarships for medical school, too, I was resigned to being a poor doctor for a while because of my overwhelming student debt. I was seriously considering getting into a debt-forgiveness program so I could go work in a rural area that really needed doctors."

I nodded. I knew about the program. I'd thought about it myself before my mother had gotten ill. "So the whole trajectory of your life suddenly changed. But that's still a positive, Owen. You can make a difference here. We don't have nearly enough facilities that provide free and low-cost services."

He pinned me with his emerald gaze. "Don't get me wrong. I'm glad I'm here. If I wasn't, I wouldn't be sitting here with you. But it's a hell of a lot different than what I'd had planned before this inheritance."

I let my hand smooth over his muscular bicep before I reluctantly pulled it away from him. "Different," I agreed. "But not bad. Please don't feel guilty because you have an astronomical amount of money when so many people don't. You deserve this after living poor for so long, and it's never going to change who you are as a person. It's just . . . money. Okay, it's a *lot* of money. Spend it. Enjoy it. And do whatever good you can with it."

Owen would never be some guy who lived in a wealthy bubble. It was his very nature to look around him, see suffering, and want to do something to help.

He smirked. "How did you know I felt guilty?"

"Because I know you."

He lifted a brow. "I thought you considered us strangers now."

"Maybe not entirely," I confessed. "There are parts of your personality that definitely haven't changed."

"So you'll give in and let me buy you a place. Come on, Layla. It's not like it would even make a dent in my bank account," he cajoled.

"Absolutely not, but good try," I said, amused. "I'm proud of everything I've accomplished, Owen. My life wasn't so great at one time, but I forced myself to overcome all of that, and now I'm doing something worthwhile that pays well, too. When I finally reach my goal for a down payment on a place of my own, I want that to be because I worked hard to do it, too. I do appreciate the fact that you care enough to offer, though. You're a pretty amazing guy, Owen Sinclair."

Honestly, I was fairly certain there wasn't another man like him in the entire world. Sure, his brothers probably gave heavily to charity, but they were still working on building extraordinary companies, too. While all Owen could think about was how to use his money to make a difference in the world, and give his services as a physician away for free now that he could afford to do that.

I folded my arms across my chest as I added, "If you aren't going to start spending more money on yourself, and doing things that *you* enjoy, I think I'm going to have to force you to do it."

"You're going to have to come up with bigger ideas than me buying you a pizza and a cup of coffee," he scoffed.

"You think I can't think bigger?" I teased.

"You've always had to watch your money, too," he reminded me. "But I dare you to try to make even a tiny dent in my bank account. You can't. It grows in huge numbers every damn day."

"Okay, fine," I said. Dammit! He knew I never backed down when he challenged me. "If we have to close down to do changes to the clinic, take me somewhere while it's being done. Someplace we never could have afforded to go three or four years ago. And I'm not talking about a hop to Catalina Island or something. Think. Big."

"Paris?" he suggested with a grin.

My heart skipped a beat. Owen and I had talked about going to Paris when we were kids. But that had always just been a discussion between two dreamers who wanted to see more of the world.

He couldn't be serious, right?

"Um . . . that might be—"

"Perfect," he finished. "Not that it's going to dent my bank account at all, but you can still work on that. You better get on getting a passport, woman."

"I-I already have one. I did a quick trip to Mexico with a couple of my classmates when we finished our master's." I was still stunned that he appeared to be completely serious about this.

He let out a whoop of laughter. "Then I guess I'd better get mine."

My heart tripped. It was the first time I'd really heard him laugh like that since we'd started working together, and it sounded so damn . . .

good. "You can't be serious," I challenged. "We can't both be gone from the clinic at the same time."

He shrugged. "Of course we can. We are going to have to shut down to get some of the renovations done. The office staff will keep getting paid, though, and so will you."

"It's not that. I have a ton of vacation built up, since I haven't really gone anywhere since that long weekend in Mexico. But taking off for a week? Two weeks? All on just a whim is . . . crazy."

"Not for me, Layla. I'm filthy rich, remember? And it isn't like Andie and Noah aren't traveling the whole damn world right now on their honeymoon. Why is it so crazy?"

Really, for him, with his circumstances, it *wasn't* crazy at all. "Okay, it's insane for *me*. I'm not a billionaire, Owen. I'm a woman who never thought she'd do any international travel until her student loans were paid and she had a home of her own. Like a couple of decades from now."

My gaze collided with his, and my heart skittered as he pinned me with his sexy green-eyed stare. "You won't spend a penny on this trip. Let's get that straight right now. I'll provide every single thing you need, right down to new underwear for this trip."

Owen actually sounded excited about seeing Paris, and I wanted that for him so much. "There really isn't anyone else you'd want to take with you? What about family?"

"They all have private jets. Billionaires. Remember? Besides, there's nobody else I'd rather be with than you," he finished huskily. "We used to dream about this, Layla. If you don't go, I won't do it, either. It wouldn't be the same without you there."

Oh, hell no. *That* wasn't going to happen. This was the first time that I'd seen Owen consider using his money for something that wasn't a home investment or something he actually needed. He deserved a very long vacation after he'd spent a decade working like a dog. "I'll go," I said quickly, before I could change my mind.

A happy grin spread across his face. "I'll do all the planning. You just work on other things on my list."

I smiled back at him because I couldn't help myself. My entire body was responding to that gloriously handsome face, and I had to cross my legs as heat spread like wildfire between my thighs.

I ached to toss myself into his arms, and work on getting that incredibly ripped body completely naked.

Maybe I had wanted him when I was younger, but not like this. I'd been infatuated, and I'd wanted to be closer to him then. All I'd longed for was a simple kiss.

Now that I was an adult, I wanted this gorgeous, intelligent, thoughtful man so much that it was nearly unbearable.

My heart wanted Owen.

My body *desperately* wanted Owen.

And my soul was screaming for satisfaction.

I jerked myself back into reality. I couldn't have Owen. I was never going to be with him the way I fantasized about.

I'm going to just enjoy what we do have right now. We care about each other as dear friends. That's got to be enough.

I *was* grateful to have his friendship back, to know that he cared about me again, and that he wasn't going to punish me for the crappy things I'd said and done to him in error.

The two of us understood each other in a way that was completely uncanny, probably because we'd had a lot of the same thoughts and experiences.

I'd missed Owen so damn much.

There was no way I was going to deny myself the opportunity to be with him as he found his footing in a whole new life.

The longing I had for more was going to just have to stay hidden.

"I'll see what I can do," I finally answered.

He winked at me. "I'm looking forward to it."

CHAPTER 11

OWEN

"I think I might need some help planning this vacation," I said to Aiden and Seth a few nights later as I tossed my fishing line back into the water.

I'd brought Layla over to Seth's place for a casual hamburgers-on-the-grill impromptu dinner, and she'd hit it off with Skye and Riley almost immediately.

Eli and Jade were staying in their place in San Diego, but I was fairly certain my sister would bond with Layla the same way if she were here.

Since the ladies had gotten into what Seth termed *girl talk*, he'd grabbed a cooler filled with beer right after dinner, and we'd gone fishing.

Not that any of us really thought we were going to catch much of anything off the dock that was on the property that Seth had designated as a wildlife sanctuary.

I had a feeling it was an excuse to hang out together, have a few beers, and catch up on what was happening in our lives.

"I'm damn glad you're even taking a vacation, Owen," Seth commented as he plopped into one of the beach chairs he kept down by the dock. "I was a little concerned that you jumped right into buying the clinic after your residency. I thought you might need to take some time to relax after working so hard to get through your medical training."

I took a bottle of beer from Aiden while he was passing them out, and popped the top off. "I don't think I know how to relax," I confessed.

Aiden lifted a brow. "What do you mean?"

After weeks of holding back on my brothers about how I really felt about my new life after school, I spilled my guts to both of them, leaving very little out as I shared my confusion and my feelings of being inept at all things that weren't medically related. As we all settled into our chairs, and Seth and Aiden got their lines into the water, I finished the explanation.

"Why in the hell didn't you tell us about all this earlier?" Seth grumbled. "Dammit! I knew *something* was wrong."

"What in the hell was I supposed to say?" I asked. "It's not like I can do some poor-me-I'm-a-billionaire thing. Hell, I know I'm damn lucky. People would kill to be in my position. But it still doesn't feel right to me."

Seth glared at me. "What? Do you really think we accepted it right away? Do you think we didn't go through some of the same things you're experiencing right now? We get it, little brother. I just don't understand why you didn't bring it up a few months ago. We're here. We can help you. But we can't get you through it if you don't fucking talk to us."

I shot him a grin. "I'm twenty-eight years old now, Seth. I'm a physician. I don't have to run to my older brothers anymore for every little thing."

"Bullshit!" Aiden exclaimed loudly. "You're *always* going to be our baby brother, grown up or not. If you have a problem, it's our problem, too. Same with Jade and Brooke. Just because they're grown, that doesn't mean we aren't still protective of them. We all took care of each other growing up. That didn't just magically end once you hit eighteen. Tell us what you need."

I shrugged. "I guess what I really want to know is how in the hell you got comfortable with having an endless amount of money."

"I'm not sure any of us really got used to it all that quickly," Aiden mused. "We all went through the same guilt, sense of unworthiness, and hesitation to accept it that you're struggling with right now. I think you were just too damn busy to deal with it earlier, so you're wrestling with all that on top of all the other changes in your life."

"You'll get a lot more comfortable with time," Seth advised. "But for me, sometimes it's still kind of surreal, but in a good way. Look at Noah. He stayed disconnected from his fortune for a lot longer than we did. And now he has a private jet, and he's traveling the world. He dealt with it when he was ready."

Aiden added, "It is your money, Owen. Hard as that may be to believe, it's not going anywhere. It makes things a hell of a lot easier, and a lot more fun if you use it to do all of the things you've always wanted to do."

"I've decided that I'm going to overhaul the clinic," I informed them. "We don't have enough free and low-cost medical access around, so I want to make those services available in the community for people who don't have insurance and can't afford regular healthcare."

Seth was close enough to slap me on the back. "You've always been the most altruistic male in this family. That doesn't surprise me at all. But let us help set it up with you. You know we're all in to donate and help you with fundraising. Eli can help with all the resources you need for that, since he's pretty heavy into that kind of thing. He's helped me a lot along the way."

"Thanks," I said, grateful that I had such an amazing family. "I think I can use all the help I can get."

"So tell us about this vacation," Aiden encouraged. "I totally agree that you need some time off, Owen."

"I want to take Layla to Paris. We used to talk about traveling the world when we were kids, but of course we never really thought we'd have the funds. Not for a long time, anyway."

Aiden pulled his line in and tossed it back out once he'd checked his bait. "That's the beauty of having money. There are very few things that are out of reach for us anymore. Maybe that's the hardest part to accept, too, since almost nothing was in our reach a few years ago. Maybe it sounds weird to say it's difficult to go from rags to riches, but it takes a long time to change a mindset you've had your entire life."

"So this thing with Layla is more than a friendship?" Seth probed.

"For me, I think it is. But she still sees me as just a friend. I'd like to change all that, but I'm not sure that I can."

"Of course you can," Seth scoffed. "Be a persistent pain in the ass like I was with Riley. She'll have no choice but to give in. And I had no choice but to change Riley's mind, since I couldn't imagine living my life without her."

I didn't miss the note of complete vulnerability in Seth's voice. "Unfortunately, I wasn't around to see that," I said regretfully.

Sometimes, it was hard to look at my older brothers as simply . . . men. Noah, Seth, and Aiden had been like father figures to me, and had been bigger than life when I was a kid. I never bucked their authority because I'd hero-worshipped all three of them. They'd *never* been capable of making a mistake when I'd been seeing them through a child's eyes.

Now, I could see they were just as vulnerable and fallible as the next guy, but I'd always look up to and admire them. Even if our relationship was shifting more toward brothers than a father-son kind of relationship, all three of them were pretty damn exceptional men.

After all, they'd taken on a huge responsibility that wasn't theirs to handle, and they'd done it without a single complaint for years.

"Be grateful you *weren't* around," Aiden said dryly. "Seth was pathetic. I was grateful when Riley finally decided to take his ass on permanently. I was sick of watching him mope."

"Do we really want to get into the lunacy of being in love?" Seth asked in a warning voice. "You weren't exactly a bundle of fun to be around, either."

"That was different," Aiden grumbled. "I was a father and I never knew it."

"There was Maya," Seth agreed. "But you fucking lost it over Skye, and you know it."

As I watched my two older brothers banter back and forth, it really hit home about just how much I'd missed. Sure, I knew the whole story of what had happened with Skye, Aiden, and the child he'd never known about until years later, my incredible niece, Maya.

I also knew that Seth had inadvertently been at fault for Aiden losing his daughter for all those years.

There had to have been a hell of a lot of pain involved for both of them, but you wouldn't really know it now. The two of them still bickered like brothers, but when they really needed each other, they were steadfastly loyal.

Somehow, they'd worked everything out, and it was pretty clear to me that they were tight now.

When they finally stopped their good-natured insults, Seth turned to me. "Please don't tell me we're going to have to go through this one more time with you and Layla. Sweep the woman off her feet and don't let her say *no*, for all of our sakes."

The warm humor in Seth's voice negated his actual words. It was a comment that told me he'd be there for me, no matter what happened. As would Aiden and Noah.

"Have I ever told you guys how much I appreciate the way you all stepped up to the plate when Mom died? You didn't have to do it. Hell, you were both still minors, and Noah was just barely over the age of eighteen, but somehow you all made it work."

If my brothers *hadn't* stepped in and taken on a shitload of responsibility while they were still teenagers, I had no idea what my life would have been like growing up.

Me, Brooke, and Jade would have almost certainly ended up in foster care, and probably would have all been split up. Maybe Seth and Aiden could have become emancipated since they'd been working, but strangely, I'd never really been worried about my future back then.

My brothers had always made me and my sisters feel secure, even if they weren't.

Seth spoke up in a nonchalant voice. "We weren't about to let our family get split up. We fucked up a lot, so I'm actually surprised that you and your sisters lived through your childhoods. We were lucky. You and the girls were pretty extraordinary kids, too. Now quit changing the subject and tell us about the quickest way we can wrap this whole thing up with Layla."

I had to try hard not to laugh. All of my brothers were the same way. They didn't feel like they'd done anything that anybody else wouldn't have done in their situation. Maybe that's what really made them so damn special.

I cleared my throat. "I don't think it's going to be quite that simple," I told him. "I've actually had a thing for Layla since high school."

I went on to tell them both a shortened version of my misunderstanding with Layla, and how I'd never told her that I was interested, even in high school.

"Okay," Seth said carefully. "Even though it pisses me off that she came to that conclusion because you're my little brother, I can't say that I wouldn't have thought the same thing if I were her. Everything kind of did fit into place. It probably wasn't a great time for you to suddenly decide that you had to back off your friendship with her."

"I don't blame her, Seth. We were stupid kids. And my innocence *was* probably suspect because of the way I was trying to avoid her. I don't care about all that old stuff. I just want her to see me as the man I am now, not the buddy I was to her back then."

"Then you'll have to make her see it," Aiden instructed. "It looks like you two are dating now."

"Uh . . . not exactly," I responded.

Even though I wasn't thrilled about sharing my desperate idea with my older brothers, I spilled it anyway.

"So she thinks she's helping you learn how to date?" Aiden asked, sounding appalled at the whole idea. "Owen, a Sinclair male doesn't *need* instructions on how to woo a female. When we find the right woman, the obsession just comes naturally."

"It was kind of a ploy," I admitted. "Although I *am* pretty inept at most things nonmedical. I didn't get around much when I was in school. I was too damn busy."

"Well, you obviously know your anatomy," Seth joked. "Even the female anatomy."

I shot him a dirty look. "I'm not *that* naive."

Shit! Were my brothers really assuming I was still a virgin?

Aiden looked relieved. "Good. We never really did have that coming-of-age discussion with you."

I grinned. "Noah tried. I knew more than he did, so he just gave up."

Aiden laughed. "Now that I do believe. But I'm not sure that doing the role-playing with Layla is really a good idea. How are you supposed to convince her that you're serious if she thinks you're just messing with her?"

"I haven't figured that out yet," I confessed. "Maybe I can convince her while we're on vacation. Or maybe we'll both find out that we were better off as friends before we get to France."

Aiden lifted a brow. "You really believe that? You're a Sinclair. Generally, it only gets worse from here."

"Hell, no, I don't believe it," I answered him gruffly. "I was so damn desperate to get her away from Jax Montgomery that I concocted this whole plan on the fly. I didn't exactly think it through, which isn't like me. At all. I'm the type of guy who likes to look at things from all angles before I make a decision on anything. Sometimes, I swear my IQ drops by at least sixty points every damn time I see her. Maybe more."

Seth smirked. "Get ready, little brother, because if Layla is the woman for you, you're going to end up doing a whole lot of things that you wouldn't usually do. And don't worry about Jax. I think he's just not used to having Hudson tied up with a woman, so he's at loose ends, and maybe rethinking his man-whore ways. I'll make sure he backs off Layla, but his intentions were probably honorable . . . for once. I think he's pretty tired of one-nighters."

I started to reel my line in to check my bait since I hadn't had a single hit. "Well, the bastard can just go *experiment* elsewhere. Layla is mine. She's always been mine."

Maybe I hadn't known that, or maybe I had since high school, which was why I'd fought my feelings so hard back then.

"Yep. You're completely screwed," Seth said dryly. "I think we need to plan one hell of a vacation. Are you chartering an aircraft, or do you want to use mine? No commercial flights, even in first class. You're going to want privacy."

"I'll take you up on your offer to use yours for now," I said. Seth had gotten himself an amazing aircraft, and I had no idea what I'd get with a charter.

"Good choice," he answered approvingly. "We have time to hammer out the rest of the details. I'm sure Skye and Riley can make some suggestions about the actual romance part. Whatever Aiden and I did, it must have worked."

Maybe an hour ago, I would have objected to telling my two sisters-in-law about my predicament, but now I really didn't care.

I'd been away for ten years, but all of these people were still my family, and I was starting to feel that bond more strongly with every day that passed.

All of them had been with me in spirit during the last decade, even when we weren't *physically* together.

I'd worried about all of them, even if I *hadn't* known every detail of their lives.

My sister Brooke lived on the East Coast, and she didn't share every detail of her day-to-day life with everybody here, but it didn't matter. She and her husband, Liam, fit right into the family, just like she always had.

I guess it wasn't the physical distance, or the number of times I saw my brothers and sisters face-to-face every week.

It was all about the way we accepted and loved each other when we were together, and when we weren't.

It wasn't about the details.

It was all about the heart.

CHAPTER 12

LAYLA

"I think I'm now spoiled for life," I laughingly told Owen as we stood beside the railing of the boat he'd chartered for a sunset cruise.

Could I really call this monstrosity a "boat"? A cabin cruiser or a yacht would be more appropriate, probably. It was approximately forty feet long, and we'd eaten a fantastic catered dinner at the bow where a table and bench seats were set up for dining. After we'd finished, we'd each snagged a glass of wine and decided to enjoy the scenery.

I'd had no idea where we were going. Owen had told me to dress casually, so I'd put on a pair of white capri pants and a summery pink top to wear with sandals. We'd both showered and changed at the clinic before we'd set off to . . . where? I'd had no idea what he was planning until he'd pulled into the marina.

For the past two weeks, every day had been another adventure. On my days to choose, I liked to take Owen to do something he *couldn't and didn't* do as a kid, like playing endless arcade games, or getting the fanciest, most expensive sundae at an ice-cream shop. Those things on his list had been easy to knock out.

His days were . . . a little bit more unpredictable, and generally more exhausting than mine.

We'd spent all of last Saturday on a VIP tour of Disneyland, which gave us priority access to both rides and entertainment.

As a local, I'd been horrified when Owen had mentioned Disneyland before Labor Day. It was crowded, and all of the lines were ridiculously long, so it sucked all the fun right out of your day to stand in line in the hot sun.

He'd told me to trust him.

I had.

And we'd had an amazing day.

What I hadn't expected was to be forced to get up early on Sunday so we could get to Aquatica in San Diego, an enormous water park where Owen and I had gone flying down eighty-foot descents while I was screaming my head off the entire way down.

He rented a private cabana, so at least we'd been able to rest between the madness, and no matter how exhausted I'd been when I'd come to work on Monday morning, I'd never forget how happy Owen had been.

I'd never seen him that way before. Even when we were younger, he'd had a lot of responsibility on his shoulders, and very little to smile about.

I'd gotten in my scaled-down activities on Monday and Tuesday; Wednesday was my evening at the shelter, and now here I was, on a fancy yacht with a glass of wine, watching the sun set with Owen on a balmy Thursday evening.

He spooned in behind me, essentially trapping me in as he put both his hands on the railing. "We wouldn't want to waste a perfectly gorgeous summer night. Monday is Labor Day. Not that we're about to start dumping in temperatures in Southern California right after it's over, but I wanted you to enjoy the rest of the summer while we still had it."

I sighed and leaned back against him, my body humming in satisfaction as I felt the warmth of his muscular chest against my back.

Not once had Owen tried to kiss me, even though he'd threatened to make it part of his deal. However, he had no problem moving as close to me as he could without locking lips.

And I certainly wasn't complaining.

Little by little, Owen seemed to be getting comfortable with himself and his circumstances.

We were planning to spend the last ten days of this two-month period in Paris. I refused to look beyond that excursion. I didn't want to ruin it by focusing on what would happen at the end of this fairy-tale time with Owen.

We'd still be friends, and that was that.

"You score really big points with this whole trip," I teased him.

"So you approve?" he said in a low, husky voice beside my ear.

I shivered at the sexy timbre of his voice, and his warm breath against my ear.

Sweet Jesus! What woman *wouldn't* approve of a romantic sunset cruise with dinner, wine, *and* the hottest guy on the planet?

"Oh, major points on this idea," I answered. "I honestly don't think you needed to learn to be romantic, Owen. I think it comes naturally for you."

"When I'm with you, maybe it does," he agreed vaguely.

I had no idea what he meant by that, but my whole body nearly went up in flames, and that damn longing I'd been trying to bury had popped to the surface . . . again.

I'd been fighting my attraction to Owen, and failing miserably.

Every time I saw his handsome face, I melted, and my body started to scream for satisfaction.

I was pulled from my thoughts as I heard a commotion coming from the bow of the boat. The deckhands were waving at something, and when I looked at the captain, he was doing the same.

"Look," Owen said quietly. "Straight out from where we're standing. It's a blue whale."

He lifted his arm, and my eyes tracked to where he was pointing. Just then, a huge spray of water rose from the sea, and underneath that stream was the biggest whale I'd ever seen.

I watched in awe as it kept coming closer.

"I think he's curious," Owen commented.

"Oh, my God. It's massive. I've never seen a blue whale before." Sightings of this breed were less common because they had smaller numbers than some of the other species of whales.

"The biggest mammal ever known on Earth," Owen commented, sounding a little bit astonished, too, but his voice was calm. "I've actually never seen one, either, so it's a first for me, too. I knew how enormous they were, but it's a whole new perspective to see a live animal in the ocean that makes a full-sized bus look tiny. Looks full-sized to me. He's got to be a hundred and ninety tons and close to eighty feet."

I nodded, unable to look away from the sight of the gigantic mammal that was twice as long as the boat we were in.

It was probably capable of swamping our vessel with one small lunge, but the captain didn't look nervous as the whale swam beside us, so I didn't worry about it, either.

Tears filled my eyes as I marveled over the strength, size, and power of an animal that we'd once brought to the brink of extinction. "We nearly killed them all, but they're still alive," I whispered.

"They're still endangered," Owen said as we continued to watch the whale swim with the boat. "But at least people haven't been able to hunt them for around fifty years because they're protected. Their biggest enemy now is getting hit and killed by container ships."

"How do you know these things?" I asked teasingly.

Owen had always been able to quote a plethora of facts on just about any subject. Sometimes I swore his brain had to be overcrowded.

His low chuckle vibrated against my ear. "I have a sister who is a big proponent of the slowdown effort to get container ships to slow down in the whales' habitat. There's no way I can be related to a wildlife conservationist and not know about most endangered species. Jade isn't exactly shy about giving *everyone* her opinions on it."

I laughed at his indulgent tone. I'd just recently gotten to know Jade, Skye, and Riley better, but I did know how passionate Jade was about her job. "She'd love seeing this," I said absently. "And why do you think this one is a male?"

"It's definitely an assumption," he said genially. "Since he hasn't accommodated us by flipping onto his back, it's just a guess. He looks like an adult, but now that he's nearer, I think he's closer to seventy feet than eighty, and males are generally smaller than female blue whales."

I bumped back against him. "Well, thank you for that short marine-biology lesson, Dr. Brainiac."

I didn't intend to ask him how to tell a male from a female if a person could view the genitals of a whale, probably because I knew he'd know the answer.

I'd always had intelligent, science-based thinking, and sometimes I could challenge Owen, but not all *that* often. His recall was phenomenal and off the charts.

Some people found it a little intimidating, but not me. It was just . . . Owen.

"You know how I am about factual stuff. It just stays in my brain for some reason," he said in a slightly sheepish voice.

Which is exactly why he knows so much about so many things, and not just medicine.

"Don't ever be sorry about being smart, Owen, or having exceptional recall ability. I think it's pretty amazing," I informed him honestly.

"That's only because you're scary brilliant, too," he said amiably.

"Not really," I answered, making light of his compliment. "I have to admit there were a few times that I wished I could remember things as well as you did, but I was never jealous. I had my own talents. I didn't need yours."

We were both silent as the magnificent creature beside us started moving away.

"He's leaving," I whispered sadly. "But it was incredible that we actually saw a blue whale."

I turned as we lost sight of the animal and held out my hand. "Look. I'm actually shaking from being so close to something that exciting."

The captain sped the boat up once the whale was out of sight, and headed back toward the marina.

Owen took my hand in his as he said, "You're way too easy to please, Layla. But that was an almost unbelievable experience for me, too, I have to admit."

As the sun began to creep lower in the sky, our gazes locked and held.

Suddenly, I felt so damn vulnerable that I wanted to turn away from him, but I couldn't. My back was literally against the wall . . . or should I say the railing?

Owen's gaze was hungry, searching, and I wasn't quite sure what he was looking for, but whatever it was, I wanted to give it to him.

"These last few weeks, everything has been wonderful," I said in a shaky voice.

This man got to me with a single look, and sometimes I felt like he could see right through me and into my damn soul.

It was as frightening as it was exciting.

I'd never connected on this level with anybody else.

Only him.

Only Owen.

My heart skittered as he moved closer and wrapped his arms around me, letting me see what it felt like to be as close to him as possible without . . .

Oh, sweet Jesus! He's going to kiss me.

"If you want me to back off, you better say something right fucking now," Owen growled as he lowered his head.

I trembled at his demanding tone, but I wasn't afraid. I was ripe with anticipation.

Was it wise to let him kiss me?

Probably not.

But I'd be damned if I didn't get a taste of Owen *right fucking now*.

I didn't say a word. I reached up, wrapped my arms around his neck, and jerked his lips to mine because I couldn't wait another damn second.

CHAPTER 13

LAYLA

Owen took control of the passionate embrace almost instantly.

And I melted down in a nanosecond.

It wasn't the sweet embrace I'd coveted as a senior in high school.

It was raw.

It was real.

And I was completely lost to the man who ravaged my mouth like he needed it to stay alive.

I opened to him like I had to have him, too, which I did. I moaned against his lips as I threaded my fingers through his hair and savored the feel of the coarse strands sliding between them as I fisted those gorgeous locks.

The kiss seemed never-ending, and I didn't want it to stop.

I whimpered as Owen backed off enough to nibble on my lower lip, allowing us both to take a breath before he covered my mouth again.

The touch of his lips was completely carnal, sensuous, and earthy. I wouldn't have wanted it any other way. Something sweet or gentle wouldn't have satisfied the craving for him that was eating me up inside.

"Owen," I whispered desperately as he finally released my mouth.

"Jesus, Layla. You're killing me," he rasped as he put his hand in my hair, pulled my head back, and started to devour the sensitive skin on my neck. "But it's not like I can fuck you right here on this deck."

He sounded profoundly disappointed about that, which made my pulse race even faster than it already was from his almost animalistic kiss.

I wanted Owen naked so I could climb up his gorgeous body and do every forbidden thing I could think of with him.

He made me want to indulge in a no-holds-barred, hot, steamy, screaming-orgasm kind of sex that I'd never experienced before.

"Son of a bitch!" he cursed as he wrapped his arms around me and just held me. "There isn't a single damn thing that I want more right now than to make you come, Layla. But I don't want or need an audience."

Tremors of frustrated lust ran through my entire body as I just held on to Owen, my arms wrapped tightly around his neck. I rested my head against his shoulder as I panted, trying to get my heart rate and breathing under control.

"I knew kissing you was going to be dangerous," he grumbled.

"Why?" I asked breathlessly.

"Because I want you way too much," he said in a raw tone as he stroked a calming hand over my hair. "This isn't pretend for me, Layla."

My heart tripped, but I knew it was just lust talking.

Owen and I had some crazy chemistry between us, and it was definitely genuine. "It wasn't fake for me, either, Owen. We really are attracted to each other."

"Fuck! Did you just figure that out? I've wanted to get you naked since the first time I saw you in the clinic. I just didn't think you felt the same way."

I disentangled myself from his arms, and stepped away to get myself together.

"We can't do this again," I said desperately. "That was the deal. No sex. I got caught up in the moment, and I'm . . . sorry."

Owen raked a hand through his hair as he stared at me with a thousand questions in his gaze. "Why can't we? We're both single. We're already friends."

I shook my head. "I can't, Owen. I'm sorry."

I wasn't a casual-sex kind of woman. I'd discovered that a long time ago. And nothing about becoming intimate with Owen would ever be *casual*.

It would be messy.

My emotions would become involved.

And I'd be screwed.

Not a single moment with Owen would be halfway, or easygoing.

For a moment, I kind of wished I *was* the kind of woman who could just have a hot fling, but it wasn't in me.

Not with him. *Not* with Owen.

I'd fall, topple completely in love with this man, and hitting bottom would be *excruciatingly* painful.

"It wasn't a good idea to get that hot and heavy," I explained in a forced calm tone. "This was all supposed to be a learning thing for us, Owen. An experiment. We just went a little too far."

Owen reached out and snagged my upper arm. "Is that really all it was for you, Layla?" he said, his tone angry now. "What in the hell are you running away from right now? Is it me? Did I scare you? Was I moving too fast? Just tell me what the hell it is, and I'll fix it. But don't back away from me."

Before I could answer, the vessel came to a stop.

We were docked in the marina, and neither of us had even noticed that we were pulling into port.

We thanked the captain and the crew, and I saw Owen slip them all a very generous tip before we disembarked.

He was silent as he opened the passenger door of his BMW, and then closed it once I slid inside.

I'd teased him just a little about his choice of vehicles, since he could afford the most expensive sports car out there.

He'd answered by telling me pricey vanity vehicles were a crappy investment.

I turned my head toward the window as I felt a tear plop onto my cheek.

I can't let him see me cry.

I swiped it away as he opened the driver's-side door, and I took several deep breaths to try to calm my nerves while I secured my seat belt.

"We have to talk about this, Layla," he said in a somber tone as he buckled his own seat belt and turned on the engine.

I suddenly realized that I'd hurt him. I could hear it in his voice. He wasn't just sexually frustrated; he was injured by the way I'd backed off.

"It's not you, Owen. It's me," I said, desperate to make him understand that nothing he'd done had scared me.

At that moment, I came so damn close to just telling him everything. I wanted to let it all out, tell him about every damn fear I'd ever had. What my life had been like as a kid, and what I'd hidden from him. And how I'd screwed up everything on my own after that.

Problem was, Owen didn't know that side of me, and I didn't really want him to see it.

He'd be disappointed, and *that* would kill me.

"Whether it's you or me, *something* is bothering you. I want to know what's eating at you. I can't fix it if you won't talk to me," he told me. "What in the hell could be so bad that you can't talk to me about it?"

Oh, Owen, you have no idea.

"If you can't leave this alone, we need to call this whole bargain off," I insisted, feeling desperate to drop the subject before I said some things I could never take back.

"Oh, no. That's not happening. I'll let you pick exactly when you want to get real and tell me everything that you never did when we were kids. But I'm not letting you walk away, Layla. Not after what just happened. I know damn well that you want me as much as I want you," he said coolly.

"I told you that it isn't you. There are things you don't know about me, Owen. Things I've never shared because I couldn't. Can't you just accept that some things are too deeply personal to talk about?" My eyes welled up with tears, and I finally just let them fall because it was dark in the vehicle.

"Yes," he said reasonably. "I *could* accept that if I didn't feel like it was eating you up inside. If it wasn't something that was affecting your life right now. But it is. So no, I'm damn well not going to accept it. I'm just going to wait until you're ready, because that's what people do when they care about each other."

I had to bite my lip so the huge sob in my chest didn't escape.

Maybe he did care about me now, but I was doubtful that he would when he found out about my past, and all the mistakes I'd made.

Better not to tell.

I listened to that annoying voice in my head, and we didn't speak until Owen pulled up to my apartment building. "I'll pick you up tomorrow morning," he said brusquely.

Since my vehicle was still at the clinic, I'd need that ride. "Okay. Thanks."

"I hate that you still live in this part of town," he rumbled. "I'll wait until you turn the light on."

A sigh escaped my lips as I released my seat belt and climbed out of the car.

Some things would probably never change. Owen was still as protective as he'd always been, and—dammit!—it still warmed my heart.

It wasn't really a bad neighborhood.

Okay, maybe it did have a higher crime rate than the beachfront area, but it was, for the most part, a middle-class neighborhood.

"I'll be fine," I said as I stood and put my hand on the door.

"You always say that. Maybe *that's* the problem, Layla. You're too damn good at convincing yourself that you don't need anyone," he replied in a disappointed tone.

God, I *hated* that particular voice.

It will sound a lot worse if you tell him.

"Good night," I told him in a jittery voice, and then quickly closed the door of the vehicle.

I knew he was waiting, so I jogged up the stairs instead of waiting for the outdoor elevator.

My actions felt so familiar, and it reminded me of every time that Owen had waited for me to turn the light on when we were teenagers.

I opened my apartment door quickly, and my hand flew to the switch before I closed and locked the door behind me.

My duty done, I slid down the door, plopped my ass on the tile, and finally allowed myself to really cry.

CHAPTER 14

LAYLA

Dark: Haven't heard from you for a while, Dreamer. Everything okay?

I'd been sitting on my bed in my pajamas reading email when I'd noticed that Dark had sent me a message on the Not-Just-A-Hookup app.

We hadn't talked in a while. Owen had kept me so busy that I hadn't really had time to talk.

Then again, Dark hadn't messaged me, either, until today.

Me: You've been a stranger, too. I'm okay. How about you?

Dark: I'm good. Everything work out okay with the boss?

I sighed. Maybe I never should have told him about that.

Me: Yes and no. Long story. He isn't the jerk I thought he was. I misjudged him, and I felt pretty bad about it.

Dark: Don't beat yourself up over it, Dreamer. I'm sure you apologized, right?

Me: I did. But it didn't feel like enough to me.

Dark: What's wrong? You don't sound like your usual chipper self tonight.

Did I really want to talk to Dark about everything? No, I didn't, but maybe I could be really general . . .

Me: Have you ever cared about somebody so much that you never want them to know about the bad things you've done in your life?

Dark: You're going to have to give me more info than that, Dreamer. I could take that a million different ways. I know we don't do specifics, but a little more insight would help.

Me: I've done some bad things, and made stupid mistakes. I have a friend who only sees the good things in me. Is it weird that I don't want that person to know that I'm not as sensible or as smart as they think I am?

Dark: Weird? Probably not. But I think if I cared about somebody, I wouldn't want them to ever think I was perfect. I think I'd want them to see all sides of me, not just the good ones, and then have them choose to like me anyway.

He was probably right, but I wasn't talking about little annoying things.

Me: What if I fess up and this person is disgusted and appalled?

Dark: Then they weren't worthy of your friendship anyway. Everybody has some kind of skeletons in their closet, Dreamer. Just be brave enough to tell them about yours, and let them decide if they can accept them. If they don't, screw them. Maybe I don't know you all that well, but I have a hard time believing your mistakes are any worse than mine. Mass murderer?

I laughed out loud.

Me: Nope.

Dark: Child abuser?

Me: Never!

Dark: Animal abuser?

Me: I'm an animal lover.

Dark: Okay. Then you're good. Anything else is completely forgivable.

I grinned, feeling a little more upbeat than I had a few minutes ago. I knew he was jokingly trying to put things into perspective. And he did. A little.

Me: Do you have skeletons in your closet?

Dark: Believe me, Dreamer, you don't want to know the answer to that question. I told you that we all have them.

Me: That bad?

Dark: Let's just say that I bet your closet isn't as full as mine.

Me: So you haven't found anybody that can totally accept yours?

Dark: I don't talk about it. It's easier that way.

Really? So why had he told *me* to take a chance?

Me: Then you aren't following your own advice.

Dark: I'm not saying I wouldn't if I found somebody I actually trusted. The desire to spill my guts has just never happened.

I had to wonder what in the world Dark was doing on this dating app. I sensed that he knew I was talking about a guy, but he didn't seem to care.

I'd suspected that he wasn't really interested in meeting the woman of his dreams online, but he was always so willing to help or just listen to me.

He had no idea what I looked like, and he only had my approximate age. I guess we'd never really thought about exchanging pictures because neither one of us cared what the other one looked like.

Me: Have you ever even thought about telling anyone?

Dark: Never. I'm not exactly a trusting soul, Dreamer. Or maybe I'm just an asshole.

He wasn't. I could sense it.

Me: You're not. I like you, and I'm not exactly fond of assholes. You've always been nice to me.

Dark: You've only seen the cyber side of me. I think we both know this isn't real life.

Me: I don't care. Until you act like an asshole, you're going to be a friend.

Dark: I think I'll take you up on the friendship offer, and try hard not to disappoint you.

Me: You haven't yet. Thanks for listening.

Dark: I'll always be around if you need anything. If you want to talk to me, I'm only a message away.

It sounded like he was backing away, but that was okay. Technically, I was fake dating Owen. So maybe it was better that way.

Me: I'll be here if you ever want to talk, too. Night, Dark.

Dark: Sleep well, Dreamer.

I waited for one of his cocky sign-offs, but it never came, so I finally dropped my cell onto the bedside table and turned off the light.

There was some comfort in knowing that Dark would answer me if I ever really needed to chat. It had been a while since I could really talk to somebody who had been willing to accept me, skeletons and all. Honestly, he was probably the only friend who ever had.

Okay, maybe Owen would, too. If only I could take Dark's advice and shed some light on the darkness of my past, but I didn't see that happening anytime soon.

CHAPTER 15

OWEN

Everything changed for Layla and me after that outrageously passionate kiss.

Three weeks later, I was *still* waiting for her to talk, but the woman had a pretty solid zipper on her mouth when it came to talking about anything really personal.

I didn't like the way she'd clammed up on me, but I didn't want her to shut me off completely. So I'd just dealt with the friendship relationship, hoping she'd eventually trust me enough to talk about her past.

I hadn't kissed her again during the last few weeks. Okay, maybe I *had* snuck in a few random touches, a hand on her back to guide her into a restaurant, or holding her hand when I could get away with doing it. Unfortunately, those things had been more like torture than a relief, but it was impossible for me to be with Layla and *not* try to find some kind of connection.

The damn obsession my older brothers had warned me about was hitting me full force now, and I was about to lose my mind.

Somehow, things needed to change between Layla and me, and I couldn't take much more of the whole polite, superficial, bullshit discussions between the two of us.

Layla and I were meant to be together. Period. No question about it.

It had just taken forever for me to see that with as much startling clarity as I did now.

I put a pod into my coffeemaker and slammed the lid down, watching the machine slowly fill the ceramic cup as I fervently hoped that the night I had arranged would lead to some kind of understanding.

Paris was completely planned, and the trip wasn't very far away. If I *couldn't* get her to talk to me, I knew in my gut that I'd end up losing the entire battle once that excursion was over.

To give her credit, she'd stubbornly stuck with her plan to finish everything on my list, whether she wanted to be with me . . . or not.

Layla never broke a promise, and she hadn't this time, either.

I'd behaved myself.

And she'd kept right on diligently checking things off the list.

I pulled the full coffee mug from the machine, smiling at the memory of the day Layla had talked me into buying it.

"Wouldn't it be nice to try something different every day?" she'd cajoled.

I'd never really thought about it before. I liked coffee. Period. I'd been fine with my regular coffeemaker.

But since she'd suggested it, I'd readily handed the clerk my debit card, and then trailed along after Layla's beautiful ass to pick a variety of coffee pods.

Turns out, she was right. It was interesting to have a different brew every day. Eventually, I'd find my favorites and stick with them, but until then, I was trying every damn flavor on the market.

And the best thing about the fancy coffeemaker? Layla loved it, too, because it made chai tea, hot apple cider, and hot chocolate. Since I'd realized *that*, I made damn sure I was always well stocked.

"Jesus! I *am* becoming a lunatic," I griped aloud after I'd taken my first sip of a Krispy Kreme Doughnut blend. "Holy hell, this one is good," I mused. "I think it's a keeper."

Note to self: Buy more pods for this particular coffee.

Once I'd inserted that data, I knew I'd remember it the next time I shopped for coffee pods.

The useless data would come out at the right time.

It always did.

I almost spilled my coffee down the front of my button-down shirt when my cell phone buzzed loudly from the spot where I'd dropped it a while ago.

"Shit!" I cursed as I narrowly escaped another stain as I tried to stabilize the mug.

I'd put the ringer on full blast now that my admitting privileges had been approved at the local medical center and I had patients in the hospital under my care.

Granted, I didn't have the kind of workload that I'd had during my residency in Boston, but I never wanted to miss or delay a call if one of my patients needed something.

I put my coffee on the island and grabbed my cell.

It wasn't the hospital.

It's Layla. Where in the hell is she?

I answered. "You should be in my driveway by now," I told her.

"I'm not having a very good day, Owen. Do you mind if we skip tonight's plans?"

She sounded completely deflated, and my heart clenched as I heard the sad inflection in her voice.

Oh, hell no. We weren't canceling. She never really had a bad day, so she wasn't going through this one alone. "Where are you?"

"I'm not far away, but I was just thinking about turning around. I don't think I'm going to be very good company tonight," she said with a tremor in her tone.

"Don't you dare turn around. Keep that ugly little compact vehicle you drive headed straight here," I demanded. "What happened? Is it one of our patients?"

Layla had finished with her last appointment before I had, so she'd taken the responsibility of doing hospital rounds after work. Since we only had a few clinic patients in the hospital, and none of them were critical, I had no damn idea what had upset her so much.

"It's not that. It's nothing like that. Our patients are all fine," she said, sounding like she wanted to cry. "Once I finished rounds, I went by the shelter. Brutus is . . . gone."

Son of a bitch! "I thought you weren't volunteering until *tomorrow*."

"I switched days," she said. "One of the volunteers had a conflict, so I took her place. I knew I'd still have time to get home and clean up to come for dinner at your place. God, I know I'm not supposed to be this upset about him being adopted, but I'm going to miss him so much."

"Don't turn around," I told her sternly. "Just get here. Now."

"Do you really want to spend the evening with a depressing, brokenhearted woman tonight? I'll probably feel better tomorrow. I think it was a shock to not see him there when I arrived tonight."

Happy or sad, *of course* I wanted to be with her. Didn't she know that? Hell, I *wanted* to be the guy she ran to when something was wrong. I wanted to be there to fix it, or just be there to hold her until she felt better. I wanted to listen, and be her sounding board. "If nothing else, I *am* your friend, Layla. I want to be there for you."

She sniffled a little before answering, "Okay. But don't say I didn't warn you."

"I definitely won't," I assured her. "How far out are you?"

"I'll be there in five minutes. I went home to shower and change before I headed your direction. I'll see you in just a few."

"Drive safe," I insisted before we hung up, not wanting her to be so distracted that she had a damn accident.

We disconnected after she assured me she was all right.

I dropped my phone on the island again, picked up my coffee, and went to flop onto my living-room couch.

"I fucked this one up big-time, buddy," I shared with the bulldog that had made himself at home on his new fluffy dog bed on my living-room rug. "She wasn't supposed to go to that damn shelter until *tomorrow.*"

Obviously, the animal shelter hadn't released the information about exactly *who* had adopted Brutus.

I'd probably been picking him up while Layla had still been doing rounds.

I grinned as the animal lifted his head and appeared to glare at me in disapproval.

"Okay, okay. Maybe I *should* have told her, but it was supposed to be a damn surprise. Since she couldn't take you home, I decided the next-best thing was for you to be here, where she could see you all the time."

Seemingly mollified, the beast dropped his head between his paws again, but he continued to watch me carefully.

"Jesus! Am I really having a one-way conversation with a dog?" I asked myself, thoroughly disgusted.

I had to admit that Brutus *was* growing on me already. All he needed to make him happy was a little love, and one of those beef-and-cheese treats I'd bought from the pet store when I'd gone for supplies.

Although I *was* starting to rethink those treats. Brutus had started to fart like a champion once he'd eaten the first one.

"Right. So you've obviously got a sensitive digestive system," I informed him. "I'm prescribing a good probiotic, a high-quality limited-ingredient diet, and treats with no lactose or fillers," I said in my best no-nonsense doctor voice. "Allergy testing, too. I'll look into that."

Maybe I wasn't a veterinarian, but I could certainly recognize a gassy disorder, even in a dog. Gas was gas, whether it was coming from a human or any other mammal.

I took a slug of my coffee, wishing I had more experience as a dog owner.

It wasn't that I didn't *like* animals, but we'd barely been able to feed the human mouths in our home growing up, so adding some canine ones to feed as well had been impossible.

I knew it had killed Noah not to be able to give Jade a puppy or a kitten, since she'd pretty much been wild about *any* four-legged creature.

I'd hardly been home long enough to sleep while I was in school, so the thought of having an animal to care for hadn't even entered my mind, and I hadn't had the extra money to feed a dog, anyway.

Now that I was capable of providing any kind of care Brutus needed, I felt comfortable about having him around. I just wasn't sure what to do with him.

He didn't look like he was interested in any of the dog toys I'd purchased, and he wasn't exactly an energetic canine.

I watched as the bulldog slowly rose, walked over to me, and promptly flopped down at my feet. He put his head on top of my foot, and then began to snore moments later.

I wondered if this was his way of thanking me for taking him out of that chaotic shelter environment, or if he just . . . liked me.

I reached my hand down to scratch his head, wishing humans could be as trusting and uncomplicated as Brutus.

CHAPTER 16

LAYLA

I swiped a tear from my cheek right after I'd pulled into Owen's driveway and turned off the motor.

Maybe it wasn't wise that I'd continued on to Owen's house after I'd talked to him.

I was feeling emotional, and that probably wasn't a good state of mind for me to be in when I was around him.

The truth was, I *had* wanted to see him, even though I was feeling sad. He was the one person who would almost always understand, and if he didn't get the reason that I was upset, he'd stubbornly keep trying.

Owen makes me . . . happy.

Maybe I wasn't always willing to admit that to myself, but right now, I was really tired of telling myself that Owen was nothing but a friend.

We connected on a level beyond friendship, beyond anything I'd ever experienced before or probably ever would.

Dammit! I knew this would happen! I knew I'd fall hard for him.

And I *had* fallen, regardless of the fact that Owen and I had conformed to an unspoken rule not to get too physically close again.

I was in love with the stubborn man, whether I wanted to admit it to myself or not.

Every part of my soul was demanding that I reach out for what I wanted.

I grabbed my cell phone from the seat, hesitating a moment to open my Not-Just-A-Hookup app and read the last words I'd gotten from Dark almost a week ago.

We still only talked in generalizations, and we'd only checked in with each other briefly a few times, but for some reason, his words spoke to me like he knew me.

But that's impossible, right? He doesn't know me.

Once or twice, I'd actually convinced myself that I was talking to Owen, but then I'd discounted the whole idea. What were the chances that he and I would find each other on a program being tested out all over the country?

I looked at Dark's last comment.

Dark: Don't sell yourself short, Dreamer. Whatever happened, whatever you did, it's past history. You're a woman any guy would be lucky to have. Don't judge yourself by the past. You aren't that person anymore. Give yourself kudos for coming so far instead of looking at all of the things you might have screwed up in the past.

I sighed as I clicked out of the app again.

Dark was right. I *wasn't* the person I'd been years ago. Not even close. Yet I was still blaming myself, and continuing to be ashamed of what I'd done a long time ago.

I thought I'd gotten over all that, until I'd seen Owen again.

Now, it would kill me to see a disappointed look on his face when he turned that sexy green-eyed gaze in my direction.

I lowered the visor and swiped at the little streaks of mascara that had melted onto my cheeks when I'd cried out all my sorrow about never seeing Brutus again.

Smudge-proof mascara my ass!

The one time I'd tested my makeup, it had failed me.

I quickly slammed the mirrored sun shield back up and opened the car door.

"God, it's warm," I said with a groan as I exited my car, which was also known by Owen as my *ugly little compact vehicle.*

I smirked as I grabbed my phone and shoved it into my purse before I closed the door.

Soon after I'd started teasing him about choosing a BMW when he could own any car in the world, he'd started to give me hell about my *ugly little compact vehicle.*

Okay, so maybe it hadn't been the most attractive car on the lot when I'd chosen it last year, and the orange shade was a little off-putting. But I knew that was why I'd gotten a good deal on it, and the gas mileage was fantastic.

Apparently, I didn't give a damn about vanity cars, either. It got me safely to any place I wanted to go, on very little gasoline.

I pushed the Lock button as I moved toward Owen's front door, trying to boost my mood before he saw me.

Brutus will be so much happier in a new home. He won't have to be crated anymore. And he'll have people around to love him all the time.

I'd done this attempted cheer-up on myself about a thousand times now, and I *was* glad that Brutus was going to have a real home.

Unfortunately, those facts did nothing to ease the pain of not seeing my buddy every time I went to the shelter.

I loved all the animals there, but Brutus was special.

I'd bonded hard with him from the very beginning, and if there had been any possible way I could have taken him home, I would have done it a long time ago.

I'll be fine. It isn't the first time I've taken an animal into my heart and watched that four-legged creature be adopted out.

That sorrow was part of volunteering for a shelter.

Animals came.

Animals went away.

But knowing that an animal was going to a good home usually overshadowed the sadness.

Almost always.

Except for this time.

I rang the doorbell and waited for Owen to answer.

Brutus had stayed at the shelter for too long, and I'd gotten too attached.

At least somebody other than me could see all of Brutus's good qualities.

Unfortunately, the director had been pretty closemouthed about Brutus's new owner.

The front door opened abruptly, and I took one look at Owen's concerned face before I crumbled. I stepped into the foyer and let him close the door behind me before I flung myself into his arms.

My grip around his neck was probably more like a stranglehold, but he didn't complain as he immediately wrapped his arms around me.

"What if he didn't go to a good family?" I sobbed. "He's been through way too much to be able to handle getting treated badly or being neglected all over again."

Poor Brutus had suffered things that no dog should ever have to experience. Ever!

"Hey, Layla. Stop," Owen crooned in a soothing voice as he stroked my back in a comforting motion. "I have a surprise for you."

I tried to get a grip. I'm sure the last thing Owen had expected was a sobbing, hysterical female rushing through his door.

He probably didn't know that I was even capable of losing it. I'd made damn sure he never saw me cry.

I let myself bask in the warmth and security of his powerful body for a moment, savoring his masculine, unique scent.

"Not that I mind having your gorgeous body plastered against me," he said, finally breaking the silence. "But I have something that will ease your mind."

I took a deep breath and pulled away from him so I could see his face. "What?"

Owen pointed toward the living room just beyond the foyer. "Him."

I let out an audible gasp as I saw the wrinkled, stout canine body wiggling around with excitement.

Brutus let out a happy whine as I exclaimed, "Oh, my God! Brutus? What are you doing here?"

I rushed to the ecstatic dog, dropped to my knees, and pulled him onto my lap as I wrapped my arms around him. I buried my face in his short, fine coat. "I thought I'd never see you again, buddy," I said tearfully as I hugged him.

I looked up at Owen in question. "Why is he here?"

He sat down beside me as he answered, "I'm sorry, Layla. I didn't know you were going to the shelter today or I never would have kept the fact that I was adopting him from you. I meant for it to be a happy surprise, but instead it ended up being traumatic for you. Brutus is going to be living with me now. Since you couldn't have him in your apartment, I decided him being here would be the next-best thing. You'll be able to see him whenever you want, and make sure he's okay anytime you want."

My mouth was still hanging open as he tried to explain his reasoning.

Bottom line? Owen had adopted Brutus to make *me* happy.

He'd done it because he knew I wanted to but couldn't.

Tired of being squeezed half to death, Brutus squirmed out of my grasp and flopped down next to me. I kept stroking his head as he rested it on my thigh.

"I think you have to be the most amazing guy I've ever known," I said, my voice quivering with emotion. "You did this for me. It was all about me."

He shot me that grin that immediately made me want to get him naked as he answered, "I have no idea when you're going to figure out that there's nothing I *won't* do for you."

His words reached right into my heart, and squeezed it so tightly I could barely breathe.

Maybe he'd said those words to me before, or had he just tried to show me how much he cared with his actions?

I'd probably been so tied up in my own insecurities that I'd just never really noticed that the man right in front of me was willing to give me anything.

I'd never even had to ask.

"Owen," I whispered as our eyes locked, and the whole damn world seemed to stand still as the vise grip around my heart got tighter and tighter.

Every ounce of my flesh, my heart, and my soul yearned for this man, yet I couldn't quite get the words out of my mouth.

Instead, I mumbled, "I can't believe you did all this for me."

He shrugged. "It's not like it's really a big deal. Brutus and I like each other, and I can certainly afford doggie daycare and anything else he might need."

"No. Don't act like this isn't a big deal," I told him as tears poured down my face. I let them fall. I didn't care anymore if Owen saw how much his actions meant to me. "It's a *very big* deal. You're the one who will have to take care of him while I just get the fun part."

Owen shook his head. "Nah. He's easy. Once I can resolve his farting issue, we'll have it made together."

Even though my face was still wet with tears, I started to laugh. "They don't call bulldogs the kings of farting in the doggie world for nothing."

He nodded. "I get it. My boy can clear a room in less than ten seconds. I guess that skill could be handy if I have unwanted company, but I think I'd rather get his gut straightened out. I think I'll take him in to the vet and see if they can do allergy testing, so I know what kind of food to get him on. I'm thinking a really good probiotic, too. I'll have to research—"

"I can help you with that," I interrupted, knowing Owen would probably dig into the research nonstop until he knew Brutus was getting the best doggie probiotic out there. "I know a really good one. I've been looking into them so that I could donate them to the shelter for Brutus."

"Of course you have," Owen said with a grin as he reached into the pocket of his jeans. "I have something else for you."

I sighed. Brutus had been more than enough of a surprise for one day.

One more, and I couldn't guarantee that Owen wouldn't completely unravel me.

CHAPTER 17

Owen

I'd never seen Layla wear a nice piece of jewelry. Ever.

In high school, when most girls had their ears pierced and were wearing some kind of earrings, Layla hadn't.

Since then, she'd obviously gotten her ears pierced, and she wore all kinds of funky, dangly earrings, but it was obviously cheap costume jewelry. I knew this because I'd never seen her freak out about losing an earring, and she'd done it twice while we'd been out doing various activities. She'd simply shrugged and said she could pick up another pair at the dollar store.

I guess her not having anything struck me as odd because, as poor as my family had been, my brothers and I had always pitched in to get my sisters something on special occasions, like their graduations and their sixteenth birthdays. Maybe those lockets and bracelets hadn't been dripping with gold and diamonds, but they'd always been a little more special than dollar-store necklaces or earrings.

Why had Layla never had *anyone* to get her some kind of trinket? To this day, I'd never seen her wear anything except dollar-store earrings.

I handed her the box. "I hope you like it."

I watched her stare at the red-velvet and gold box for a moment like it was a snake that was going to envenomate her.

"What is it?" she asked in a timid voice that I'd never heard from Layla before.

I released a pent-up breath when she took it.

"It's just a gift. No strings attached. I just wanted you to have it. I guess you could call it a . . . memento."

I crossed my legs and watched her face as she popped open the box, hoping I hadn't made a mistake.

What if she didn't really want to remember that particular day? At all.

"Please tell me this isn't real," she said in a rush. "It's a Mia Hamilton box."

I nodded, knowing she was looking at the fancy gold script underneath the top of the box. It wasn't like she could miss it. The writing on the red velvet boldly declared the work *A Mia Hamilton Original.* "It's real. Did you really think I'd give you something that wasn't authentic in a Mia Hamilton box? I'd have to be a total dick, since I definitely have the money for the real thing."

"How is this even possible?" she said breathlessly as she continued to gawk at the branding. "Her stuff is really exclusive and really, really expensive. Most people can't get one, even if they can afford it."

I knew people were clamoring to get an original from Mia, which was why my first gift to Layla had to be a Mia Hamilton. Hell, she'd waited long enough. Her first jewelry gift needed to be special.

"Eli is acquainted with Max Hamilton," I explained. I'd been ecstatic when I'd found out that Eli had actually rubbed elbows and worked on some charity projects with Mia's billionaire husband. "He introduced me so I could ask Mia to do this piece for me."

The necklace was unique, and that was probably what I liked best about getting this from Mia Hamilton.

Once I'd explained to Mia that I desperately needed it for a woman who was twenty-eight years old and had never had a real piece of jewelry, she'd caved in pretty fast. The woman definitely didn't need the money, but she had a good heart.

Layla's face turned ghost white as she gingerly lifted the necklace from its bed of red velvet.

"Oh, my God!" she said, sounding like every ounce of air had *whooshed* out of her lungs along with those words.

I wasn't quite sure whether that was a good "Oh, my God!" or a bad one, but I was sincerely hoping it was the former.

"Breathe, Layla. It's not going to bite you. It's just a piece of jewelry."

I had to admit, Mia had done an incredible job, and I could see why her jewelry was so sought after and coveted.

Even the platinum chain had been carefully encrusted with tiny diamonds, so it sparkled in the light, but not nearly as much as the artisan blue whale at the end of the pendant.

Layla put a hesitant finger to the tiny whale. "Are . . ." She coughed and tried again. "Are these sapphires?"

"No," I explained. "They're blue diamonds. They're kind of rare, so Mia wasn't sure how long it would take her to get them, but she came through. I wanted you to have this before we left for Paris, but Mia was insistent about not using sapphires. She said the whale wouldn't be as lifelike without blue diamonds."

"It's incredible," Layla said, still sounding like she'd been mesmerized by the gems. "It's almost exactly the same color as the blue whale we saw. I didn't even know that blue diamonds existed."

"They only exist in a couple of mines in Australia, South Africa, and India," I said.

I stopped myself from explaining that the mesmerizing blue color came from traces of boron in the carbon composition of the diamonds.

Layla looked like she needed resuscitation more than she needed geological information.

"Owen, this gift is way too dear to give to me. I don't think I even want to know how much it cost."

"Layla, I'm a billionaire. It doesn't really matter how much it cost. And it wasn't my purpose to make it the most expensive jewelry money can buy. I just wanted it to be special. I wanted you to be able to see it around your neck every day and remember how incredible that experience was for both of us. And fuck yes! I wanted you to think about the guy who gave it to you every damn time you felt it against your skin or saw it in a mirror. Look, it's not exactly something I can take back or return at a department-store counter. So you're just going to have to find a way to accept it, whether you like it or not. It would mean nothing to anyone else."

Her head jerked up, like she'd awakened from her trance, and she pinned me with those beautiful baby blues that were so full of emotion that I couldn't decipher all she was thinking.

"Owen, are you under some kind of assumption that I *don't* like it? God, it's probably the most beautiful thing I've ever seen. Do you know I've never had a single person give me any kind of jewelry? Honestly, I've had so few gifts in my life that I can count them on one hand. And now this . . . It's a little much to take in for a woman like me. It's incredibly thoughtful. And generous. But I've never owned something this nice."

Well, okay, then. I guess I could deal with that explanation. If she liked it, she could get used to wearing it. "Do you want me to put it on?"

She looked so torn that I simply reached out and snatched the pendant from her, put it around her swan-like neck, and fastened the catch.

"Does it have a safety lock?" she said, sounding half-panicked.

"Yes. I fastened it. Layla, that sucker isn't coming off. Mia makes high-quality jewelry. She knows how to keep it around a woman's neck," I assured her.

"It looks good on you," I added once I'd leaned back to have a look.

"Seriously, Owen? A Mia Hamilton piece doesn't just 'look good.' It looks absolutely spectacular. I've never seen her work in person, but

I've seen pictures. I'm so flabbergasted right now that I'm not even sure how to thank you."

I could think of any number of ways she could thank me, but they involved the two of us being naked and sweaty. "Then don't thank me. I wanted to do it."

She looked at me with suspicion in her eyes. "How did you know?"

I lifted a brow. "What?"

"How did you know that I'd never gotten a single piece of jewelry?"

"Maybe because you never wear any?" I suggested. "Except for your dollar-store earrings. In high school, you didn't even have your ears pierced."

She put a hand to her throat and stroked it over the blue diamonds. "Maybe one of the most touching things about this gift is the fact that you noticed that. Honestly, I think I would have been devastated if you'd taken it back, even though I wasn't sure how to accept it. I'd never want you to think I didn't love something that you put this much thought and effort into for me. But I know it was expensive, and it's a really big gift for a woman who has rarely had any gifts at all."

Most other women would have easily accepted that jewelry and more, and it killed me that Layla apparently didn't feel like *she* deserved it.

I made a mental note to myself to buy her gifts more often until she could take them in stride.

Where in the hell had her parents been all these years? I knew she was left to her own devices a lot, but hadn't they bought her birthday presents? Christmas gifts? Anything?

"I'm sorry, Layla. I'm sorry for every damn gift you didn't get as a kid, and as an adult," I said huskily, wishing I could erase whatever had happened in her past and fill it with everything she should have had.

How had such an incredible woman come out of what I suspected had been a pretty joyless childhood?

I got up and pulled her to her feet. When she collided with my body as she came up, I could barely stifle a groan.

"I'm sorry," she said as she stumbled to her feet. "Did I hurt you?"

I couldn't tell her that it hurt every time I looked at her but couldn't touch her. In fact, it was fucking agony. "No. I'm good. Let me put the burgers on the grill."

"Wait!" she entreated. "I want to figure out how to thank you for the most thoughtful gift anyone has ever given me."

Just hearing her say that was more than enough thanks for me, but I turned my head and pointed to my cheek. "Thank me here," I suggested.

Her smile lit up the entire room as she moved forward, put her hands on my upper arms, and planted a lingering kiss on my cheek.

"Thank you, Owen," she murmured in a husky, sexy alto that made me want to hear *that voice* thanking me for making her come a dozen times or more.

I gritted my teeth while I fought every instinct I had to wrap my arms around her, push her up against the nearest wall, and bury my tormented cock inside her until we were both satisfied.

"I'll help you," she offered as she stepped back.

Unfortunately, making burgers wasn't exactly the type of help I needed right now.

CHAPTER 18

LAYLA

I have to tell Owen everything.

I wasn't quite sure when I'd made that decision. Probably somewhere between him ripping my heart out by adopting Brutus, and giving me a piece of jewelry some women would gouge their own eyes out to own. As a memento.

I fingered the beautiful blue diamonds like I'd been doing most of the evening, knowing that Owen had no idea what he did to me with every thoughtful gesture he performed with simply my happiness in mind.

I hated the tension that flowed between us, and it wasn't something he deserved.

Like it or not, fearful or not, I *did* want Owen to see my present and my past, and if he didn't look at me any differently after that, I was going to strip his clothes off and explore that gorgeous body of his all damn night.

We were friends, but we were both feeling the stress of keeping it that way.

That painful lust was always there.

I felt it, and I knew he did, too.

It was a throbbing ache for me that never went away, but lately, not being able to give everything to Owen was nearly killing me.

It didn't matter that I wasn't a casual-sex kind of woman. Nothing with Owen would ever be that way, and if we didn't explore this chemistry between us, I knew I'd always wonder what it would have been like if we had.

I didn't want to have regrets.

What I really wanted was to break free and be exactly who I was with Owen, and he really needed to know the truth before we could move forward . . . or not.

A lot of my lingering insecurities came from my past, so he really needed the whole picture.

I stroked my hand over Brutus's deformed ear as he sat at my feet.

"Coffee?" Owen asked from the kitchen.

I already had a Diet Coke beside me in the living room. "No. I'm good," I called back from my position on the couch.

Owen entered the living room with a big mug in his hand, and Brutus rose and waddled across the room. The bulldog flopped onto his comfy bed, and let out a low moan of satisfaction.

Owen sat on the other end of the couch. "You sound like I feel, buddy," he said jokingly to Brutus. "I think I ate one too many hamburgers. I'm stuffed."

I smiled as I looked at Owen. The man could put down a lot of food, but there wasn't an ounce of fat on his body. I knew he did a rigorous workout every morning in his home gym, and it definitely showed. He was far from the slender teenager I'd known, but I certainly couldn't mourn the loss of that boy when such a devastatingly gorgeous male body had taken his place.

"It will wear off. You'll be hungry in a few hours," I teased.

He grinned wickedly. "Maybe I'm still a growing boy."

Oh, Owen Sinclair was no boy. Not anymore. He even had the scruffy jaw to prove it. I knew he shaved every morning, but by dinnertime, he had that sexy five-o'clock shadow going on.

I had to tear my eyes away from him so I'd stop fantasizing about what it would be like if we were both completely naked instead of sitting in his living room on opposite sides of the couch.

"I want to talk if you're willing," I said, trying to keep my voice calm.

"Willing?" he said huskily. "I've been waiting for weeks now. I want to know what happened on that boat, Layla. Mostly, I think I really want to know why you backed off when we're so damn attracted to each other that we can't think about anything else when we're together. Well, at least I can't."

"I think you already know that I'm attracted to you, too. But I can't sleep with you knowing that you really don't know me, Owen. I want you to see all the dark parts of me before you make a decision about whether or not you want our relationship to continue." I couldn't look at him. If I did, I might decide to play it safe.

"There isn't a damn thing about you that's dark, Layla. You're all light."

"No!" I denied, my voice desperate. "I'm not. That's what you think, but it's not true. I think I honestly wanted you to keep thinking that, but I really need you to know all of me, the good and the not so good, too."

"Talk, Layla. Nothing you can say is ever going to make me feel any differently than I do now. Quit tormenting yourself," he said in a low, earnest baritone.

I took a deep breath. "Remember when we were teenagers, and you wanted to know why I was alone a lot?"

"Yeah."

"God, you'll never know how much I actually liked it when my mother wasn't there. It was preferable to the times she was home. My mother was a raging alcoholic, Owen. And when she drank, she was violent. It got worse after my father left. But even as I grew, I was still afraid of her, so I took every single punishment she dished out, desperately hoping for another one of those times she'd disappear. I was never brave enough to fight back." I paused for a moment, trying to get my emotions under control.

"So those bruises that I saw sometimes . . . they weren't accidents, or bumping into walls in the dark?" he asked in a hoarse voice.

I shook my head. "Never. I tried as hard as I could to cover them up. I think you were the only one who ever noticed. When I got older, she started using a belt instead of her hands, so that's where those weird welts came from that you noticed our senior year. And those times that I told you I was sick, I wasn't. Those were particularly bad beatings, so bad I couldn't get out of bed because I was hurting. Rather than getting angry, I got more terrified, and I was really embarrassed. I mean, what girl wants to tell her friends that her mother is a violent, crazy alcoholic who doesn't have an Off button? Most of my friends were planning proms, dances, and graduation with their mothers. I was just trying not to piss mine off enough that she'd leave me disabled for a week or two."

"Fuck!" Owen exploded. "I should have looked harder. I should have known what was happening. We were best friends, for fuck's sake."

"No," I answered calmly. "You couldn't have known, because I was a master at hiding it. Nobody knew, and I was willing to suffer in silence to make sure that they didn't. I wanted to be normal, Owen, so I did as much as I could to be an ordinary kid."

"Why didn't you tell me?"

"What could you have done?" I questioned. "My mother would have denied it. Believe me, she was a master manipulator. She screwed with my head until I actually believed that I deserved it."

"Where in the hell was your father?" Owen said angrily.

"He paid his child support faithfully because he didn't want to get into trouble, but he didn't give a damn about me. When he left my mother, he left both of us. All he wanted was his freedom." My father had been perfectly aware of my mother's abuse, but he'd never once stepped in.

"You said he traveled," Owen growled.

"He did. But even when he wasn't on the road, he never answered my calls. We were never close. He rarely even spoke to me when he was home, but after the divorce, I called him. Several times. At some point, I just gave up."

"Layla, how could you think for a single moment that any of this was your fault?"

I shrugged. "I don't think that anymore, but I was seeing the whole situation through the eyes of an adolescent, Owen. I thought I was a bad daughter. I was ashamed that I wasn't normal, which is why I tried so hard to pretend that I actually was ordinary. Don't think that you didn't help me back then, even though you didn't know. You and Andie kept me relatively sane."

"Bullshit! Somebody needed to be there to protect you," Owen exploded.

I nodded. "Once I graduated from high school, I knew I had to get out."

"Please, fucking say that you did," Owen said gruffly.

"I did," I answered obligingly. "I moved in with a female roommate after you and Andie went to Boston, and I tried to get ready to knock out as many classes as possible so I could get into nursing school. But somewhere during that summer, I lost . . . myself."

"What do you mean?" Owen rasped.

"I got . . . really depressed."

"Understandable," Owen said. "Tell me everything, Layla."

"I did all kinds of things I can't really explain that summer," I said, my voice shaking with emotion. "It was like I was searching for something I couldn't find. You asked me if I was a virgin. I'm not. But I've only had sex with one guy, and it was the most horrible experience of my life. I just lay there, hoping I'd feel *something*, but all I felt was even more ashamed. I think I'd been looking for some kind of attention, but I didn't get it. The only thing I got was pain, and some guy I barely knew grunting on top of me to get himself off. I spiraled downhill after that. I pulled myself out of bed to go to work because I knew I had to, but every day got darker, and eventually, I just didn't care what happened to me anymore because I thought nobody else did. After years of nothing but abuse or indifference, I thought I was just . . . totally unlovable."

"What happened?" Owen prompted.

"I took a razor blade, crawled into my bathtub, and tried really hard to just die."

"What the hell?" Owen growled.

"In other words, I tried to kill myself, Owen. I was so fucked up that I really didn't want to be alive anymore. At that point, it wasn't a cry for help. When I slashed my wrists, I couldn't wait to die. Sliding into that darkness from losing blood was nothing but a relief for me. I lay there bleeding out, and I didn't even give a damn. That's the part of me you don't know, Owen. I just gave up. I quit. I actually hated my roommate for coming home and saving my life that day." Tears were coursing down my cheeks, but I didn't care. I finally let go in front of Owen, and I didn't care if he saw this side of me, the side that wasn't very pretty.

"Jesus, Layla. I don't even know what to say."

"Don't," I pleaded. "Don't say anything. Just let me finish. Later, I finally realized that I'd been sliding into major depression for a long time. But once my life started to change after I finished high school, I was really lost. I wasn't me anymore. I wish I had reached out for help, but I don't think I even knew what was happening. I got better once I got on medication and started going to intensive counseling. I was able to get off the antidepressive medication when I was in nursing school, and I haven't ever gone into another major depressive episode like that again, but it took a lot of work to get my shit together. I try to take care of myself and my mental health now. But even after years of counseling, I still have some insecurities that pop up sometimes, Owen. I don't talk much about that part of my life, because you and I both know there's still a mental-health stigma in medicine, even if medical people swear that there isn't. Some people still judge, so I've tried to just close the door on that period of my life and move on. I've worked through all my issues in therapy, but sometimes I'm just not comfortable talking about it."

I took a deep breath, waiting for him to say something, but he didn't.

So I waited a little longer.

But the living room stayed dead silent.

I swallowed hard. Maybe I *had* my answer about whether or not Owen would see me differently if he knew everything about me.

The quiet lasted so long that it got uncomfortable.

I hopped to my feet. "Okay, well, so that's everything. I guess I better get home."

I couldn't look at him as I scooped up my purse and walked to the door, tears flowing even faster as I realized that he wasn't going to say . . . anything.

Maybe he couldn't deal with the fact that the woman he'd been lusting after had once lost her mind, and could possibly do it again someday.

I saw myself out, not releasing a painful sob of sorrow until I'd closed the front door.

I'd gambled on Owen, and I'd lost, but I refused to believe that things would have been better if I *hadn't* tried.

I was tired of only letting Owen see what I wanted him to see because I was afraid of his reaction if he knew the truth.

None of the bad things in my past had really been my fault.

I made it to my car, put my head against the metal, and cried like my entire world had just ended.

Maybe I'd *thought* I was ready in case Owen decided that he couldn't deal with my crazy past, but I hadn't been. At all.

I fumbled for my keys, digging into the bottom of the purse, my hands shaking so badly that I couldn't find them.

Before my fingers connected with my keys, a solid, bulky form wedged up behind me, and I saw a pair of hands slap onto the ugly paint of my vehicle.

"Where in the fuck do you think you're going?" Owen growled against my ear.

"Home," I squeaked, startled by the intense fierceness in his voice.

"Not. Happening. You nearly gave me a damn heart attack, and I have questions. About a million of them," he warned.

I took a deep breath and closed my eyes. "Look, I'll be okay if this freaked you out. I get it. To be honest, sometimes it seems surreal, even to me, that it happened."

So much of that summer and fall was still a blur. I couldn't connect with how I was feeling then, because I hadn't really been feeling . . . anything. I'd been completely empty.

"Stop running away, goddammit!" he said angrily, slamming his fist against the metal of my car. "There's nothing I can't handle as long as it doesn't involve seeing your backside in the distance. I need time to take everything in, but never at any damn time is it going to change the way I feel about you. When in the fuck are you going to understand that the way I feel about you *isn't* going to change? What else do I have to do to make you understand that? You're beautiful to me, no matter what happened to you a damn decade ago, after you'd been through hell and back. Jesus, Layla, just give me a damn chance, would you? Just for once, trust that from now on, I'm always going to have your back."

I lifted my hands and rubbed them down my wet face, my heart pounding so hard that I could feel the deep contractions.

I had no reason *not* to believe him, but I turned so I could see his face.

That action nearly destroyed me.

My handsome, gorgeous Owen looked like he'd been through a devastating trauma, his expression ravaged and defeated.

But underneath all the pain on his face, I could still see tenderness in his dazzling, opulent green eyes.

Oh, God. He's hurting. I did this to him by running away.

"Owen, if that's true, I'm warning you, you're never going to get rid of me," I said in a voice that was hoarse from shedding so many tears.

"Thank fuck!" he said with a groan. He picked me up, and without saying another word, he carried me back into the house.

CHAPTER 19

OWEN

"I guess I've gotten all my answers, but that doesn't mean I have to like *any* of them," I told Layla as my arms wrapped a little tighter around her waist.

I had to give her credit, she hadn't avoided a single question, no matter how uncomfortable it was to answer.

After she'd been brave enough to put everything out there, I still hadn't forgiven myself for going silent and giving her the impression that she'd freaked me out.

Jesus! How could she ever think that what she'd been through would even be an issue for me?

Okay, maybe it *was* an issue, but only because I was so pissed on her behalf.

"What do you mean?" she asked as she put a hand over mine.

I had her reclined back against my body and between my legs on the sofa. My arms were wrapped around her from behind. She'd promised she'd never run away again, but I wasn't taking any damn chances.

"I mean that I hate every single thing that happened to you, Layla, and I really despise your asshole of a father who could have made it all go away if he'd wanted to intervene. I also detest the fact that you ever felt even the tiniest bit of shame for something that wasn't your damn fault. Come on. We're medical people. You and I both know that major depression is the same as having diabetes, or any other medical issue. You needed help, and you didn't get it. I don't want to think about how close you came to dying. I guarantee I'll have nightmares about it. I don't know how you felt, but I can empathize. Your medical issue was in control at that moment. You couldn't save yourself. Nobody is going to blame you for that."

"Do you really think you'd talk about it if it happened to you? Most reasonable and good medical professionals know that it's chemical, but there are still judgmental assholes in our field, Owen."

"But you never even told Andie," I argued.

"Because I was afraid she'd tell you," she explained. "I will tell her when she gets back from her honeymoon."

I reached out, threaded our fingers together, and lifted both her hands. Why had I never noticed the scars? "If I sit and really look at your wrists, I can see the cuts, but they're barely visible," I said huskily as I kissed both of her wrists, right on top of the barely discernable scars. I closed my eyes as I dropped our hands back to her waist, trying to clear my head.

"I got lucky in that respect," she explained. "There was a plastic surgeon in-house at the hospital that day. He repaired the exterior after the internal work was done. He did a really good job, and I use a concealer-type makeup to hide the rest. Somebody would really have to study my wrist like you just did to notice them now."

I opened my eyes, and tightened my arms around her waist again in a protective hold.

I can't think about that night. Not until I can do it more rationally.

"You told me that your mother got sick, and I assumed you had to care for her," I said, suddenly remembering that her mother had died less than a year ago.

"I did take care of her," she answered. "She reached out to me at the end stage of her liver disease. Her alcoholism caught up to her, and she didn't have long to live. I can't say that we were ever able to make amends, but I was her only child, and I didn't want her to die alone. I had to ask myself if it was something I really wanted to do. In the end, I stayed with her at the nursing home whenever I could simply because she wasn't the all-powerful, violent, terrifying mother I once knew. She was sick, weak, and dying. I was at peace with not letting her go alone."

Christ! Even after the abuse and neglect Layla had suffered as a kid, she was *still* there at the end for her mother. "You know that's way more than she would have done for you," I commented.

She nodded. "I knew that. But I wasn't her. I didn't allow myself to think that she was sorry for what she'd done, but she was the woman who had given me life, so it didn't feel right to just abandon her when she was dying. I was sad when she passed, but I didn't grieve for her. I think I was mourning the mother I wish I could have had. In some ways, it was probably a good thing for me to see that she wasn't scary to me anymore. She was just a very flawed person with a disease that she couldn't conquer. Seeing her like that kind of put everything into perspective for me. It probably helped me heal any of the wounds that hadn't completely closed."

Honestly, knowing Layla, if she hadn't been there, it probably would have eaten her up. She was the type of person who couldn't hear a cry for help and not answer it, even if it had come from the mother who had made her life miserable.

I moved on to another topic, since she didn't seem like she had any more to say about the last one. "So tell me more about this guy you met that summer."

"A complete stranger," she said flatly. "I never saw him again. I think I wanted . . . something, but I didn't need . . . that. Maybe I thought if I could just get close to someone, I'd feel better. I'd feel something. But I think that incident did me a lot more harm than good."

"So you haven't been with anyone since you were eighteen?" I asked curiously.

"Nope. I've never found anyone that I wanted to try it with again. What about you?" she asked.

"Definitely more than once," I confided. "I didn't feel great about one-nighters, but a guy has to get laid occasionally."

She laughed. "I'm definitely not going to judge you," she said. "So where do we go from here, Owen? I don't think it's possible to keep pretending like I'm with you because of some favor. I want us to be honest with each other. I'm pretty much done pretending that I just want to be your friend, too. Honestly, I had a pretty big crush on you during our senior year, too."

My heart sped up. This was a discussion that was long overdue. "I can't do it, either. Let's make it real, Layla. If we're really putting the truth on the table, I didn't just ask you to help me because I wanted to learn how to date or to check things off my list. I think I was trying to figure out a way to get close to you without scaring you off."

"I want that, too," she said with a sigh. "I know I've been sending you some mixed signals, but I think I'm just really scared."

Christ! I hated hearing apprehension in her tone, but I knew she was being brutally honest.

I didn't want her to be afraid of anything, especially me.

"We'll just take it slow and see how it goes," I said, trying to calm her fears.

She slowly turned in my arms until she was straddling me. "Exactly how slow are you planning?"

"Do you really expect me to think rationally when you're in this position?" I asked in a strangled voice. "Layla, you're too damn

151

vulnerable right now. You just spilled your guts and told me everything. I'm not sure you're ready for me to drag you off to bed like a damn caveman."

I wanted her so desperately that I nearly did just that.

But I couldn't.

I wanted more than just her body.

Her eyes widened. "Is there a caveman inside you somewhere? That's kind of a hot visualization."

"Woman, if you don't stop grinding down on my cock, you're going to be introduced to that caveman way sooner than you want to be," I warned, my patience hanging on a very thin thread.

She stared down at me with a wanton look in her gorgeous eyes. "Owen, I told you that I'm done pretending. Yeah, I don't really have experience seducing a man, but I'm ready to give it my best shot. I'm laying myself bare to you, which I should have done a long time ago. You've never given me any reason to think you'd take advantage of it. If there was ever somebody I should have trusted . . . that man was you. I'm just sorry I wasn't completely honest with you from the start. But I'm done with half truths and avoidance. I want you to know me. All of me. *Intimately.*"

That last word had been like a low, steady purr, and I nearly lost it.

This was my fantasy.

This was my deepest fucking desire.

All I'd wanted was for Layla to look at me with the same crazy, out-of-control lust that I felt for her.

And damned if I couldn't see that same carnal desire in her eyes.

She wanted me as much as I wanted her. Okay, maybe not quite as much as I wanted her, because my need for this woman was tearing my guts out, but I did know that she wanted me. Badly.

The lust-filled male inside of me wanted to drag her off to my bed and show her just how good hot, sweaty sex could really be.

But the guy who cared about Layla so much that it physically hurt wanted to protect her from any further emotional damage.

Which essentially meant I was fucked all over again.

She leaned down and put her forehead against mine. "I'm ready, Owen. Can't you see that? I want to be with you. No holding back for me anymore. I want to see where all of this takes us. I have to know what it's like to be with someone who actually gives a damn about my pleasure."

Oh, I gave a damn, all right. Maybe too much. Everything she was saying was like a goddamn aphrodisiac I sure as hell *didn't* need. I reached up and threaded a hand through the glorious mass of her silken blonde hair. "Once I take you to bed, it's going to change everything," I told her in a hoarse tone of desperation. "I won't be able to go back to a friendship, Layla. For me, it's all or nothing. I have to be honest about that. I plan on giving this relationship everything I have."

I couldn't pretend that once she was mine, I might be able to let her go if she decided our relationship wasn't working.

I'd fucking find a way to make it work.

Layla was mine.

She was probably always meant to be mine.

Just the fact that we were both single and had never found anyone we wanted to share our lives with seemed like a damn sign. And I didn't even believe in fate.

She smoothed a gentle hand over my hair, an action that felt so good it was pathetic.

"Owen, I'm not going into this halfhearted, either. Now that you know everything, the good and the bad, I'm all in. Meaning I'm not the least bit hesitant to let you carry me off to your caveman lair." She pulled back and shot me a quizzical look. "Or do I need to drag you to bed this time?"

She looked so damn sure about what she wanted that I almost threw my reservations to the wayside.

I curled my hand gently around her neck to bring her face to mine. "Don't you know you're worth waiting for, Layla? We're going to do it right this time."

Before she could say another word, I put my hand behind her head and jerked her mouth down to mine.

If I couldn't fuck her, I was willing to take the next-best thing.

CHAPTER 20

Layla

His lips were demanding, sensual, and a bold promise of things to come, and I felt those assurances of future pleasure beyond imagination slither like a jolt of electricity down my spine.

Now that there was no misunderstanding between us, and I knew he'd care about me no matter how many skeletons I had in my closet, I was more than ready to give a relationship between us my all, too.

I closed my eyes and just absorbed the sensuous embrace.

His scent.

The touch of his lips.

The feel of his fingers in my hair.

And the heated emotion that flared between us as he slowly devoured my mouth like it was a feast for a starving man.

I'd hurt this loving, incredible man, and I wanted to make up for every time I'd doubted him.

I slowly stretched my body out on top of his.

I needed more.

So much more.

I wanted to be connected to Owen from my mouth to my toes.

I moaned against his mouth as I absorbed the pleasure of his muscular form beneath me.

Owen was strong and powerful.

Yet as he wrapped his arms around me, he was also the sweetest security I'd ever known.

Heat flooded insistently between my thighs, and my need to be even closer to him was relentless.

I reached between us, desperate to undo the buttons of his shirt and explore his bare skin.

He caught my hand as he lifted his head. "Don't, Layla. Not right now," he said gutturally.

I was so desperate my entire body was shaking. "Owen, I need . . ."

He shifted our bodies until I was suddenly looking up at him as he said, "I know what you need, sweetheart. Trust me."

"God, yes," I moaned as he pinned me beneath him and started to explore the sensitive skin of my neck.

I tilted my head, eager for him to have access to everything he wanted.

My need for Owen was a hell of a lot more powerful than any kind of fear I had about my lack of experience.

He'd teach me, and relish every damn minute of it.

I needed him inside me, surrounding me, drowning me in the passion that had been growing in intensity since day one of seeing him again.

"Fuck me, Owen. Please. I want that. I need it."

I knew he wanted to protect me, but I didn't need to be sheltered.

Not when I was with him.

Never when I was with Owen.

My nipples abraded against his chest, and they were almost painfully hard and sensitive.

He nipped at the skin below my ear before he growled, "Do you know how damn long I've wanted to hear you begging me to fuck you, Layla?"

"Probably not nearly as long as I've wanted you to do it," I panted. "Owen, I can't take this anymore."

"The only thing I've wanted more is to watch you come for me," he rasped as he changed positions slightly, until he was half on and half off my body.

I whimpered in disappointment until I felt his hand slide down my neck and then under my flimsy cotton shirt. I gasped as he repositioned my bra above my breasts, and stroked over one of my tight nipples, sending a lightning bolt of pain and pleasure through my entire body.

"Yes," I hissed, my body arching in need. "Touch me, Owen."

His mouth came down on mine, and the never-ending desire that was constantly tormenting me boiled over.

He teased both of my nipples, pinching and then stroking, while I was helpless to scream like I wanted to because he was ravaging my mouth.

I needed . . .

I wanted . . .

I tried to wrap my legs around his waist in an attempt to relieve the yearning that was all but consuming me, but he pulled his hand from my breasts, lifted my leg, and pulled it back down as he released my mouth. "Easy, sweetheart," he said in a rough voice right next to my ear.

"I can't take it easy. I need you," I whimpered.

"You have me," he said in a graveled voice as his big hand cupped the quivering flesh between my thighs, and then gave it a hard squeeze.

I yelped in relief, and pushed my hips up, needing more pressure than he was giving me.

As he lowered the zipper of my jeans, and his fingers found their way inside my panties, I threw my head back and released a long, hungry groan.

I fell completely into the mesmerizing, explosive heat that he was deliberately creating.

I fell into Owen, and let myself lose control as he nipped at my earlobe, and his skilled fingers played in the heat of my pussy.

"Jesus, Layla! You're so damn wet," Owen rasped into my ear.

Of course I was. How could I not be when he was doing his best to make me completely insane?

I jerked when his finger stroked over my throbbing clit.

When he did it again and again, harder and harder, I screamed, "Yes, Owen, yes! Please make me come."

He pressed his face against my neck. "Well, since you asked so nicely," he said in a smug, satisfied tone. "I think I will, although I'd really like to bury my face between those sexy legs of yours."

Just the mere thought of Owen going down on me stripped me of any semblance of rationality.

When he slipped his entire hand inside the denim material of my jeans, and doubled his efforts to make me come, my climax ripped through me almost immediately. "Owen! Oh, my God. Owen." I screamed his name with an abandon I didn't realize I was capable of, and I couldn't have cared less if his neighbors heard me.

All I felt were the drumming pulsations that pounded at my body as Owen kissed me like he wanted to absorb every ounce of my pleasure.

I wrapped my arms tightly around his neck, kissing him back with equal ardor as my body shuddered.

I love you, Owen. I love you so damn much.

I ached to say those words aloud, to tell him over and over how much he meant to me. How much he'd always mean to me.

Unfortunately, it was way too early to say that to him, so I tried to put everything I was feeling into our fierce kiss.

When he finally released my mouth, I said breathlessly, "Is this the part where you carry me off to your lair, caveman?"

He grinned. "No. This is when I savor the memory of you coming so hard that you screamed my name in complete ecstasy."

Owen looked as satisfied as a cat with a bowl of cream, and I'd never had the chance to touch him.

I stroked a hand over his hair. "I want to learn how to please you, too."

"Sweetheart, you just made me happier than I'd ever thought possible," he said blithely as he zipped my jeans and closed the button.

I frowned at him as I snuggled into the warmth of his body after he'd pulled my bra back into its previously supportive position. "How is that possible when I'm the only one who had a screaming orgasm?"

Owen was a giver, but for once, I wished he'd take . . . me.

He pinned me with his sharp gaze. "I just fulfilled one of my fantasies, which was to hear you scream my name while I made you come."

The tone of his voice was wicked and hoarsely erotic, and the fact that I could see this side of him was incredibly humbling, but also so freeing that I felt giddy. "Maybe I have next to no sexual experience, but I am a medical practitioner who is very familiar with bodily reactions and human anatomy. I think you'd feel a lot more pleasure if you fucked me."

There was a pleading note in my voice that I didn't even try to hide.

Owen had given so much to me. The man really did need to look after his own interests once in a while. And I planned to make damn sure he did.

I was in love with Owen, and more than anything, I wanted to see him happy. All the time.

My days of inadvertently causing him hurt or pain were over.

Causing him injury was painful to me, and I was going to do everything in my power to make Owen smile every single day.

He didn't need to worry about my psyche. Now that I'd plowed through my confessions and he'd chosen me anyway, nothing could drag me away from him.

I cupped the side of his face, a face that was decidedly different from the one I'd swooned over when I was eighteen, but familiar at the same time.

I brushed his whiskered jaw with my thumb. "Now I have to ask you what I can do to make you realize that you're never going to see the backside of me again."

He shot me a mischievous smile. "Whoa, sweetheart. I didn't say I didn't want to see that shapely ass of yours, I just want to see it bared and in my bed instead of walking away from me."

I snorted. "You aren't exactly trying very hard to get me there. Maybe I'm sexually inept, but I'm more than ready to start burning up the sheets while I learn. And I'm pretty eager to move on to the next phase of this relationship, all that adoring-you-without-pretending-it's-a-game thing."

"I think you and I both know that nothing between the two of us was ever a game," Owen said huskily as he tightened his arms around me protectively. "Now quit trying to tempt me, or you'll get more than you bargained for, Layla."

I let out a frustrated sigh. "Promises, promises," I teased.

I was more than ready to drop any pretenses I had, but I wasn't going to push Owen. He'd waited for me, so I could do the same for him. Eventually, he'd realize that my past didn't define me. Yes, an occasional annoying voice popped into my head sometimes, but I'd always managed to overcome and squash it.

I'd smashed the hell out of it tonight by facing my fears, and I'd do it again and again.

I wasn't fragile or helpless.

I was a woman who needed a man like Owen, and after tonight, I'd never have a single doubt about him abandoning me because I wasn't perfect.

"So, what can I do to convince you that you'll never see me walking away?" I asked softly as I looked into his endlessly tender eyes.

Owen looked at me like I was the only woman in the world who existed for him, and I found it strange that I'd never noticed it before tonight.

"Right now, you can kiss me," he answered throatily.

I immediately gave him exactly what he wanted.

CHAPTER 21

OWEN

"Tell me again exactly why you're dragging us through this hellish San Diego traffic when we could be back home with our wives in Citrus Beach," Seth requested dryly from the back seat of my vehicle.

Aiden was riding shotgun beside me, and Seth had hopped into the back when I'd told them I needed them.

Neither one had even questioned why I needed them at the time.

"Because if you're not with me, I'm very likely to kill somebody, and I'd rather not. I'm a doctor, and I took that Hippocratic oath pretty seriously at the time. I'm just not sure I can uphold it if I don't have anybody to hold me back," I told them bluntly.

It hadn't taken me long to track down Layla's father, which I'd been itching to do since the moment she'd told me everything last night.

I'd wanted to rant, rave, and lose my shit over all the crappy cards she'd been dealt in her life, but in the end, the most important thing I could do was to protect her so they never fucking happened again.

If I thought too much about a confused, lost, helpless, adolescent Layla who had been submerged in so much darkness that she climbed into a bathtub and slit her wrists, I'd completely lose my mind.

After I'd taken her home last night, I hadn't slept much. My mind had gone over and over everything I could remember in high school, trying to figure out how I'd missed the fact that she was being tortured by her violent, alcoholic mother.

I had noticed some marks on her a couple of times, but she'd explained them away with so much nonchalance that I hadn't even questioned whether or not she was telling me the truth.

By the time the sun had risen, I'd decided that she was right. I hadn't known because she'd become a master at hiding what was happening to her at home.

Did I hate the fact that I hadn't known? *Yes.*

Did I understand why she'd hid it? *Yeah.* How could I not? I was a physician now, somebody who was fully trained to recognize how an abused child became codependent and actually tried to cover up for an alcoholic parent. I got why she'd been ashamed, and how she'd spiraled down into major depression, too.

It was just a hell of a lot harder to handle when that person was somebody you cared about. A lot.

"You planning on sharing with us about why exactly you want to commit this homicide?" Aiden questioned.

I wasn't about to share all of Layla's secrets, but I gave my brothers the brief version of what she'd been through as a child. Her mental breakdown was private, and not something they needed to hear unless Layla someday decided she wanted them to know.

"How in the hell does that happen?" Aiden said, sounding infuriated. "If somebody messed with a single hair on my daughter's head, I'd kill the bastard."

Shit! Wasn't that the truth? Aiden was an extremely protective father. I wasn't sure he'd even let Maya date until she was over the age of thirty.

"He knew," I explained. "The asshole knew that Layla was being abused, but he never lifted a hand or even a damn telephone to make it stop. She called him, begging him to help her, and he never even called her back. Yeah, maybe we all had an absent father, too. But we had a mother who loved us, and did her best to take care of us. Layla had nobody. No siblings, no close family who wanted her. Nowhere to run. Nobody she could turn to about it." My voice cracked with emotion, but I wasn't concerned about hiding shit from my brothers. They understood how pissed off I was, because we were all Sinclairs, and no Sinclair in this generation would ever abandon their child.

"If I'd known, I would have done everything in my power to help her," Seth said, his voice dripping with regret.

I shook my head as I pulled into the parking area of the office building where her father worked. "I didn't know, and Layla and I were close friends."

I felt slightly guilty about leaving the clinic a little early, and asking Layla to do rounds again, but she'd cheerfully assured me she didn't mind if I had errands to run.

Because that's just the kind of woman she was: always willing to help somebody with anything if it made their life easier.

"Hell, I'm not sure I want to hold you back," Aiden grumbled from the passenger seat.

"Me either," Seth seconded.

"I want answers," I explained. "I want to confront him so he can't forget the girl he abandoned. But I'm also not willing to throw my life away on somebody like him. I need to be around to make damn sure that Layla is never alone again. She came through everything okay, and she's the most extraordinary woman I've ever known. Now that I finally have a chance with her, I'm not losing it because of a lowlife bastard," I said irritably.

"You're right," Seth agreed. "No murder."

"Got it," Aiden concurred as I parked, and we all exited the vehicle.

During my research into Brent Caine, I'd discovered that he'd been an international tour guide for years with a big tour company. Eventually, he'd landed a management job in their home office in San Diego, a position that didn't require him to travel anymore.

He'd been close to Layla for years, and had never even checked up on her.

To make things even worse, he'd remarried, and had two more children with his current wife.

I really hoped that the mother of his other children was a hell of a lot better than Layla's mother had been.

As we exited the elevator, the receptionist sitting right next to the office entrance inquired, "Do you have an appointment?"

"I need to see Brent Caine," I answered abruptly, annoyed that my mission had been delayed.

Seth elbowed his way in front of me and gave the older woman a charming smile. "Seth Sinclair," he said as he handed her a business card he'd pulled out of his pocket. "I'm the CEO of Sinclair Properties. My brothers and I need to have a meeting with Caine. I'm thinking of doing a very large destination celebration for my company's anniversary. I need to get things going on that immediately."

The woman sat up straight so abruptly that the glasses perched on the end of her nose nearly hit the floor. "Mr. Sinclair," she said, sounding flustered as she glanced at the card. "Oh, you are the Citrus Beach Sinclairs."

If I hadn't been so full of rage, I probably would have laughed at the expression of awe on her face.

Never in a million years had I ever thought that one of my brothers would command that kind of reverent greeting, but she was looking at Seth like he was a god of some kind.

Really, maybe he deserved it. He'd made a damn good reputation for himself with Sinclair Properties already, and it was hardly a secret to the world that our entire family had inherited billions from the already well-known East Coast Sinclairs.

Obviously, the woman knew exactly who was standing in front of her as she said, "Oh, I'm sure Mr. Caine would be happy to see you. Go right on in. He's not in with another appointment right now."

Seth nodded. "Thank you. We'll do that," he told her as he headed straight for the door she'd pointed toward.

I moved in front of him and barged through the heavy wooden door first.

I wasn't sure what I'd expected, but Brent Caine looked like any other middle-aged guy as he rose from the office chair behind his desk. "Can I help you gentlemen?" he asked, sounding confused, but amiable enough.

Layla has his eyes.

The guy was average height and a little bit overweight, and he had ever-changing, deep-blue eyes that I'd only seen on one other person in the world.

"Owen, Seth, and Aiden Sinclair," Aiden said flatly. "That's all the greeting that you're going to get. I don't shake hands with shitty fathers."

I knew Layla's father recognized the Sinclair name, because I could suddenly see green dollar signs where those blue eyes like Layla's had been just seconds ago.

"I'm in love with your daughter," I informed him.

He looked taken aback. "My daughter is only ten years old."

Christ! Was he serious? The bastard wouldn't even acknowledge the fact that Layla existed?

I crossed my arms in front of me. "I'm talking about Layla."

The dollar signs disappeared, and his eyes became an icy blue. "I wrote her off a long time ago," he said in a chilly tone. "She was destined to become just like her mother. It was in her genes. If she's not an alcoholic slut, she probably will be."

"She's not!" The words exploded from my mouth like a shot from a cannon. "She's a beautiful, successful nurse practitioner who cares about other people more than she gives a damn about herself. Regardless of the fact that she never had anyone who gave a damn about her. She called you, asked for your help. How can any father deny a child that he knows damn well is suffering in an abusive atmosphere?"

"I sent the damn child support. That should have been enough. Her mother was a whore who was never sober, so I assume every penny of my money went toward alcohol. But I sent it until the day that Layla turned eighteen. I did my court-ordered duty. All I wanted was to never see either one of them again."

"Layla was a good kid," Aiden said furiously.

"She had the alcoholic genes. I knew she was going to end up just like her mother."

Seth spoke up, his jaw tight. "She was being abused, you asshole."

Caine rolled his eyes. "And what did you expect me to do? Her mother was a crazy bitch. She assaulted me, too. It wasn't just Layla who had to deal with her abuse. Getting out of that situation and anything associated with it was the best thing I could do for myself."

"You were a fucking adult," I growled. "Layla was a defenseless kid. *Your* kid."

"She was a teenager by then," he argued. "She could defend herself, but she did anything her mother asked her to do. Layla was a lost cause. She was already brainwashed."

I gritted my teeth. "She was terrified, not brainwashed. You should have taken her out of that whole situation."

"I had my own issues to deal with," Caine said, his tone full of hostility and self-pity. "I had child support to pay. I couldn't get out of that. How was I supposed to start over with that payment always squeezing me?"

"You didn't need to start over. You needed to take care of the daughter you abandoned to a violent alcoholic," I told him vehemently. "Christ! Didn't you feel anything for her?"

"Never," Caine replied coldly. "I never wanted her. Didn't want anything to do with her. I was ready to leave Layla's mother when she got pregnant. Because of Layla, I ended up stuck in that marriage years longer than I wanted to be. I don't even know if she's mine. Her mother was cheating on me almost from the very beginning."

I pulled my phone out of my back pocket and brought up a recent picture I'd taken of Layla. I held it right in front of him. "Those are your eyes you see looking back at you."

Would the man finally see all of the damage he did to his own child? Honestly, it shouldn't matter whether Layla shared DNA with him or not; he'd been the only father she'd had.

Caine looked for a brief moment, and then looked away. "Maybe she is mine, but she looks a lot like her mother."

So that was it?

No remorse?

No regret?

No kicking himself in the ass for never realizing that Layla was his biological daughter?

Nothing?

He still couldn't see Layla as a separate person who was totally innocent of her mother's crimes?

Brent Caine was a whiny, self-centered bastard who should have been castrated and never allowed to have another child.

Just imagining Layla as an innocent girl, stuck between a violent, alcoholic mother and this monster who wanted to deny she was ever born, was enough to make me totally lose control of the blinding rage that I'd managed to keep reined in . . . until now.

"You failed her," I accused. "Every single person in her life failed her. I don't know how, but she still managed to become the most amazing woman I've ever known. I think you knew damn well she was your kid, but you wanted to find a reason to hate her from the time she was born. What in the fuck is wrong with you? You're a father the second that baby is conceived, and you act like that child's father until you die. Layla didn't ask to be born, and she sure as hell didn't ask for an asshole like you to be her father, but you were all she had. You could have saved her from those beatings and the horrific verbal abuse she had to take day after day. I don't give a shit what kind of feelings you had about her mother. Layla was just a kid, you bastard, and were her only possible protector back then."

"I didn't want to protect her," he shot back. "She was like a rope around my neck that kept me with—"

I snapped, and went for the bastard's throat. I couldn't listen to another word without tearing his ass apart.

I'd barely made a leap toward Caine when something hit me from behind. *Hard.*

"Don't do it, little brother," Seth rasped into my ear as he wrapped his arms around me from behind, essentially immobilizing me with a gigantic, powerful bear hug. "You were right. He's not worth it. The guy is a sociopath. He's fucking twisted, and he doesn't know how to love anybody. Layla is better off without him. Don't risk the medical license you worked so hard to get on a shithead like him."

I sucked air in and out of my lungs, trying to see through the red haze of fury that was blurring my vision.

"He fucking hurt her, Seth," I spat out between breaths.

"I know. And I know exactly how you feel. Been there. But the man who hurt Riley was already dead. Be happy together. You can't change the past, Owen, but you *can* make an amazing future together."

I stayed locked in Seth's hold as I watched Aiden walk up to Caine, pull his arm back, and slam his fist into Caine's face.

When the older man fell on his ass, Aiden said calmly, "That's for every father out there who would sacrifice anything for their kid, when you wouldn't even lift a finger to help a daughter who was in real danger. I guarantee every one of those dads would like to hurt you."

"I think you broke my nose," Caine whined from his position on the floor. "I'll sue you for this."

Aiden lifted a brow. "Try it, asshole. You won't come out looking very pretty in court."

As my breathing calmed, I stared at Aiden, astonished.

He looked back at me. "What? I didn't repeat any Hippocratic oath, and I'm a damn father." He grabbed me by the upper arm, and Seth took the other side, both of their grips tight, probably in case I decided to try again.

By the time they got me down to the car, I wasn't sure if I was glad they'd held me back, or pissed off because they had.

Aiden fished my keys out of my pocket and got into the driver's seat, while Seth pushed me into the back seat. As he slid in beside me, Seth commented, "You'll thank us for this someday, even if you're pissed off right now. Shit hits the fan with brothers sometimes, but there's no way we aren't going to try to protect each other anyway."

My body was still surging with anger, but I knew both of them were just trying to cover my ass.

I only wished they hadn't been as efficient as they'd been in holding me back.

"Do me a favor," I requested. "Don't tell Layla about any of this. She already knows that her father is an asshole. I don't really want to have to confirm that pain for her by having to explain to her what happened today."

"It never happened," Aiden confirmed readily.

"What never happened? I know nothing." Seth echoed Aiden's feigned ignorance.

I crossed my arms over my chest. "Good. Keep it that way."

It wasn't Layla who had needed answers, it was me, and the last thing I wanted was to open a wound that had already closed for her.

My brothers would keep their word.

All I'd had to do was mention causing an innocent person pain of any kind, and their lips were zippered.

Even though I wasn't ready to tell them right at the moment, a guy really couldn't ask for better brothers than mine.

CHAPTER 22

LAYLA

"I think maybe we should hit a different mall for clothes," I told Skye and Riley as we had lunch at a little café near the entrance of the expensive mall where I'd taken Owen for our first coffee date.

I'd become close to both of these women, and I'd finally felt comfortable sharing my story about what had happened to me when I was young, and about my severe depression as a teenager.

They'd showed nothing but empathy and understanding, and in turn had shared their own horrific backgrounds with me.

Both Riley and Skye had been through more trauma in their lives than I had, but they were both incredible women, and an inspiration to me.

Skye shook her head. "Not happening. They have beautiful clothing here. The other places aren't as good."

"Don't you think it's a little pricey?" I asked, realizing a bit too late that I was talking to women who were wives of billionaires.

Skye grinned as she chewed a huge bite of her sandwich and swallowed. "Don't you worry, girl. Owen gave me his shiny new black card, and I know how to use it. Yes, they are pricey, but you're going to Paris. Owen wants you to have anything and everything you need without spending a dime. He said that was the agreement."

I rolled my eyes. "I don't really need clothing, and I feel guilty enough about him paying for everything. I have a good job."

"A good job is one thing," Riley replied. "Having billions of dollars is another. We could swipe that beautiful black card over and over for weeks, all day long, and it would still be a pittance to him, Layla. Just give up and let him do things for you. It makes the Sinclair men happy when they can give stuff to the people they care about."

Skye held up her hand. "No. I totally get it. I used to feel really guilty, too. Maya and I didn't have much money when we moved to Citrus Beach, and we were on a budget. It's not that easy to get used to being involved with a billionaire who can buy something you could only dream of, with a single quick phone call. But I'm telling you right now, woman to woman, get used to it. You'll hurt Owen's feelings if you don't. He has the money, and he's never going to understand why you won't use it, so save yourself the headache and just swipe the damn card."

My hand went to my beautiful blue-whale necklace, just like it did several times a day because I didn't ever want to lose it. "I accepted a really expensive piece of jewelry. I couldn't give it back. It was too sentimental."

Riley nodded. "Okay, I'll give you that. Owen has damn good taste in jewelry. No one I know has a Mia Hamilton Original piece. The poor guy must have jumped through some hoops for that one."

I sent her an admonishing look. "You know it was really expensive, too."

"Oh, hell yes," Skye said cheerily. "It probably set Owen back by about—"

Riley clamped a hand over Skye's mouth. "Let's not go there. You know, sticker shock and all," she said in a warning voice. "We've had time to get used to it, Skye."

Skye pulled Riley's hand down. "Sorry," she said sheepishly. "I guess I've gotten used to having money. But I feel for you. It really wasn't easy."

I made a goofy face. "It feels weird to have a guy offering to buy my clothes."

"Girl, he wasn't offering," Skye said with a laugh. "He was very insistent. Just roll with it. We'll find you some gorgeous stuff for Paris. And they have some beautiful lingerie at that exclusive little shop near the end of the mall. Classy, and not trashy."

I shrugged. "I don't usually worry too much about that. I've never had a hot guy in my life."

Riley wiggled her eyebrows. "Well, you have one now, and he's loaded, too. He's worth a couple of new pairs of panties, wouldn't you say?"

I laughed. "He's worth a lot more than that. I hate to say this, but I have no idea how to seduce a guy."

"Oh, my," Riley said with fake alarm in her voice. "You mean you haven't succumbed to the Sinclair alpha-male charm yet?"

Skye beat on her chest. "'You my woman, me your man. Come to my bed or I'll carry you there.' Is that the *charm* you mean?" she asked Riley dryly.

Riley grinned. "Sometimes that take-charge thing is pretty adorable. And you know they aren't always like that. Seth can be . . . incredibly romantic when he wants to be."

"Aiden, too," Skye said with a flustered smile on her face.

"Okay, ladies. No swooning at the lunch table, please. I'm eating," I teased them both right before I downed the last of my soup.

Skye took a sip of her soda before she said, "Okay, so here's the thing . . . There really is no such thing as seducing a Sinclair male. They're pretty much ready to go from the second they see you, whether you're having a really bad hair day or not."

I snorted. "That's really not helpful, Skye. I'm not sure exactly why, but Owen seems . . . hesitant to make his move. I think he's afraid of moving too fast after I told him about all the stuff that happened to me when I was younger. But he's not moving fast enough for me."

Riley's face was thoughtful as she said, "Then I guess you're going to have to seduce him. Be bold, Layla. The guy is crazy about you. It doesn't surprise me that he worries about everything. He's quieter than the rest of his family, and pretty damn sweet. But take my word for it, he's still a possessive, protective, obsessive Sinclair male. I think he's just a little less aggressive about it."

"Owen has always been like that," I told the women with a sigh. "He's always had a gentle, forgiving soul and a tender heart. I think that's one of the reasons he wanted to be a doctor. He really wants to make a difference in the world through science. Maybe he's a little different because he was the youngest, and he didn't have to grow up as fast as his older brothers, but all of the Sinclair male traits are present, too. He can be really stubborn when he wants something, which is how he managed to get through medical school and his residency."

"Well, he was definitely stubborn about me using his card for every single thing your heart desired," Skye joked.

"He's so amazing," I said with intense longing threading through my voice.

"Hey, hey," she said as she snapped her fingers in front of my face. "Who's doing the swooning now, Layla?"

I pulled myself from my thoughts about Owen, and chuckled. "What other man would put up with Brutus stink bombing his house just because Owen knows that I love that dog?"

"I don't think he minds," Skye said gently. "He takes Brutus everywhere, much to my daughter's delight. She loves it when her uncle Owen and Brutus come over to our place. He might have initially got him for you, but I suspect he's pretty attached to Brutus, too. I think they've . . . bonded."

"He still calls my poor Brutus the ugliest dog in town," I reminded them.

"But he does it fondly," Riley said. "And that dog follows him around wherever Owen goes."

I knew they were right. Owen was a sucker for Brutus now, and he spoiled the English bulldog shamelessly. Brutus had been allergy tested, and he was a lot less gassy now that he was on a good probiotic and a healthier diet. "I love that he fell in love with the ugliest dog in town," I said with an enormous smile on my face.

"Brutus isn't ugly," Skye insisted. "He's got character, and his scars are proof of that."

I nodded. I definitely agreed.

Skye put her spoon down beside her empty plate. "So are you ready to go find the perfect clothes for Paris?"

"Do I really need them?" I asked. "Paris might be a fashion-design city, but from what I've read, it's pretty informal most of the time. And we were planning on a lot of walking tours."

"There's casual dress, and then there's sexy casual dress," Skye considered. "How many pairs of jeans do you have at home that make your ass look amazing?"

I thought about her question. "I don't know. I don't look at my own ass in a mirror."

"Okay," Skye said indulgently. "I'll take that to mean you have zero pairs of hot-butt jeans. We've already discussed the incredible lingerie shop. It's October. So I think you need to look at layering if you're going to be going on tours. And what do you have for jackets?"

I shot her a dubious expression. "I have a raincoat. It's Southern California, Skye. I'm not one of those people who are freezing when it gets to sixty degrees. I like the winter weather here."

"You still need a light coat," she argued. "Walking shoes, and probably boots, too."

I sighed. "I'm a woman who lives in a pair of scrubs and lab coat most of the time. I'm not really all that into clothes. I like to look decent, but I don't worry about all that stuff."

I'd never really felt like it was necessary to spend a fortune on clothing. Not when my goal was to get to what I needed for a down payment on my own home.

Riley crossed her arms in front of her. "I don't think any of us are fashionistas," she commented. "But sometimes it really feels good to have something other than cotton against your skin, and to watch the man you love while his eyes pop out because you're wearing something new and sexy, because believe me, he *is* going to look at your ass. Owen, Aiden, and Seth are pretty special, because I believe they think we're beautiful no matter what we're wearing. But sometimes it feels good to know I look sexy. It makes me *feel* sexy."

Did I want to feel that way? For most of my career, all I'd wanted was to be taken seriously, so I'd actually downplayed anything that would make me look like a dumb blonde.

I was established in my career now, and I was starting a whole new chapter in my relationship with Owen. So yeah, maybe feeling like I was hot once in a while wouldn't be a bad thing.

I had two women as friends now who could probably guide me in the right direction.

"Nothing super fancy," I warned them. "It's not my style."

Skye nodded. "That's not my style, either, so I get it. We'll figure out your style as we go along."

"Then I'm in. Let's do this before I change my mind."

Riley and Skye jumped to their feet like their chairs were on fire, and I knew our adventure was about to begin.

CHAPTER 23

Owen

Brutus released some kind of doggie sound that was something between a sigh and a moan as I rubbed his belly.

"I kind of feel the same way, buddy," I said, commiserating with the canine because Layla should have gotten to my place by now, and I was still alone with the ugliest dog in town.

I raised a brow. "You know you shouldn't be on the couch, right? I mean, I know I pulled you up here, but you should really be on your bed or the floor. Layla said you could puncture the leather furniture with your claws." Brutus sat up and shot me the nastiest sideways glance that I was convinced only a bulldog could do right.

"Don't give me that look," I warned him. "You've been fed, walked, and petted. What else do you want?"

Brutus looked longingly at the front door.

"Yeah, I want the same damn thing, buddy. But she's worth waiting for, trust me on that one."

It was Saturday, but I'd decided to go into the clinic to wrap up some things with my patients before the clinic closed down for expansion.

Layla had gone off shopping and to lunch with Skye and Riley. Jade had called me earlier and mentioned something about meeting all the other ladies at the spa when she and Eli got home from San Diego.

Still, it was almost eight o'clock now. What could she be doing with the girls for this long?

The doorbell rang, and I lugged Brutus from the couch to the floor, and then practically sprinted to the front door.

Maybe my actions were a little too eager, but I didn't give a damn. I hadn't seen Layla since we'd left work the day before, and it felt like it had been way too long.

"It's about time—" I stopped my joking comment abruptly as she smiled at me like she was just as happy to see me, too.

Fuck! That gorgeous smile was going to be the death of me someday.

"You cut your hair," I said, dumbfounded as she strode through the door in the sexiest pair of black leather stiletto boots I'd ever seen.

"I did. I ended up going to the spa with your sister and sisters-in-law. I ended up getting it cut and highlighted. Do you like it?" she asked as she sashayed her sexy ass over to Brutus to give him some attention.

My cock strained against the buttons of my jeans, pleading to be set free. When she bent over to love on Brutus, I had to tamp down a groan. The woman could fill out a pair of jeans with her gorgeous curves like no female I'd ever seen before. But I wasn't sure I'd ever seen her rock a pair of jeans quite like she was doing tonight.

The denim stretched lovingly over her ass, thighs, and slender legs, hugging her body until the material disappeared into those cock-teaser boots she was wearing.

I cleared my throat and finally answered her question. "You look absolutely beautiful."

The style suited her. It still fell to her shoulders, but they'd removed some length to make it sleeker, and the highlights were subtle, but they made her beautiful blue eyes seem to pop richer, and deeper.

She straightened up again, and turned to face me. "So how was your day?" she questioned.

I looked her up and down, stopping at what looked like a red angora sweater. Or at least . . . half a sweater. The garment was off the shoulders, and it was the first time I'd had a glimpse of that creamy skin since the day she'd worn that sundress. Today, she was showing just a little more skin than she had before. The sweater was cropped, but it ended right at the waistband of her jeans, so it flirted with showing skin, but didn't quite get there.

Is it possible to wear a bra with that kind of top? Or is she not wearing one?

"It was good," I said huskily. "I went to the clinic this morning, and then Brutus and I had some guy time. I was starting to miss you, though."

I couldn't take my eyes off that damn sweater.

She moved forward and put her arms around my neck. "I missed you, too."

Christ! Was she really talking to me in her *fuck-me* voice, or was I having happy hallucinations?

She kissed me softly, and then pulled back. "Are you okay, Owen? You're so quiet tonight."

I buried my face in her neck and took a deep breath. "What is that amazing smell?"

The woman had her own unique aroma, a faint floral scent that had always sent my testosterone into overdrive.

But now, all I wanted to do was take a bite of her.

She smelled like . . .

"Sugar cookies," she said with a chuckle. "I guess I discovered I wasn't into heavy perfume, but I really like this body mist. Is it too much?"

"Hell, no. But it does make me want to devour you in a couple of bites."

She perched on the arm of the sofa. "I had a lot of fun today," she said wistfully. "Thank you for buying me new things. I feel really good.

Your sisters-in-law helped me find my own personal style without getting anything fussy."

"What else did you get?" I asked, still trying to take in how beautiful she looked.

It wasn't just the clothing, it was Layla. She looked so vibrant and happy that she was mesmerizing.

If this was her personal style, I fucking adored it.

"Do you want to know if you're broke now?" she said cheekily.

"If it makes you happy, I don't give a shit if you take every penny I own," I told her honestly.

She snorted as she reached into the pocket of her ass-hugging jeans. She handed me my card. "I didn't do too much damage. Although I did do a significant spend at the lingerie store. Would you like to see that, too?"

Goddammit! That *was* definitely her *fuck-me* voice, and I couldn't handle much more of it.

I'd decided to wait until we got to Paris, give Layla more time to get comfortable.

She deserved to be romanced, and what was more romantic than Paris, right?

"You know damn well I want to see it," I growled. "But if you make a single move to show me, I'll have you pinned to the wall and my cock inside you so fast you'll never see it coming."

She rose and toed off her boots as she shot me a hungry look. "Is that so?"

I nodded sharply, but she didn't seem the least bit intimidated.

I couldn't speak as she took the hem of her sweater and pulled the garment over her head as she said, "Maybe I'd like that. In fact, I think I'd probably love it."

She was wearing a bra, but it was a strapless, silky garment that barely covered her nipples. There was a front tie, and her breasts seemed like they were ready to overflow the material.

Maybe blush pink shouldn't be the sexiest color in the world, but on Layla, it was the most sensual thing I'd ever seen.

My eyes lowered to the place where her fingers were working to lower the zipper of her jeans.

Fuck! Don't do it! Do. Not. Do. It.

But in a matter of seconds, she'd shimmied out of her jeans, revealing a pair of panties that matched that barely there bra. The delicate panties were lacy and silky, and the tiny little bow at the very top was so . . . it was so Layla.

"Um . . . this is the part where you really need to help me, Owen," she said in a low murmur. "That pretty much does it for my seduction skills."

Our eyes met, and I could see a small glint of uncertainty in her gaze.

She's waiting for me because she doesn't know what to do now.

Jesus Christ!

I was done waiting, done trying to convince myself that I could wait until Paris.

I couldn't.

I moved until I was right in front of her. "I warned you, right?"

She nodded. "You did. Do you like the new underwear?"

I swung her up and into my arms. Much as I wanted to fuck her up against the wall, I wanted her in my bed more. "You know it made me hard enough to cut through granite," I accused.

Her happy grin was like a sucker punch in the gut.

"I didn't know, but I'm not about to say that I'm sorry."

"You don't have to," I told her in a hoarse tone as I started up the stairs. "Your fate was sealed the second you took off that sweater, and started to talk to me in that *fuck-me* voice that makes me crazy."

"So no wall sex?" she queried.

"Not this time," I told her as we hit the top of the stairs.

I wanted her to be comfortable, because it was going to be a while before I'd ever let her go.

CHAPTER 24

Layla

I was completely relieved that Owen had finally given up the idea of waiting any longer to take me to bed.

However, I was just the tiniest bit nervous.

My one attempt to enter the world of sensual pleasure had been one of the worst experiences of my life, and really, it hadn't taught me much of anything.

We entered Owen's bedroom, a space I hadn't ever seen before because I'd never had a reason to go upstairs.

It was dark, but I could hear the rustling of sheets as he pulled back the comforter, and then he tossed me onto the bed.

I blinked a couple of times after Owen turned on the bedside lamp, and I could suddenly see again.

My mouth went dry as I noticed that he was unbuttoning his shirt.

"You do realize that you're going to have to lead me through this whole . . . process, and show me what you want," I said, my voice soft and low. "I really don't know how to turn you on."

His eyes locked with mine. "Baby, you won't need anybody to lead you. That seduction scene downstairs was the sexiest thing I've ever seen. And you don't need to lift a finger to get me turned on. My dick gets hard just from watching you fucking breathe."

My heart skittered as he finished with the buttons and his shirt fell open. As he took it off, my body shuddered at the sight of his gorgeously formed, muscular chest and well-defined six-pack abs that I suddenly wanted to trace with my tongue.

Sweet Jesus! The man was hot everywhere.

I licked my dry lips as he removed his shirt and then reached for the buttons on his jeans.

Owen Sinclair had suddenly become a sex god, and I was savoring every moment of this new side of him.

His eyes were infused with heat as his focused gaze remained directly on . . . me.

"I wanted to wait, to make sure that changing our relationship completely wasn't going to mess with your head. But I think it's screwed with me even more than it's affected you," he said as he popped every button on his fly. "I told you that this was going to change everything. There is no going back. You get that, right? The moment I get my hands all over that gorgeous body of yours, you're mine, Layla, but maybe it doesn't even matter. You've been mine since the second I saw you again. That striptease downstairs was just the final straw."

My breathing grew heavier as his jeans came undone, and his mammoth erection strained to get completely free of confinement.

Moist heat flowed between my thighs, and I ached to touch him. His words of possession didn't faze me one bit, because I knew that he was mine, too. Every glorious inch of that mesmerizingly masculine form all belonged to me.

Every ounce of Owen's attention was focused on me, and for now, we belonged to each other, and I was trembling with need to claim what was mine.

He was the sexiest man alive, and when he shucked his jeans and his black boxer briefs without a moment of hesitation, all of the desire I'd been holding back flooded my body with intense heat.

"I-I really need to touch you," I stammered. "Please."

His cock was standing hard and proud against his lower abdomen, and even though I knew the male anatomy well, I'd never seen anything like *that*.

My one brief sexual experience hadn't allowed for touching, or for seeing my partner's male form. We'd been mostly dressed, and there had been no foreplay. At all.

Owen came down on top of me, completely nude, and I hissed at the feeling of our bodies plastered against each other, skin-to-skin.

I wrapped my arms around him, stroking every inch of him I could reach. He was all heated skin over hard, uncompromising muscle, and I savored every touch.

"Not now, beautiful," he said in a coarse, raw voice. "My first priority is to see your new lingerie up close and personal."

He kissed me, and the embrace was languorous, thorough, and hotly erotic.

Our urgency was there, but Owen seemed determined to make sure I knew that he was claiming me.

I was panting when he lifted his head and traced his lips and tongue down my neck until he could nuzzle my breasts.

"You look like a fucking goddess," he rasped against the exposed portion of my cleavage. "Innocent and sexy as hell at the same time."

"I told you that I'm not innocent," I said on a gasp as he figured out exactly how to get the lingerie off, and tossed the pretty bra aside.

"You are," he argued. "But I'm having a damn hard time remembering that."

I spread my hands through his hair as his mouth came down on one of my peaked, hard nipples. "Owen," I said in a tormented moan

I couldn't control as he nipped and stroked both breasts, moving back and forth until I felt like I was losing my mind. "Please."

My head thrashed mindlessly as my brain willed him to stop before I went insane, yet I held his head against me for more.

Owen moved down my body slowly, branding every inch of bare skin he could find with that wicked mouth and tongue of his, and I whimpered from the loss of them on my nipples.

Until he parted my legs and licked right over the thin barrier of fine silk between him and my bare pussy.

"Oh, God," I moaned. "No more, Owen. I can't handle it."

The lingerie fabric was so thin and delicate that it provided me little protection against his hot, marauding mouth.

And then, the flimsy barrier was gone. One strong jerk of his powerful hand and arm completely tore the fabric away from me. "I'll buy you more, hundreds of them in every available color," he said in a raspy, grumbly voice overflowing with lust.

I didn't have a chance to respond before Owen buried his head between my thighs.

And then, I was lost.

He wasn't teasing anymore; he was deadly serious and erotically aggressive as his mouth, tongue, and lips worked together to drive me mad.

No man had ever had his head between my thighs, and the sensation of Owen greedily lapping the liquid heat there was mind boggling.

The pleasure was so intense that it was almost painful.

I fisted his hair, holding on tight to the mass of coarse locks, not knowing whether I wanted to tug him away or press his head hard against me.

"Owen," I moaned as I lifted my hips. "It's-way-too-much-but-it-feels-so-good."

I was babbling mindlessly, awash in a sexual pleasure I'd never experienced before.

I had no idea how to handle the massive climax that was building, and rushing toward me.

"Owen," I screamed, the sound bouncing off the walls of the silent room. "Oh-my-God-I'm-not-sure-I'm-going-to-live-through-this."

He didn't even pause. He doubled his efforts to make me completely come undone.

I was panting and moaning, arching as I lost every fear I had about my enormous climax as it seized my body in spasms. "Owen! Oh, God. Owen!"

I let go, allowing the sensual pleasure and my release to completely consume me, knowing that Owen was here to catch me if I fell.

I'd never known the sense of freedom that grabbed hold of me in those moments. I felt like I was flying, floating completely unfettered without another thought in my head except the sensations and the man creating them.

I came down from my intensely pleasured state slowly, dizzy from the powerful event, as Owen drew out the postorgasmic bliss by savoring the liquid heat of my climax before he prowled up my body.

"La petite mort," I whispered as I continued to pant, trying to catch my breath. "It's just like that."

The French described orgasms and the brief time afterward as *la petite mort*—or in English translation, "the little death"—and now I knew exactly why they did.

I'd been completely ripped from normal consciousness for a moment, but the experience hadn't been scary.

It had been pure bliss.

"As long as you don't really leave me completely, I think I'm okay with that," Owen said huskily right before he kissed me. I tasted myself on his lips, and it was the sweetest aphrodisiac I'd ever known. When he finally lifted his head, he pinned me with a fierce, emerald-eyed stare that caused my heart to do a complete somersault inside my chest.

I smiled at him as I stroked a hand over his hair. He was obviously familiar with the French expression, which didn't surprise me at all.

Owen looked tousled and barely controlled, like a conquering warrior who was just starting the fight. His expression was fervid, harsh, but adoring at the same time.

I love you. I love you so much.

The words were caught in my throat, demanding escape, but I swallowed those emotions.

I wasn't about to ruin this moment, this whole experience, by babbling something that Owen didn't want to hear.

But God, I could *feel* them so acutely that I could hardly keep those words contained.

"I need to touch you," I demanded.

He shook his head sharply, and I heard the crinkling sound of a condom wrapper as he started tearing it open.

Thank God!

I'd started on birth control, but wasn't quite completely protected.

Owen rolled it on like a madman, but hesitated slightly as he covered me, and was poised to give us both something we'd been anticipating for what seemed like years.

"What?" I breathed out slowly, stroking my hands over his back until they landed on his tight glutes. I squeezed his perfectly formed ass to encourage him.

"I don't want this to be like the last time for you," he grumbled, his voice tight.

I felt a viselike grip around my heart as I heard a note of vulnerability in his tone.

He's still afraid for me. He's actually worried that I'll be disappointed.

I wrapped my legs tightly around him and lifted my hips. "It won't be," I assured him. "But if you don't fuck me right now, I swear I'll never speak to you again. I can't wait anymore, Owen," I entreated.

I heard a strangled laugh escape from his lips right before his hips surged forward and he buried himself to the hilt inside me.

"Fucking hell!" Owen cursed loudly. "You're so damn tight."

I tightened my legs around him because I knew that fact was driving him insane.

I was half-crazy from the feeling of Owen stretching me almost to the point of pain. He was a big man, but I wanted every inch of him. "Fuck me," I pleaded beside his ear. "Fuck me hard like I know you want to. I need it that way, too."

I wanted every bit of Owen's fierce possessiveness.

Like my words had made him come unglued, he pulled back and plunged in again with a powerful thrust.

"Yes," I hissed. "Just like that. Show me that I'm yours," I begged.

"You will *always* be fucking mine, Layla. Mine. All mine," he rasped harshly as he put one hand under my ass, forcing me to meet every single hard, hot stroke.

I moved my hands up his back, and my fingernails gripped his upper back so hard they'd probably leave marks. "That means you're mine, too, Owen. All mine, too," I moaned, half out of my mind as he was pounding into me relentlessly.

"Fuck, yeah, I'm yours. Always have been," he said on a long groan of satisfaction.

As I caught the technique of meeting his every powerful downward thrust by raising my hips, Owen pulled his hand from my ass, and threaded it into my hair to jerk my head back, exposing my neck to his hungry mouth.

He licked and nipped at the tender skin, bringing a yelp to my lips, an animalistic sound that echoed the forceful, completely carnal instincts that had taken over my entire body and mind.

My back arched in mindless pleasure, trying to get as fused to Owen as I could possibly be.

"Harder," I demanded.

I'd waited too damn long to feel this man completely lose it, and for him to take me until I felt thoroughly consumed.

The freedom I'd felt when his mouth had been ravaging my pussy was nothing compared to how I felt with him fucking me like he was in a frenzy.

He was wild, untamed, and dominated by lust.

All of those emotions filled my senses until I wasn't sure if it was me or him who generated the feral instincts, but it really didn't matter.

We were tangled up, and in the throes of this crazy, frantic turmoil together.

"Owen," I moaned in anguish and pure bliss. "I need you."

He shifted his massive body slightly, until every volatile stroke of his cock brushed along my clit. "Come for me, baby. Let it go."

The tension inside me was coiled tight, and it wound into an ever-more-inflexible state.

He filled me.

His cock teased me with every brush against the sensitive, hard bundle of nerves between my thighs.

I could feel Owen's warm breath landing in forceful wafts against my ear.

"Come, Layla! Come hard for me. I have to see it," he demanded in a bossy tone that set me off.

There was something about Owen's alpha-male side that made me raw, and completely turned on.

The snugness of that coil inside me suddenly released, and I shattered.

I started to come. *Hard.*

And it was even more powerful when, right before I closed my eyes from the force of my climax, I could see that Owen was watching my face. He was greedily savoring every second of my climax.

I could feel the caress of his gaze even after my eyes were tightly shut.

"Owen," I cried out in a strangled voice as my inner muscles clamped down strong and tight around his cock as his pace became almost frantic. "I-need-this-so-much-I-need-you-so-much-I-can't-stand-it."

Words poured out of my mouth completely unchecked. I babbled, and they made completely no sense to anybody but me.

When I reached the pinnacle, I simply screamed his name. "Owen!"

"Layla. Fuck!" Owen's voice was vibrating with an emotion I didn't recognize.

I opened my eyes as he closed his. He buried himself deeply inside me while my contracting muscles milked him to his own heated release.

I watched Owen as I slowly drifted back down, savoring the tormented ecstasy on his handsome face.

He rolled to my side, but he pulled my sated body against him like he couldn't stand to be parted from it for very long.

Neither of us spoke for several minutes because we were busy trying to catch our breath.

"Nothing like the last time," I murmured once my heart had stopped racing and I was able to take a deep breath.

"Thank fuck for that," Owen grumbled as he wrapped his arm tightly around my waist with a grunt of satisfaction. "Especially since I plan on being the only guy who ever touches you again."

I burrowed into his warmth, and smiled against his chest.

His comment warmed my heart, because I felt exactly the same way.

CHAPTER 25

Owen

"What in the world did you do?" Layla said, laughing in my ear as she answered my phone call.

We were escaping a rainy day in Southern California for Paris, but I didn't give a damn what the weather was like here.

I was on my way to Layla's apartment, and all I cared about was finally getting her to Paris.

"I have no idea what you're talking about," I managed to answer in a puzzled voice.

I knew exactly what she was talking about, but I wasn't ready to proclaim my guilt quite yet.

I could feel Layla's laughter down to my bones.

She wasn't mad.

Just surprised.

And I'd damn well find something to shock her every single day if she continued to sound this flustered and giddy.

Dammit! She deserved to be completely spoiled.

"I got another delivery this morning," she informed me, knowing very well who had sent it.

For the last few days, I'd been sending her any number of things I thought she'd like for our Paris trip. "It was only one delivery today," I reminded her.

"Because it's only nine a.m.," she answered, laughter still ringing in her voice. "Owen, you have to stop this."

"Why?" I challenged.

"Because you've sent me a ridiculous amount of stuff. My apartment isn't that big. Although, you had already promised all the panties that were delivered this morning." Her voice got lower and softer during that last sentence.

Holy crap! It was her *fuck-me* voice. Again.

Maybe she didn't *intend* for that husky, beckoning timbre to be a *fuck-me* voice, but it didn't matter.

When *my dick* heard anything close to the husky inflection she used in the bedroom, *anything* she said was immediately interpreted as "You're such a stud, Owen, please take off my clothes and do me *right now*."

Layla started to speak again since I hadn't responded. "No woman needs over three hundred pairs of panties."

"You do," I informed her. "I hope you packed extra. You'll probably only come back with half of them since your boyfriend is a little rough on your underwear."

I heard her breath catch before she said, "Certainly you'll slow down on that eventually."

Oh, no, I certainly *wouldn't*.

We'd had sex on several different occasions now, and she'd lost a pair every single time. When I finally got to those silky, translucent panties, I didn't have the desire or the patience to be extra careful.

I didn't see that changing anytime soon.

"I wouldn't count on that, sweetheart," I warned her.

Layla seemed to enjoy our sexual activities as much as I did, so she'd be absolutely no help in the save-the-panties effort.

Not that I cared about that. My goal was to make her happy, even if that meant buying her a million pairs.

I was getting a lot more comfortable with my billionaire status these days. Not that I'd ever forget those poor-student days of not knowing where my next meal was going to come from sometimes, but remembering that would keep me humble.

Otherwise, I really had no problem with spending my money, and with the help of my savvy, business-minded family, I was learning to handle most of my investments myself.

Eli and Jade had made themselves available to help me get the clinic established as a not-for-profit operation, so that transition was going a lot smoother than I'd thought it would.

"I can't believe I'm actually going to get on a jet and fly to Paris," Layla said chirpily.

I chuckled, my heart a lot lighter just because I knew she was genuinely happy. "It's not like you haven't known about it for a while now, sweetheart."

She sighed. "But now it's happening. And I'm going to see it with you."

My chest ached from her words. I had no doubt Layla cared about me, but when she said shit like that, I could almost imagine that I meant as much to her as she did to me.

Hell, I'd always been way ahead of her in the area of obsessive affection. I wanted to put an enormous diamond on her finger, hustle her to the altar, and call it done so that the craziness inside me to call her mine would abate just a little. Although I wasn't entirely sure that would help, either.

"I'm looking forward to it, too, Layla," I told her honestly. "The best part of it is being with you."

She let out a breath. "So does that mean you'll slow down on buying me stuff, so my apartment isn't cramped? I love everything you got me, but I'll be sleeping outside if you don't stop."

"It just so happens that I have an extremely large home with an abundance of unused space," I hinted.

I didn't realize I was holding my breath while I was waiting for her response. Maybe I was moving too fast, but dammit, I wanted her in my bed every single night.

I wanted her to make my sheets continue to smell like sugar cookies.

I wanted her damn toothbrush in the same bathroom as mine.

I wanted to open my dresser drawer only to find out that she'd taken it over with a million pairs of her sexy panties.

To hell with personal space, I wanted Layla to invade mine.

I wanted her to come home with me every damn night after a rough day at work so we could talk about it and decompress over dinner.

I wanted to walk Brutus together, when I could actually get my big boy up and moving.

I wanted to fall asleep to her warm breath on my neck, and wake up every morning to her beautiful face smiling at me as we greeted another day together.

Okay, yeah, I wanted it all.

But it was all too soon for that.

I was more than ready for a lifetime commitment.

But I didn't think Layla had quite caught up with me yet.

Maybe after Paris . . .

"Well, my apartment is pretty small," she said, not taking the bait.

The air *whooshed* out of my lungs.

Okay, so much for the possibility of getting her to move in with me. *For now.*

"I buy you that stuff because whenever I pass by a store, or even get online, I see things that remind me of you," I told her.

"Yeah," she answered softly. "I think that's why I really love *everything* you've sent. Because I know you're thinking about me even when I'm not around. Could we at least bargain on the food and sweets? I think I've gained three pounds in just a few days, and it's all gone directly to my rear end."

"You won't hear me complaining if your ass is a little plumper," I said hoarsely.

"Oh, God, you're impossible, Owen Sinclair." The fondness in her tone took any of the sting out of her words.

"We missed a lot of holidays, birthdays, and special occasions together, Layla. Give me a break. I have more money than I could ever possibly spend, and all of my family is in the same situation. Who in the hell do you think I'd want to spend it on?"

"I really did love the watch," she said softly. "And all of the gorgeous earrings and clothes. I'm thinking you did a consult with Skye and Riley on those."

"Nope," I informed her, slightly offended that she'd think that Skye and Riley knew her better than I did.

"Seriously?" she asked, still sounding doubtful.

Did she really think I couldn't pick out her gifts myself? "You seem to really like sexier stuff than you used to wear, but nothing too overtly revealing. You like to feel comfortable and together in what you wear, and you aren't crazy about anything fluffy, ruffled, furred, or otherwise gaudy. You prefer jeans or casual pants to a dress, but you like to style it up a little, and every once in a while, you like something quirky if you're in that mood. Overall, classy is the goal, but a *relaxed* classy is more your style. You like colorful, crazy earrings, the bigger the better, but *only* with earrings, because you'd rather have silver, white gold, or platinum for any other type of jewelry because it's something you're not going to lose or throw away. You've pretty much decided that perfumes are too strong, so you'll stick with a body mist and fragrance lotion. Oh, and you've developed a fondness for black leather boots, although heels are optional, depending on how much walking you plan on doing that day. I guess I'll have to see what direction you go after boot season is over. How am I doing so far?"

"I'm . . . stunned," she muttered.

"I'm observant," I answered. "Especially when it comes to you. What guy wants to send a woman something she *won't* like? And I sure as hell don't want to ask somebody else what to get my girlfriend. If I have to do that, then I'm not paying attention."

She sighed. "You're probably the most thoughtful guy I know, so I guess I shouldn't be surprised. But we still need to talk about your, um . . . generosity."

"It's just a few gifts, Layla," I told her. "It gives me more pleasure to give them to you than you probably get by receiving them, so work with me here. Don't make me give up doing something I've just discovered I really like."

"What am I going to do with you?" she said with what sounded like a mix of exasperation and adoration.

Love me?

That sounded like the best idea I could think of at the moment, but I wasn't about to say that out loud.

"You're going to Paris with me," I said as I pulled into the driveway of her apartment. "I'm here. I'll be right up."

"If you come in, we'll end up late for our flight. You know we will," she said firmly.

I grinned as I locked my vehicle and sprinted toward the stairs so I wouldn't end up drenched with rain. "Sweetheart, we're taking a private jet. *They* wait for *us*, not the other way around."

I heard her suck in a sharp breath. "Okay. Then hurry. Maybe we won't get too late of a start."

Fuck! I love this woman.

I took the stairs two at a time instead of waiting for the elevator.

I didn't give a damn how late we were, but I knew I couldn't wait another second to get my hands on her.

CHAPTER 26

LAYLA

"I have no idea how something so small can hold so much magic," I said to Owen several days after we'd arrived in Paris, as I stared at the *Mona Lisa* painting by da Vinci that was hanging on the wall in the Louvre museum.

I tilted my head to get another angle, but it still seemed just as surreal, any way I looked at it.

We couldn't get extremely close to the work of art. The wall area was roped off, but I was close enough to be awed by the masterpiece.

Yes, I'd *known* it was small, only approximately thirty inches by twenty-one inches, which *wasn't* very big when one was considering priceless paintings, but size didn't seem to diminish the piece. It just made it more . . . unique.

It still seemed crazy that I was actually staring at the *Mona Lisa* in person. In the Louvre, for God's sake. The world-famous museum would have been extremely high on my bucket list later in life. Honestly, I'd wanted to come here since I was a child. I just hadn't expected to actually see these masterpieces before I was thirty.

Truthfully, all of my days in Paris had been miraculous.

Owen and I had spent the first several days just walking to as many famous landmarks as possible, and getting waylaid by chocolate croissants, French pastries, crepes, and delicious coffee along the way.

Somehow, he'd found us an elegant, detached, fully furnished home for our stay near the Champ de Mars in the seventh arrondissement, *with* an unobstructed view of the Eiffel Tower. So even our accommodations were extraordinary.

The City of Lights had enchanted me from the first day I arrived, and I fell more in love with it every single day.

"It is pretty amazing," Owen said from behind me. "I think I expected to be disappointed because it isn't a very big painting, but it still packs an enormous punch."

He'd taken up a position behind me to try to protect me from getting trampled by an enthusiastic crowd.

Our trip hadn't been quite the serene experience I'd expected, at least not when we were visiting huge tourist attractions. In fact, the tourists got downright pushy to get their photos and move on to the next work of art or historical landmark.

Then again, a massive amount of people came from all over the world to see Paris. There was only so much space for the thirty or forty million visitors who came to see this amazing city every year.

When we were ready, Owen plowed his way through the crowd, holding my hand and making a pathway for me to get through.

I was laughing by the time we'd exited the large crush of people clamoring to see the painting.

He grinned at me. "What famous work of art do you want me to get you to next?"

I smiled back at him. Owen was acting as my personal bulldozer, and for some reason, he seemed to enjoy helping me get near every piece I wanted to see.

God, the man looked as happy as I felt right now. "Is there anything else *you* want to see?" I asked.

Owen and I had covered a lot of territory today. Since there was no possible way to see the entire museum in one day, or even a week of continual visits, we'd decided on our must-see list before we'd even left the house early this morning.

We'd seen the Venus de Milo, the Winged Victory, *The Dying Slave*, *The Raft of the Medusa*, and so many other pieces we'd pegged as *absolutely necessary*, and our list had been so long that we'd done it without much time to spare. I knew the museum would be closing soon. "If you're game, I wouldn't mind just seeing more of da Vinci's work," I suggested.

"I'm right behind you," he said agreeably as he gently squeezed my hand. "Or maybe I should be right in front of you to get us through the crowd."

"I'm not in any hurry," I assured him as we started to stroll. "I've seen all the stuff on my wish list, and we still have the Musée d'Orsay later in the week."

I was really looking forward to the Musée d'Orsay. It was known for its large section of impressionistic work, which was my favorite, and it housed a lot of Monet's paintings.

"You're itching to get to that museum," Owen teased.

I bumped his shoulder playfully. "I'm eager to see everything, and I'm thankful for everything I've already had a chance to visit. The Arc de Triomphe, the Panthéon, the Eiffel Tower, even though I can actually see that landmark from the house. I wish we could have gone into Notre-Dame, but from what I've heard, it may not be open for another five years."

"Notre-Dame may have been spared from some of the flames of the fire, but it's unstable," Owen said grimly. "We'll be back one day, Layla. We can see it next time."

My heart jumped at the knowledge that Owen expected us to be together for a long time. We hadn't really discussed the future much. We'd just enjoyed being together as a couple. And really, it was probably too soon to plan a future together, but I couldn't deny that my heart didn't think it was too soon.

"I'm not disappointed," I told him. "How could I be, when everything else has been so wonderful, and we still have so much more to do?"

He pulled me aside from the crowd and wrapped his arms around me. "Do you want to know what I'm looking forward to the most?"

His voice was husky and low, and his hooded gaze told me exactly what he was thinking.

Maybe the two of us should have been completely sated by now. We'd been together 24/7 for days, and had spent a significant amount of those hours indulging in ways to try to satisfy our insatiable hunger for each other's bodies.

I could never get enough of Owen's smoking-hot body, or the things he could do to me with a single touch.

Rather than appeasing my crazy need, every time he touched me, I got more addicted, and I craved that *next* caress, that *next* sensuous kiss, that *next* mind-boggling climax.

It just kept getting more intense as Owen and I grew closer and closer, and got familiar with exactly how to make each other crazy.

I put my arms around his neck. "I don't know. But I'm sure you're going to tell me."

He put his mouth beside my ear. "I can't wait to get you back to the house, take off your clothes, and find out what color panties you're wearing today."

I snickered as I looked into his eyes, my heart accelerating in anticipation.

Owen was absolutely relentless about finding out what color panties I was wearing, since he'd given me about a gazillion to choose from.

I playfully refused to let him see every morning, so he teased me about it all day.

"Why?" I asked him. "Every time you see a new color you tell me *they're* your favorite. What happens when I run out of new colors?"

"Then I guess you're going to have to find another sexy style so I can get some different shades," he suggested.

"Or, we could just start all over again from the beginning with the ones that I have," I teased.

He put his forehead against mine. "I wouldn't mind seeing every one of those colors again, just to make sure all of them are my favorites," he readily agreed.

"You're such a pervert," I accused.

"And you love every minute of it," he shot back flirtatiously.

"Oh, God. I do," I confessed with a quiet groan. "Does that mean I'm just as depraved as you are?"

"Probably, but you won't hear me complaining, sweetheart," he answered in a heated voice that never failed to make me twitchy to get him naked.

"Cherry red," I blurted out.

He pulled his head back and lifted a brow. "What?"

"My panties. They're cherry red and I love them," I said, my face turning the same color as my underwear.

I might have loved to play with Owen, but I wasn't quite used to our frequent sexual banter yet.

Maybe this was commonplace for most couples, but I was sadly behind my age group when it came to all things sexual, or having someone look at me with the kind of raw desire that Owen did.

It was new.

It was exciting.

It was a little terrifying.

And oh, God, it was thoroughly intoxicating.

Owen was completely overwhelming sometimes with his sweet compliments, his willingness to do anything and everything to please me, and his testosterone-fueled desire to watch me come over and over again.

"You're blushing," he said in a surprised tone.

"I know."

"Don't tell me you're still shy with me, Layla. After all the things we've done."

"I'm not . . . shy," I insisted, even though I could feel the heat on my cheeks. "I'm just not entirely used to discussing my panties with a guy."

"Woman, we've had sex in every possible position, and you're blushing over underwear?" He sounded more delighted than confused.

Every so often, I did feel myself getting flustered. I could go toe-to-toe with him on dirty talk one moment, and the next, I'd wonder what in the hell I was saying.

"Layla, if something is wrong, talk to me," he rumbled, every bit of playful humor instantly gone.

I shook my head immediately. "No, Owen, nothing is wrong. Everything is perfect. Please remember that all of this is new for me. I'm not used to having someone who cares about how I feel, and honestly, I've never had a serious boyfriend. I'm not used to playing with someone, or having them tease me. I love it, but it's still different for me. I just . . . Oh hell, sometimes it feels so unreal that you want me this much that I get a little flustered. But for God's sake, don't stop. Because it's also the best feeling in the world to me."

He put his forefinger on my chin and lifted my face to his. "It's kind of new for me, too," he said, his voice gravelly as his eyes met mine. "Don't ever think I take *any* of this for granted, Layla. For me, just *you* being with *me* is like a goddamn fantasy that I *never* want to end. It's not like I've engaged in much dirty talk myself, and fuck knows I've never had the kind of mind-blowing sex that we have. I've never had a serious relationship, either. Never wanted one until you."

Why was it so hard to believe that Owen, for a guy his age, probably was inexperienced, too? "I think being a pervert just comes naturally for you," I teased, trying to lighten the conversation since we were alone in the middle of a huge crowd.

"I think it comes naturally to most guys, whether they can back up all their trash talk or not."

Owen knew how to make me feel comfortable and not make a big deal out of nothing. He'd acknowledged my quirk, related to it, and then brushed it off.

His ability to accept any weird stumbles that I made while I was getting used to this new relationship between us was one of the things I loved about him.

We'd probably both screw up while we were figuring everything out, but at the core of *us*, we were best friends.

I'd always have Owen's back.

And he'd always have mine.

There was just a whole lot of adoration, lust, chemistry, and for me, romantic love tossed into that mix, too.

"Baby, you have no idea how badly I want to see those cherry-red panties, and then rip them off your body right now," he said in a low, seductive baritone next to my ear.

I pulled his head down and gave him a sweet, brief kiss. "Come on, Tarzan. We have some paintings to see."

Either I needed a distraction, or I was going to drag him outside, call an Uber to get us home as soon as possible, and strip him the second the door was closed.

"Later," he said in a warning voice as he led me back into the stream of people.

I laughed as I tripped into the crowd with him.

I could hardly wait.

CHAPTER 27

LAYLA

I sank into the bathtub with an enormous sigh, my body exhausted, but my head still buzzing with activity.

It's my last night in Paris.

Owen had taken me to the Jules Verne, the restaurant on the second floor of the Eiffel Tower, for our last dinner in Paris. The views had been breathtaking from the panoramic windows there, and the food had been absolutely delicious.

When we'd arrived back at the house, Owen had needed to answer some important emails about the progress on the clinic, so I'd wandered into the spa-like master bathroom, and finally decided to take advantage of the massive bathtub that I'd been eyeing since we'd arrived.

Honestly, we hadn't really had a free moment until now.

I felt like we'd hiked halfway across France over the last nine days, and it felt good just to let the warm water relax my muscles.

There hadn't been a single moment in Paris that I wouldn't cherish for the rest of my life.

Owen and I had been busy every day, trying to take in all the magnificent history of Paris, and at night, we burned up the sheets together.

"No wonder I'm so damn tired," I muttered as I sank into the relaxing bath until the water was touching my chin.

Probably some of my favorite memories of Paris would always be just walking and exploring with Owen. Paris was a city where people walked and took in the ambiance. It was those quieter, softer moments that I'd miss the most.

I grabbed the brand-new loofah that I'd left at the side of the tub, put some of the mild soap I'd purchased on the sponge, and began to stroke it over my skin.

"I'm the first in line to volunteer to wash your back for you, or any other part of your body, for that matter," Owen offered from the entrance on the other side of the room.

My breath caught as I saw him leaning against the doorjamb, still dressed in the charcoal-gray suit he'd worn to dinner.

Owen always looked comfortable in his own skin, but he looked equally at ease in a suit and tie.

With his white dress shirt and striking navy-and-gray tie, my eyes had hardly left him the entire night.

I'd worn a classic little black dress that I'd brought with me. I'd told Owen to remember it, because he probably wouldn't see me in another dress for a long time.

He'd listened.

And he'd looked until I thought the heat in his eyes was going to incinerate me, and I'd squirmed in my chair. A lot.

"I think you'd get that gorgeous suit all wet." I was hoping he'd take the hint and take it off.

He did. Almost immediately.

"You are looking a little lonely," he observed as he slid the tie off his neck. "It's a pretty big tub."

It was gigantic, probably big enough to have a pool party. "I can definitely make room for *you*, handsome."

He'd just taken off his suit jacket when his cell phone blasted from his jacket pocket. I watched as he pulled it out to look at the caller ID.

"Fuck!" he cursed loudly. "It's Seth. I forgot that he wanted to talk to me by the end of day about a couple of things on the clinic remodel. It's after three in California."

"Answer it," I told him, pointing at the bedroom to let him know I was heading that direction.

He nodded and answered Seth's call on his way back to his computer in the living room.

I sighed as I got out of the tub before I pruned, brushed my hair out, and wandered into the bedroom. I left the bedside lamp on for Owen, and slid between the softest sheets I'd ever slept on.

I was exhausted, but my body and mind were still very much awake.

As I turned my head, I caught a whiff of Owen's scent, pulled his pillow toward me, and inhaled. I tried not to think about what he and I would be doing right now if Seth hadn't called.

And I failed.

I'd spent the entire evening squirming under Owen's lustful gaze, and just when I'd thought I was getting satisfaction, I didn't.

Not that my endless desire to ravish my boyfriend came before the clinic, but I was hoping Owen would come to bed before I started nodding off.

After a few more minutes of breathing in the scent of Owen's pillow, I felt so sexually frustrated that I ran my hand softly down my naked body, opened my legs, and touched myself.

I was perfectly capable of getting myself off. Maybe if I did, I could sleep.

It wouldn't be the same, but Owen was busy, and we'd had a really long day and evening.

I was already wet from that whole bathroom anticipation scene, so I let my eyes drift shut, picturing how Owen's face had looked earlier that evening.

I released a quiet moan, and then a little whimper as I let my imagination go completely wild.

"I guess you couldn't wait for me?" I heard Owen's baritone inquire.

My eyes flew open, and I was mortified when I saw Owen watching me intently, his hip propped against the dresser, only four or five feet from the bed.

I opened my mouth, but couldn't get a single word out.

"Keep going, Layla. I want to watch you make yourself come," he demanded, his voice low and commanding.

Every hormone in my body came to life. Owen and I had done a lot of sexual exploring, and he knew bossy-in-bed did it for me.

I might not like it in everyday life, but when he started issuing orders in the bedroom, I was more than okay with that.

"Look at me," he said huskily. "Are you embarrassed?"

I nodded as I met his hungry gaze.

"Don't be," he insisted. "You're so damn beautiful. I will fuck you, but I'm going to watch you come first when I can see the whole picture."

Heat infused my entire body, and my fingers went back to work.

Watching him standing there like a sexy god, his eyes all over me, had my body coiled tight.

I sensed that this game had him incredibly turned on, too.

Since I couldn't stand to see him and not touch him, I closed my eyes.

"Do not close your eyes. Look at me," he instructed. "Do you want me, Layla?"

"Yes." I released the one word with a moan, and met his eyes again.

My hand moved faster as he started to undress, his eyes never leaving me.

"Fuck me, Owen. Please," I entreated.

My body was about primed to implode.

"Not yet," he said when he was completely nude, his clothes in a heap at his feet.

That gorgeously masculine, hot body of his made me crave his touch so badly I could hardly breathe, and I needed him so much that I couldn't stand it.

"Imagine me with my head between those gorgeous legs of yours, and make yourself come," he ordered as he stroked a hand up and down his beautifully hard cock.

I did imagine it. Between that visualization and the sight of Owen touching himself, it was only a matter of seconds before I started to climax.

"That's right, baby, bring yourself off," Owen demanded sharply.

"Owen!" I screamed at the top of my lungs as my body shattered.

Before my orgasm was over, Owen was inside me, his massive body on top of mine.

"Fuck!" he hissed. "Condom."

"I'm protected now," I told him breathlessly.

Owen and I had already had the new-couple-having-sex discussion, and there was no reason . . . "Don't stop," I added.

"I've never had sex without a condom, and you feel so damn good that I'm not going to last long," he said with a groan as he started to move. "I don't know what the fuck I'd do without you now, Layla," he ground out as he buried himself inside me again and again.

"You'll never have to find out," I moaned, clinging to him like he was a lifeline in a very rough sea as I closed my eyes.

Owen had been so aroused that I could tell that he was already close.

His breathing was ragged, and it wasn't from exhaustion.

When my body finally reached its breaking point, my orgasm was even stronger than the last one.

"Oh, God, Owen, I'm coming again," I said, completely mindless as I closed my eyes.

"I know," he grunted. "And it's the sexiest thing I've ever seen."

I wanted to open my eyes, but I couldn't.

His mouth came down on mine, and I wallowed in his sensuous kiss as we both drifted back into the real world.

He landed on his back a few seconds later with a grunt.

I almost purred as I burrowed into his warm body, wrapped my arms around him, and rested my head on his shoulder.

He entangled our legs, and his muscular arms wrapped around me, one hand on my back, and the other on my ass.

It was an intimate position, and my heart and my body were rejoicing because we were so entwined.

He put a hand in my hair, and moved it in a tender, gentle, relaxing motion.

It was absolute bliss to be held like this by Owen.

I felt safe.

I felt needed.

I felt protected.

But most of all, I felt . . . loved.

CHAPTER 28

LAYLA

Owen and I attended a Saturday-night barbecue at Seth's place several days after our arrival back to the States.

The clinic wasn't officially reopening for a few more weeks, but Owen had been in the thick of things, making sure everything was going to be completed on time.

He included me like I actually *was* a partner, rather than just an employee, and had enthusiastically implemented all of the things I suggested.

Owen had even insisted that I sit in on interviews for new clinic staff. He was adamant that he needed my input since I'd worked with our existing small team much longer than he had. According to him, I was a lot more knowledgeable about what kinds of personalities would be a good match with our current crew.

Although I'd told him dozens of times that he was perfectly capable of making those decisions for *his* clinic on his own, I secretly loved the fact that he treated me like a valuable medical associate. I was so excited about how much good the new clinic was going to do for the community, and I was thrilled to be consulted in all of the planning.

By day, I was his colleague.

But once we left work behind, we were lovers who could never get enough of each other's bodies.

Since we'd returned from Paris, I'd spent my nights with Owen at his house. He'd told me it was way too difficult to say goodbye to me at night after we'd spent every moment together in France.

Little by little, a lot of my things were finding their way to his beautiful home on the water, and my apartment was feeling less and less like my real home.

"Thanks for all your help," Owen said to Seth and Aiden as we all sat around an outdoor table at Seth's place after dinner. "I owe both of you for helping out with the changes I'm making at the clinic while Layla and I were in Paris."

Seth shrugged. "I haven't really done that much," he denied. "You've gotten pretty damn good at time management and cracking the whip when you see that something is behind schedule. All I've done is kept an eye on things while you were gone, and you were long overdue for some time off, little brother."

Aiden added, "And all I did was keep the ugliest dog in town at my house while you and Layla were away, which ended up being no work at all since Maya adores the mutt. She pretty much took care of Brutus on her own."

I smiled. Aiden's daughter was such an exceptional kid. Maya was wise and intelligent way beyond her years, and as kindhearted as her mother and father.

Owen and I had dropped Brutus off to stay with the little girl tonight since she'd stayed home with a sitter. We'd started the evening late, and past her bedtime.

I think she'd been way more delighted about keeping the dog and sleeping with Brutus than she would have been about joining an adult gathering.

"Anything else I can do to help?" Eli inquired from his seat next to Jade.

Owen shook his head. "God, no. You and Jade have done enough. I've got all the legal experts I need in place for the rest of the details. I owe you guys, too. A lot."

"I haven't done a damn thing," Jaxton Montgomery said from his place beside me. "Probably because nobody even asked me. But I'd do anything possible to help out. You're doing a hell of a lot to help out the people who need it the most in this county."

"I'm good," Owen muttered as he shot Jax a look of displeasure.

It wasn't the first disgruntled expression that Jaxton had seen from Owen this evening.

Jax had wandered into the gathering alone right before dinner. Owen had pointed to the empty seat at the other end of the table, but Jax had just grinned and plopped down on the vacant chair on the other side of me instead.

Owen had muttered, "What in the hell is that bastard doing here?"

I'd replied, "He's Riley's brother, and she doesn't see him that often. He's family."

"He could have sat closer to her," he'd grumbled. "And he's not *my* family."

I'd let out an exasperated breath before I'd dropped the subject.

No matter how many times I'd told Owen that Jax and I weren't the least bit attracted to each other, he gave me the same answer. "I trust you, but I *don't* trust him."

I jabbed Owen playfully in the arm when I noticed he was still glaring at Jax.

He obligingly looked away from the man he saw as some kind of rival, but he still didn't appear to be happy as he resumed his discussions with his brothers, his sister, and their partners.

I picked up the glass of white wine that Seth had handed me earlier, and took a sip.

Eventually, Owen was going to have to at least be civil to Jax. Riley always invited her brothers to join us at any of our gatherings at her place, and rightfully so. They were the closest and the only real family she had. Hudson and Cooper were often too busy to come, but Jax seemed to be showing up more and more often, according to Riley.

Now that Jax wasn't occupying his free time with a different woman on his arm all the time, Riley joked that he had more opportunity to be with family.

"What's going on in that intelligent head of yours?" Jax asked quietly.

I turned to him as I pulled myself out of my thoughts. "Nothing, really. I was just thinking about Owen." I wasn't about to tell the man that he'd busted me when I was wondering about his life and his motivations for spending more time in Citrus Beach with Riley.

He drained his own glass of wine before he asked, "You guys really are an item now, right?"

Jax's tone was low and quiet as Owen continued to have an animated discussion with the rest of his family about Jade's research project.

Obviously, Jax wasn't averse to poking Owen occasionally, but he evidently didn't want an all-out war with Riley's brother-in-law, either.

I smiled at Jax. "We definitely are. I guess sometimes things don't always work out the way you thought they would. We went from friends to enemies to friends again, and then our relationship took a whole new direction. But I'm certainly not sad that it did. He's the most incredible person I've ever known."

"He doesn't seem like he's ready to embrace me as family," Jax said dryly. "But I do admire all that he's doing for the community."

"He will eventually," I assured him, without any further explanation. I wasn't comfortable talking about Owen with Jax. "And I admire what he's doing, too. He busted his ass to get a medical degree. But the minute he became way beyond financially secure, his first thought was who he could help. I wish every rich person in this world thought the way he did."

Jax shrugged. "Some do, and many don't. There's good and bad in any income bracket. Don't give up on all rich people. You are dating one of the good ones."

"Oh, I don't think they're all that way," I hurried to tell him. "All of Owen's family are deeply involved in their own charitable projects, and look at you and your brothers. Instead of just signing a check, you guys went to work to make a difference in the world."

He smirked. "Yeah, and we nearly lost our legacy because of it. We put the wrong people in charge while we were out saving the world. We were pretty much forced to reinsert ourselves back into the ultrarich bubble we'd escaped. It was either that or lose Montgomery Mining."

Riley had touched on the reasons her brothers had left the military, but I didn't know all that much. "Was it that bad?" I asked Jax quietly.

He nodded sharply. "Really bad. Hudson, Cooper, and I had to work eighteen-hour days for a long time just to get Montgomery Mining back on track. But we're back in shape now. We're doing better than we ever have. I've been looking at those rare blue diamonds you're wearing around your neck. Most likely they came from one of our mines, since we own every blue-diamond producer except one."

My hand crept to my neck, and I fingered the beautiful blue-whale pendant that rarely came off it. "It's the most precious thing I've ever owned," I confided. "Not due to the rare gems, but because it reminds me of how lucky I am to have a guy like Owen."

"He's pretty fortunate, too," Jax responded smoothly. "So you're really happy, then, Dreamer?"

My entire body froze as Jax called me by the nickname only one person in the world used. "You called me Dreamer," I whispered as I gaped at him. "Oh, my God, are you Dark?"

His face went blank. "What? I have no idea what you mean."

God, he was good. I nearly fell for his innocent facade. Except . . . I knew better.

"You don't want me to know," I accused. "Please take that innocent look off your face. There's no way that name was a coincidence. It's not like it's some kind of common nickname. You *are* Dark, and you've always known I was Dreamer. What were you thinking? Why did you string me along like that? Were you trying to screw with my head?"

"No," he said in a harsh whisper. "We can't talk about this here and now. Meet me down the beach by the fishing dock in five minutes. I can explain."

Still stunned, I watched as Jax excused himself and went inside the house.

My brain was still reeling in shock as Owen bent his head down. "Everything okay? He left kind of abruptly. And you've been kind of quiet, sweetheart."

I forced myself to smile at him. "I'm fine. Just listening. Do you want another drink?"

"No, but I can get you one," he offered as he started to stand up.

"No!" I said with a little more force than needed. "I'll grab it. I need to hit the bathroom while I'm inside."

He nodded, and then responded to something that Eli had asked.

I relaxed for a minute to try to get my whirling brain to think logically, but really, there was no logical explanation for what Jax had done.

Dark and I hadn't spoken for several weeks.

I hadn't messaged him.

He hadn't messaged me.

It was kind of like we'd both just moved on with our real lives, and I was okay with that. Now that I could talk to Owen about anything, I didn't need an anonymous confidant, and I'd just assumed Dark had outgrown me, too.

In the end, I'd decided to let it go because it just didn't matter, and neither had Dark's real identity. Whoever he was, and for whatever reason, Dark had given me the encouragement I'd needed to be truly free of the horrible things that had happened to me a decade ago. He'd helped me take back my life and my confidence again when I'd been so torn about telling Owen the truth.

I'd been at a crossroads, and Dark had been there to nudge me in the right direction, and I knew I'd always be grateful that he was there when I needed him.

I'd been just fine with letting go of my anonymous friend.

Until. Right. Now.

Now that I knew exactly who Dark was, I wanted to know why in the hell Jax had been playing that game.

I wasn't some stranger to him. Just the fact that he'd referred to me as Dreamer told me he'd known who I was all along.

I shouldn't go meet him. I should just let it go.

Problem was, now that I knew the truth, I wanted answers.

I had to know why Jaxton Montgomery had targeted *me*.

CHAPTER 29

LAYLA

"Jax!" I called out angrily as I stood on the sand near one of the local fishing piers. "Where in the hell are you?"

Since I'd just excused myself from the table to get a drink and use the bathroom, I didn't have a lot of time before Owen would start worrying.

I'd wanted to tell him exactly what had happened, but since it was a long story, that would have to wait until we got home later this evening.

It was dark, with just enough moonlight for me not to be stumbling around in complete blackness, but I was still cursing myself for not grabbing my purse and my cell phone.

As of yet, I hadn't seen a single shape or form near the damn pier, and I started to wonder if this was another one of Jax's twisted ways of messing with my brain.

He apparently wasn't going to show, and I wasn't wasting my time on another round of silly games.

As I went to make my way back down to Seth's place, I let out a loud yelp of surprise as I felt something grip my upper arm.

"I'm here, Dreamer," Jax said calmly. "No need to yell."

"Shit!" I cursed as my hand went to my chest like *that* would slow down my racing heart. "You scared the hell out of me."

I'd never spotted him, but he must have been behind one of the pylons that stabilized the wooden structure, hiding in the shadows.

"Come with me. Let's sit down," he suggested.

He let go of my arm, turned, and strode toward a bench that sat right near the entrance to the beach, away from the noise of the waves hitting the pier.

He walked like a man who expected me to follow him.

And grudgingly, I did, because I wanted answers.

"Why?" I blurted out the moment we were sitting side by side on the wooden seat. "I just want to know why you targeted me, or was this all some kind of big joke for you? I don't get it. You always knew it was me. So why me?"

Jax put his arm along the back of the bench as he said, "It was never a joke, Dreamer. And I wasn't trying to upset you, nor does it give me any kind of sick pleasure to play games with innocent people. Noah asked me to be in the beta testing, and I reluctantly agreed because I wanted to help him out. The only interesting person I talked to was you."

I snorted. "Yeah, that's what I thought about you, too, until tonight. I dropped every other person that I started a conversation with on that app. I should have dumped your ass, too. And how is it *not* twisted that you knew me, but I didn't know you? And how did you know my app name to seek me out, anyway? God, you didn't even know *me* at the time, but you did know Owen's family. Did you know, when I was complaining about my boss, that he was your sister's brother-in-law?"

He had to have known, but nothing made any sense right now.

"I didn't know," he countered. "When you and I first started chatting, I had no idea who you were. All I knew was that I enjoyed a lot of those conversations. I knew you were smart. And funny. One of the highlights of my day was touching base with you. I didn't know your identity until the night of Noah and Andie's reception. Your phone was on the kitchen island. You once told me that you had a weird purple phone case so you could recognize your phone anywhere, but you never told me that you actually had your screen name on that case. When I put the fact that the phone on that island had *California Dreamer* scrolled on the back of a pretty distinctive phone case Dreamer had once described to me, it didn't take much brainpower to figure out that my anonymous friend was one of the guests at that reception. It didn't take much casual asking around to find out who that phone belonged to, or who you were."

My head was spinning as I tried to recall every detail of that evening.

I *had* probably left my phone on Owen's kitchen island. I did it all the time.

"If what you're saying is true, then why didn't you just tell me as soon as you found out?" I questioned. "I was at that party. We even had a fairly long conversation."

"I'd intended to, but Owen spirited you away before I had a chance, and he was on guard for the rest of the night. I asked you to dance, and I was going to tell you that I was Dark."

He had said that there was something he wanted to talk to me about.

He'd been staring at me, but I probably would have been gawking at him, too, if I'd just found out that somebody I'd been talking to online was at the same party I was.

"You could have just ended our communication once you knew who I was," I mumbled.

"I could have," he agreed amiably. "But to be honest, I didn't want to do that. Not entirely. I wanted to make sure that you were okay first."

I turned my head sideways and looked at Jax for the first time since we'd seated ourselves on the bench. We were almost directly under a streetlight, and I could see his face just fine.

But . . .

His expression told me nothing.

"I don't understand. Why wouldn't I be okay?" I asked him, still confused.

His eyes locked with mine, and his gaze didn't waver. "Because a little over ten years ago, I lifted you out of a bathtub filled with blood after you tried like hell to make sure that you died."

I looked away from him.

He knew. How in the world . . . "You were there? Why?"

"One of my casual one-night dates, I'm afraid," he explained. "Her first name was Charlene, and that's pretty much all I knew about her. I met her in Coronado, where I was stationed and living at that time, but she lived in Citrus Beach. Charlene and your roommate, Megan, were friends, and we ran into Megan and her date at the local bar here. When the ladies wanted to head out for a bigger club in San Diego, I was game. Hell, back then, I was generally up for just about anything. On the way out of town, Megan wanted to stop and change at the apartment before we headed to San Diego. Except we never did make it to San Diego that night."

My heart was racing as I asked, "What happened?"

"Like I said, I got you out of that bathtub, and since I was the only one of the four of us with first-aid training, I did my best to make sure you didn't get your death wish," he explained in a matter-of-fact tone of voice.

I was silent for a minute, thinking about what I knew about that night, which wasn't really all that much. "The doctor told me later that a Good Samaritan had almost stopped the bleeding, and made pressure bandages out of a T-shirt to help until I could get to the hospital. Was that your handiwork? I'd always assumed it was Megan, but she wasn't exactly the type to know what to do in an emergency."

"She screamed a lot, and very loudly," Jax said dryly. "It *was* my handiwork, and one of my favorite T-shirts, too."

Jax might have been responsible for keeping me alive until I'd gotten to the hospital. By the time I'd arrived in the ER I'd already lost a critical amount of blood. Without his strictly coincidental presence that night, I could very well not be talking to him right now.

Every bit of my anger dissolved almost instantly. "I had to have been a mess that night. How did you recognize me ten years later?"

"I never forgot your face," he answered in a troubled tone. "Jesus! All I could think about was how damn young you were, and then I had to wonder what in the hell had happened to somebody your age to make them want to die so damn badly. Those were no shallow wounds, Dreamer. You did some serious damage, and I know damn well that you didn't plan on living through that suicide attempt."

I probably should have been mortified that Jax had been there to witness the darkest day of my life, but I wasn't. Instead, I felt some sort of kindred connection to him because he *had* been there, and he'd never judged me for what I'd done. He obviously hadn't then, and didn't now. "I was very serious. Without going into the details, my life was pretty rough as a kid. I was depressed, and it escalated so quickly over a period of a few months that I didn't even think about or want to reach out for help. Once I was recovered physically, I got the help that I needed and started a pretty long road to recovery. I never did speak to Megan again. I went to a mental-health facility once I was discharged from the hospital. It's never happened again, and I'm grateful every damn day that I didn't die, even though I desperately wanted to at the time."

Jax released a long breath. "Damn glad you recovered. I've actually thought about you a lot over the years, and I wondered what happened to you. I got deployed a few days later, so I was never able to get any follow-up, and I never saw Charlene or Megan again."

"Bad date?" I joked halfheartedly.

"I guess she wasn't thrilled about spending the rest of the night with a guy who had no shirt and bloody pants," he answered in the same sarcastic tone.

"Yeah, well, sorry about that," I mumbled.

"Don't be," he insisted. "I think she only agreed to go out with me because I was a Montgomery with a lot of money. I can assure you, I didn't miss anything meaningful."

I smirked at him as I asked, "So once you knew I was the same girl that you'd helped, why did you keep on talking to me?"

He shrugged. "I liked you, and after I recognized you, I admired you, too. You got through all of that, plus you're pretty damn successful, too. You should be proud of yourself, not beating yourself up for mistakes you made as a kid. I wanted to make sure you were solid before I cut you loose completely."

"You were never going to tell me the truth, were you?"

"Not once the reception was over. Really, there was no point. When I talked to you that night, I was only going to own up to being Dark and seeing your phone. I didn't plan on dragging up something from the distant past that you'd rather leave behind you. But you looked so betrayed tonight when I slipped up, I figured I should own up to everything. I know you're happy now, Dreamer, and that's all I really wanted to know. That's why I haven't messaged you in a while. You don't need me anymore. I think you've got it all figured out."

Really, Jax's actions had been completely selfless. "So what did you get out of those conversations?"

He grinned. "The satisfaction of knowing that a girl that I'd once helped, and had thought about over the years, had turned into an amazing woman. I enjoyed talking to you, Dreamer. Don't start thinking that I'm somebody I'm not. I'm pretty much an asshole most of the time."

I didn't believe him. Maybe that was the only persona that Jax allowed most people to see, but in my eyes, he was pretty damn special. "I don't think that's true at all," I said adamantly.

"Believe it," he said flatly. "Other than Riley, my relationship with you is the longest one I've ever had with a female."

I snorted. "Only because you want it to be that way. And we'll still be friends, Jax. We just won't have to anonymously cyberchat anymore. Thank you. For everything you've done for me. Years ago, and recently when I needed to talk things out with someone."

My heart swelled with gratitude, and I impulsively threw my arms around Jax's neck to hug him.

"Easy, Dreamer," he drawled. "Let's not get all emotional and sappy."

Even as he said those sarcastic words, he pulled me in for a bear hug.

"I think we found her," I heard Seth say in a startled voice from right behind me.

I pulled away from Jax, and turned around.

While Seth looked puzzled, and Aiden looked confused, Owen's eyes were full of anguish, hurt, and crushing disappointment that nearly brought me to my knees.

CHAPTER 30

OWEN

"I hate to say this, because you know I'm *always* going to be on your side," Seth said carefully from his position in my living-room recliner. "But I bought every single word of Jax's and Layla's explanation. When we dragged you away so you *didn't* do something stupid to Riley's brother, we just meant for you to cool off and see some sense. I didn't expect you to leave."

I *had* left. After my older brothers had yanked me from that scene at the beach to cool off and think, I'd needed to get away. I'd been pissed off, but I hadn't wanted to do or say anything I was going to regret later. Especially since I knew Layla wasn't far behind us. Seth and Aiden had just followed me and made themselves at home in my living room.

Aiden spoke up from the other side of the sofa we were sitting on. "I believed them, too," he said with some regret. "She didn't have her tongue down his throat, Owen. It was just a hug. It looked pretty innocent. Jax didn't even have a hand on any of her private parts. And there's no way you could ever believe that Layla has a thing for Jax. Not with the way she looks at you, Owen. She's fucking crazy about you."

"I thought she was," I grumbled.

"Don't do this, little brother," Aiden said, his tone ominous and full of warning. "I mistrusted Skye at one time, and it tore her up. I was damn lucky that she has a good heart, and we were able to get through it, but it took a toll on her, Owen. Don't fuck up this relationship because you lost your shit when you saw another guy touching her. Both of them explained, and you know why they're connected now. You know Jax's motivations. Deal with it. If I were you, I'd be damn grateful that Jax saved the woman I loved so she could be there for *me*."

"She had her arms around the bastard. Layla was all over him. Don't tell me you wouldn't be pissed," I said, irritated with both of my brothers right now.

Seth shrugged. "Riley hugs you, Noah, and Aiden all the time. If it's not really a threat, it doesn't matter. Look, I get that you see Jax as an outsider, but I don't. He's Riley's brother, and his womanizer reputation aside, he's a decent guy, just like Hudson and Cooper. I don't doubt for a minute that he jumped into a mess, and did everything he could for Layla years ago, or that he's making sure she's okay now. All three of the Montgomery brothers seem to want to save the whole damn world. Honestly, I never once saw Jax look at Layla like he wanted to nail her. In fact, he looks at her like he looks at Riley."

Aiden released a long breath. "I have to agree. Think about it, Owen. Do you really think that Layla *wanted* to spill her guts about something really bad that happened to her years ago? But she did. Because of you. Skye told me before we left that she, Jade, and Riley knew, but do you really think Layla wanted to reveal all that to me, Seth, and Eli? And she did it without hesitation, because she wanted you to understand that there was absolutely nothing going on between her and Jax."

Goddammit! I knew they were right, and really, Layla shouldn't have to explain herself to me, or anyone else.

I'd seen red when we'd stumbled upon the two of them while we were searching for Layla. I'd wanted to beat the hell out of Jax, and the circumstances had made me question whether Layla *was* as committed to our relationship as I'd always been. "We've never really talked commitment," I said absently. "Or our future."

"Don't be a damn idiot, Owen," Seth said sharply. "Maybe you haven't talked about it, but open your eyes. That woman loves you just as much as you love her. She doesn't exactly verbalize how she feels, and neither do you, but it's pretty damn clear that you're committed."

"I love her, dammit!" I said roughly. "I love her so much that I'm not rational about her most of the time. What if she *doesn't* love me? What if everything *doesn't* work out? What if she's not happy? What if something fucking happens to her? I'm a damn doctor, and if she so much as breaks a fingernail, I'm sweating. I have nightmares about what happened to her when she went through that major depression, visions of her in a goddamn bathtub bleeding out and all alone. And if she's not there when I wake up from those dreams, I have to talk myself down from calling her at three o'clock in the morning just to hear her voice. Almost every single person in her life who should have been there for her let her down. What if I somehow let her down, too?" I took a deep breath before I added, "I haven't been myself since the day she walked into the clinic, and in my gut I knew that she was still going to get to me, just like she did in high school. And I was right. But nothing could have prepared me for the crazy way I love her now."

The living room was silent for a few minutes after my tirade, until Aiden spoke in a low, serious tone. "I never got over Skye, either. We were both young when we fell for each other. Because I was heartbroken, I managed to put all those emotions away for a long time, but they were still there. I know you weren't here when Seth and I went through exactly what you're going through now, but it does get better. When you love a woman, and that woman becomes your entire world, there's never a day that you don't think about her security and her happiness. But the near-insanity does settle down a little after you've been together for a while. You start to have faith that she's not going anywhere, and you have proof that she's happy every single day with the decision she made to take your ass on for a lifetime. It's the uncertainty in the beginning that makes you crazy."

I raked a hand through my hair in pure frustration. "So what in the hell am I going to do?"

"Just love her," Seth suggested. "Marry her. Give everything you have to that relationship because you know you'll be fucked if she's not happy. Live through the hard shit because you know a bad day with her is better than any day without her in it. In the beginning, keep reminding yourself that she feels as crazy as you do sometimes, and roll with it together."

"And for fuck's sake," Aiden said in a disgruntled tone. "Don't ever accuse her of cheating on you unless you know you're one hundred percent correct, because once you do it, you can never take it back."

"I didn't accuse her of that," I said defensively.

"You didn't say it," Seth agreed. "But you were thinking it, and she knew what was in your head when you left without a single word to her. Listen to your gut and your heart, instead of your obsessive mind."

I banged my head against the back of the sofa. Maybe I *hadn't* said it out loud, but I *had* let my insecurities about our relationship get to me.

Never once had Layla given me any reason to think she wasn't faithful to our relationship. Hell, we spent most of our time together.

"I want her to live with me," I confessed. "I want to marry her. I want all of those things you said. I'm just not sure she's ready."

"She's ready."

"She's ready."

My two brothers made their assessment almost simultaneously.

I was going to have to lay all of my cards on the table with Layla, whether she was ready or not. If I didn't, I'd end up losing her because of something stupid, like jumping to conclusions just because she was hugging another guy who didn't have my DNA.

"*Logically*," I said, "I know damn well she isn't interested in Jax. She's told me that before. And maybe it bothered me that she'd never told me that she was talking to somebody on Not-Just-A-Hookup, too, but she has a right to have her own friends. She sure as hell doesn't need my permission. Maybe what really gets to me is that Jax was there for her when I wasn't. But *logically*"—I stressed that word again like it would magically make me think with a rational brain—"my being there for her wasn't even possible. We weren't even speaking because of that whole scholarship misunderstanding."

Aiden's expression was troubled as he started to speak. "Owen, you can 'what if' yourself to death, but at some point, you have to leave all that shit behind. Been there. Done that. Drove myself nuts about the years I lost with Maya and Skye. Don't let your past define your future."

"You can be there for her *now*, Owen, if you really want to be," Seth pointed out. "You can't change the past, so find a way to let it go, and plan your future. *Logically*, it's a lot more constructive."

"Thanks. I think that's exactly what I need to do," I told my brothers gratefully.

They were both trying to use their own experiences to save their little brother some pain, and I finally understood that. Very clearly.

The doorbell rang, and when I didn't move, Aiden got up to answer it.

"I need to talk to Owen," I heard Layla say in a clipped tone after Aiden had opened the door.

She strode inside like a woman on a mission, walked to the couch, folded her arms in front of her, and stared down at me with a determined—and maybe a little bit angry—expression on her face.

"So I can't show *you* my backside, but it's perfectly okay if I see yours?" she asked in a no-nonsense voice as she raised an eyebrow. "Well, guess what, Owen Sinclair. You held on to me when I tried to walk away, and I'm going to hang on to you until we get through this.

I'm camping out at this damn house until you completely understand that I don't even see any other men except you."

Aiden cleared his throat. "I think Seth and I will just be going now. Call you tomorrow, Owen. Okay? Right. We're out of here."

Out of the corner of my eye, I saw my two older brothers leave like their asses were on fire.

But right in front of me, there was a magnificently bold blonde woman who was staring at me like she wanted to hug me and punch me at the same time.

I grinned at her like an idiot, and got to my feet.

CHAPTER 31

LAYLA

I wasn't entirely certain if I wanted to rip his clothes off, or slap some sense into Owen.

Maybe a little of both.

Okay, mostly, the tearing-his-clothes-off urge *was* stronger than my compulsion to smack him alongside his head, but that was going to wait until we got several things straightened out.

Failure was not an option.

I loved Owen way too much for that.

I took a deep breath. "If you think, for one single second, that I felt anything for Jax Montgomery except gratitude, then you and I are not on the same page, and we need to straighten this out. I'm not leaving, Owen, and I'm not letting you walk away, either," I informed him.

I looked up at his face, only to see him smiling.

How dare he smile about this!

There wasn't a single amusing thing about him walking away from me after Jax and I had *completely* explained everything.

For God's sake, I dragged every damn skeleton out of my closet and paraded it in front of his whole damn family because I had *nothing* to hide anymore.

Nothing was more important to me than Owen.

"I love you, dammit!" I told him angrily. "I love you so much that you make me completely insane. I don't care if you're not ready to hear it, or if it's too early to say it. You're just going to have to deal with it, because it's not going away."

He put a gentle hand on my shoulder. "Layla—"

I cut him off. "Your behavior tonight was unacceptable, Owen. What else do I have to do to convince you that the only man I love, and ever will love, is you?"

He wasn't smiling anymore.

I poked my finger into his chest. "I'm pretty sure I've always loved you, even years ago. Maybe that's why there's never been another guy for me. Maybe that's why I'm still alive today. Because I was *always* supposed to be with you."

I started to unbutton his shirt.

"What exactly are you doing?" Owen asked huskily.

"Ripping your clothes off," I snapped back at him. "We're having sex right here, right now. I'm going to get so close to you that you won't be able to peel me off your gorgeous body," I warned him as I yanked his shirt off, and then started on his jeans.

He cleared his throat. "Won't that require you getting naked, too?" he asked gently.

"Probably so," I said in a clipped voice.

In seconds, the two of us were tearing each other's clothes off like we had only seconds to have sex, and then we'd never have the opportunity again.

I felt desperate, needy, and completely out of control. "I'll make you beg for it, Owen Sinclair," I threatened as I dropped to my knees, wearing only the panties he hadn't had the chance to tear off my body yet.

I jerked down his boxer briefs, the only article of clothing left until he was completely nude, left them around his ankles, and went after the part of him that I wanted inside me.

"Layla—"

Owen stopped talking abruptly as I practically swallowed his cock. I'd gone down on Owen before, but never with this much determination.

I wanted him to feel me.

I wanted him to need me.

I wanted him to realize that I was never going to love anyone but him.

"Layla. Baby," Owen groaned.

Because that hungry tone in his voice was *exactly* what I wanted to hear, my body relaxed slightly, and I pulled back and teased him by running my tongue along the underside of his massive shaft. I took my time, licking the sensitive tip before I sucked him back into my mouth again, and set a fast rhythm that I hoped would practically make his head explode.

"Jesus, Layla! Fuck!" Owen shouted in a raw voice.

My hand was on his upper thigh, and I felt his body tighten.

"Layla, fucking hell! Stop!" he demanded as he pulled me to my feet.

He kicked out of the boxer briefs, and then lifted me until I had to wrap my legs around his waist to stay balanced.

My back came up against the living-room wall, and both of us were panting when we finally locked eyes, and then . . . the whole damn world seemed to stop.

Just like it always did whenever Owen looked at me.

"I wasn't finished," I told him obstinately.

"Oh, we're not finished," he said, his chest still heaving. "But I need to tell you something before I demolish another pair of your panties."

"What?" I spat out.

"I love you, too, goddammit!" he rasped. "Always have, always will. And I don't have the words to tell you how sorry I am right now."

I searched his beautiful eyes, but there was nothing there . . . but love.

No pretense.

No anger.

No distrust.

I couldn't see anything except my own feelings reflected back at me.

"Don't worry about finding the words right now. Just fuck me," I said breathlessly.

One tug, and I was saying goodbye to another lovely pair of underwear, but I didn't have time to mourn them.

Owen lifted me by my ass, and was buried to the hilt inside me with one powerful thrust.

I tightened my legs around him, and moaned as my head hit the wall behind me.

"Oh, God, Owen. I love you." It was the biggest relief I'd ever known to be able to say those words out loud.

"I love you, too, baby," he said in a raw voice as he gripped my ass harder, and sped up the motion of his hips until he was fucking me like a man possessed.

My body was so pumped with adrenaline that it didn't take long for me to reach the point of climax.

"Don't ever try to walk away from us again," I said fiercely as I fisted his hair and tugged. "Because I'll always find you, Owen. Always."

I was done being hesitant, and pretending that if things didn't work out between Owen and me, that I'd be okay with it.

I wouldn't.

Ever.

And just like he'd been willing to pull me back to him, and never walk away, I was just as stubborn, and I'd do the same for him.

If Owen and I loved each other, we could get through anything that came our way.

"Owen!" I keened his name as my orgasm took over my body and shook it to its core.

His mouth came down on mine, muffling his groan as he found his own release.

We devoured each other's mouths as our bodies rocked together in the aftermath of our passion.

Both of us were out of breath as we landed on the sofa together in a tumble of entangled legs and arms.

I just lay there panting, my body completely spent, as Owen straightened us out until we were lying side by side. He pulled me against him, and I rested my head against his chest, able to hear his racing heart as I tried to catch my breath.

He threaded his hand into my hair and gently stroked my scalp.

"That whole bossy thing you had going on was pretty hot," he said huskily a few moments later.

I snorted, because it was so like Owen to try to make me smile when that was the last thing I wanted to do.

"But," he added, "completely unnecessary since I was about to come find you. What happened tonight was all about me, Layla. Not you. I let myself give in to a knee-jerk reaction, and I'm not proud of myself for that. And you're right. It was bullshit. I feel so off balance sometimes when it comes to you, but those are my issues. My insecurities."

My heart completely melted. I pulled back to look at him. "What can I do to help?" I asked him softly.

He shot me a mischievous grin. "Love me. And keep on loving me. Even when I'm an asshole. I'm learning to leave the past behind, but I might fuck up another time or two before I get it right."

I put my palm to his scruffy cheek. "Owen, you're the most amazing man I know, and you're rarely an asshole. In fact, I'm pretty sure this is the first time you've ever really been a complete jerk."

Like I hadn't made my share of mistakes in the past with him? I could forgive him some mistakes, too.

"I've wanted to tell you how much I love you for a long time," Owen said earnestly. "I just wasn't sure you were ready to hear it. Or if you felt the same way."

I smiled. "Same here. I knew that you cared about me—"

"Baby, I more than cared," he interrupted. "I've been completely, madly in love with you since the first time I saw you at the clinic. It was like that old high-school crush went into overdrive the minute I saw you again."

"I don't think mine ever really ended," I explained. "It just got put on hold for a very long time." I let out a long sigh as I added, "Jax was there for me when I needed a friend, and now I know he was there on the worst night of my life. He helped me, he encouraged me, but there's nothing else there, Owen. The conversations we've had are still in the app. You can read every one of them."

He shook his head. "I don't need to read them. In my heart, I knew the truth, but I'm so damn in love with you that he just seemed like a threat. Someday, I'm sure I'll thank him for what he did. Just don't ask me to do it right now."

I laughed because he seemed so disgruntled. Maybe he wouldn't warm up to Jax tomorrow, but I had a feeling they would be friends someday. "Just don't kill him. That would *definitely* cause a huge rift in the Sinclair family."

"I love you, Layla," he said huskily. "Granted, I was crazy about you in high school, but the way I love you now isn't an infatuation." He paused before he rasped, "Marry me, Layla. Put me out of my misery and promise me forever."

My heart stopped, and then it started again at a frantic pace.

"Okay," he rumbled. "I think I did that all wrong. I know it was *supposed* to be a question, not a demand, and I should have the ring in my hand right now, but I really wanted to give you something that was one-of-a-kind—"

I stopped his flow of words with my mouth. I couldn't speak, but I gave him a kiss that told him what my answer was going to be.

"Yes," I said as I finally released his lips. "I don't need a ring right now, Owen, and I'll pretend it was a question. I want to be with you for the rest of my life. I don't even want to imagine a future without you in it."

He shot me what looked like a very relieved smile. "You *won't* have a future without me in it. The moment you told me that you loved me, you were pretty much doomed."

I sighed as he gave me a sweet, tender kiss of promise.

He promised me laughter.

He promised me love.

He promised me passion.

He promised me respect.

He promised he'd never want anyone else.

Owen had promised *everything* in a single kiss.

As he slowly lifted his head, I murmured, "I love you, Owen Sinclair. Take me to bed and I'll show you just how much."

"Dammit, Layla. Please. Not the *fuck-me* voice. It kills me," he grumbled as he hopped up and lifted me gently off the sofa.

As he cradled me in his arms softly, I swatted him on the shoulder. "That is not my *fuck-me* voice," I informed him. In a gentler tone, I murmured, "That's my *love-me* voice."

Our gazes locked as he carried me up the stairs. His eyes softened as he answered, "You'll never need that voice, because there will never be a moment during any day in our future that I *won't* love you, Layla."

My heart was skittering as he put me gently on the bed. "What if I use that voice accidentally?"

As he stretched out next to me and pulled me in to him, he said, "Then I'd have to assume that you need reassurance. In which case, I'd have to carry you off somewhere and *love you* until you were totally convinced."

God, how could I *not* love this man with every beat of my heart when he said things like that?

I fell into his fiery emerald eyes as I wrapped my arms around his neck. "I don't really need reassurance, but I'd really like it if you *loved me* right now."

And just like that . . . Owen very eagerly complied.

All. Night. Long.

EPILOGUE

LAYLA

Eight months later . . .

"Owen, tell me again exactly why we're here when we could be home instead. You could have destroyed a perfectly nice pair of my panties by now," I teased.

I blinked as he turned on the lantern he'd brought with him from the house, and waved me toward one of the swings in the very same park we'd often escaped to when we were teenagers.

He turned and laid his devastatingly gorgeous smile on me as my ass plopped into the seat.

I put the swing in motion, enjoying the tranquil sway as Owen sat down next to me and pushed with his foot to get his seat moving.

He reached out his hand, and I took it, sighing as he threaded our fingers together.

Suddenly, it really didn't matter why we were here, or why Owen had been so insistent that we make the drive tonight, after we'd had a really long day at the clinic.

The park was quiet.

It was a beautiful night.

And I had Owen next to me.

Everything was right in my world, as far as I was concerned.

It was Owen who finally broke the silence. "I haven't been here since that last night we were here together, senior year. I know we both agreed to leave the past behind, but sometimes it feels good to go back and see what it feels like to do things right."

My heart skittered as I realized what he was trying to do.

He's looking for some kind of closure.

For the most part, Owen and I *had* left the past behind.

Since the night he'd asked me to marry him, we'd both looked forward, instead of behind, and Owen had learned to stop asking "what if."

Instead, he'd just spoiled me rotten in the here and now, and I'd done the same.

I'd finally gotten him partially on board on my save-the-panties mission, meaning he only destroyed one or two pairs a week. Okay, maybe he *wasn't* all that on board with it, but I'd discovered a way to cut down his consumption: sometimes I just didn't wear any panties at all.

So now, instead of wondering what color panties I was wearing every day, his main goal was to figure out if I was wearing any, or if it was a commando day.

I took a deep breath. "Some things are still the same, though," I told him.

"And what would that be, beautiful?" he asked huskily.

"I thought you were the hottest guy in the world back then, and I still do. All I wanted was for you to kiss me, and I still want that now, too," I told him in a much more wanton voice than I'd ever used as an adolescent.

He leaned toward me, and our lips met, our swings still in motion.

After he slowly released me, Owen said earnestly, "I did ask you to come here for a reason."

I sent him a questioning gaze. "I thought we were just being nostalgic."

He shook his head, stopped his swing, and brought mine to a halt. "I didn't really do a very good job when I asked you to marry me eight months ago, so I'm going to try it again."

My heart skittered wildly as Owen pulled a box from the pocket of his jeans, and dropped to one knee.

Oh, God, he really is going to do it all over again.

He cleared his throat. "I should have had the ring last time, and I should have asked the question, Layla, but I didn't. So now I'm asking. Layla Caine, will you make me the happiest guy in the world, and say yes to a real proposal this time?"

I let out an audible gasp as he popped the box open, and I saw the ring.

It was made of the same beautiful blue diamonds as my pendant, and was also a Mia Hamilton Original.

"Yes. Oh, God, Owen. You knew I was a sure thing," I murmured as I speared a hand through his hair and started scattering kisses all over his handsome face.

He finally grinned. "Maybe I did, but I wanted to do it anyway. I did screw up the first time, and since I'm never letting you go, it's the only proposal you'll ever get." He handed me the jewelry box and slid the gorgeous ring on my finger. "Mia designed the ring, but I have to admit that Jax helped me out with getting the blue diamonds this time."

I studied the ring I knew I'd be wearing forever, and let out a happy sigh. As usual, it was perfect, just like every gift I'd ever gotten from Owen.

I threw myself into his arms as he got up. "I knew you'd eventually become friends with Jax," I said as I wrapped my arms around his neck. "The ring is absolutely beautiful. I love it."

"I'm glad you love it. And I can't say Jax and I are really friends, but he's tolerable. I can't hate the guy. He was there when I couldn't be, and I'm not even pissed off about *that* anymore, because you're mine *now*, and that's really all that matters," he rumbled as he kissed my forehead.

My heart danced as he gave me a longer and much more satisfying kiss.

There had been a *lot* of changes in the last eight months.

Skye was sixth months pregnant, so she and Aiden would be welcoming their second child into the world just three months from now, and Riley and Seth were starting to seriously consider a family.

Despite Andie's concerns, it looked like having a child would be an option if she and Noah decided that was what they wanted someday. Right now, I wasn't sure either of them were ready to make that commitment, since they were planning their next world travel right after Owen and I got married in February.

Eli and Jade were going to hold off a little while longer, because Jade had so much going on with her research.

Brooke and Liam were currently hoping for a positive pregnancy test in the near future, too.

As Owen lifted his head, I said dreamily, "You do realize that you're going to be welcoming a lot of new nieces and nephews into the family soon. I think everyone is ready to start the next generation of Sinclairs."

When our gazes locked, I melted as I saw the serious look in his eyes. "We haven't really discussed kids very much. We did both say we want them someday," he said huskily.

I laughed. "I think we should let everyone else go first. We have time. Besides, it looks like there are going to be plenty of kids everywhere at the family gatherings five years from now."

"Is it selfish that I'd like to keep you all to myself for a while?" Owen asked.

I shook my head. "I feel the same way."

After so many years in school for both of us, we were career focused, but I knew there would be a day in the future when we'd be ready.

"I love you, Layla, and right now, you're all that I need," Owen declared as he nuzzled my ear.

My body responded instantly. "I think we should go home," I suggested, edgy because I was more than ready to get Owen naked.

He put a hand on my ass and pulled my hips forward, until I could feel exactly how much he wanted me.

"Owen," I said breathlessly as he held me there.

"I want you, Layla," he said hoarsely. "Right fucking now."

And oh, God, I wanted him, too.

"Sex in the park?" I asked, knowing I'd be game for anything if I could just get Owen inside me.

"I don't think so, baby," he said regretfully. "It wouldn't look good if anybody saw us. Besides, I'm pretty sure we've both outgrown this place."

"Let's go home," I urged.

He was right. We didn't belong here anymore.

This place was our past, and I got why Owen had wanted to propose here.

This was really where we'd started.

And now, we'd come full circle by having a very happy moment here as adults.

But both of us were ready to say goodbye to the past, and move on without a backward glance.

Owen picked up the lamp, turned it off, and handed it to me.

I shrieked in surprise as he picked me up and cradled me against his body. "You're crazy. We're too far from the car."

There was enough light for him to get to his vehicle without the lamp, so I just held it as he ate up the distance between us and the parking lot.

"I think I've been crazy since the first day I saw you in the clinic. Why should today be any different?" he answered gruffly.

Owen *was* different than the first day he'd come to work at the clinic, and he was far from crazy.

Every day, he got more comfortable with himself, his place in this world, his change in circumstances, and being an active part of his family.

He was catching up with the world he'd left behind when he started college, and the confidence looked damn good on him.

I rolled my eyes as I saw the vehicle come into sight. "You could have saved some energy for later. I can walk."

"I thought I was saving *your* energy for later," he said roughly.

My heart started to flutter. "Planning a long night?" I squeaked.

"It's Friday," he reminded me in a very wicked tone. "When is it ever a short night?"

No clinic tomorrow.

"Okay, then, hurry," I told him.

He chuckled as he opened the passenger door and gently put me into the seat of the vehicle. "No hurrying," he said, his voice warm. "You're going to marry me in February. We have forever now, Layla."

I sighed as he kissed me, one of those tender-but-passionate kisses that made my toes curl.

As he settled into the driver's seat, I said casually, "It's a *no under-wear* day."

Before the light in the car dimmed, I saw the muscle in his jaw twitch, and his features harden with anticipation.

We have forever, but why not start forever just as fast as we can.

"I'm not going to speed, but I'll take every shortcut I know," he said in a raspy, turned-on voice that I knew very, very well.

I smiled as he started the engine, put the car in gear, and made it back home in record time without speeding . . . much.

Neither one of us gave the park we'd just left a second thought.

We raced into the house laughing, took another step into our future, and let our forever begin.

AFTERWORD

Even after so many advances in modern medicine, there's still so much we don't know about clinical depression. It can happen once in a lifetime or a few times, and for some, it can be a debilitating and chronic condition that never goes away. What we do know is that neurotransmitters are naturally occurring brain chemicals that likely play a role in major depression. Imbalances and deficiencies can cause problems in the area of the brain responsible for mood stability.

For teens, there are way too many risk factors for me to list here, but let's just say that Layla would have checked a lot of boxes on that list.

Maybe we don't know everything there is to know about clinical depression, but there are effective treatments out there. Medications, therapy, lifestyle changes, and tons of support can help. If you suspect that you or someone you love is suffering from depression, please reach out for help. You can start with your doctor, or use one of the multiple resources available online to start on your journey toward a better life.

ACKNOWLEDGMENTS

Like with every other Montlake book I've written, I want to thank the Montlake team, and my senior editor, Maria Gomez, for being behind every Sinclair book I've written for them. As a mainly self-published author, it's not easy to go hybrid with a traditional publisher, but you've all made this journey a lot easier by treating me like a partner.

As always, a big thank-you to my personal KA team, for all of the effort you all put into every single new release, whether it's Montlake or self-pub.

Thank you a million times to my readers! I wouldn't have this writing career I love if it wasn't for you. Although Owen was my last Sinclair, my alpha-male billionaire journey is already continuing with Hudson, Jaxton, and Cooper in my long-running self-published series, The Billionaire's Obsession. Thanks so much for all of your support on every book I write. I couldn't do what I do without all of you!

Xxxxxxx Jan (J.S. Scott)

ABOUT THE AUTHOR

Photo © 2013 Carrie Herzog

J.S. "Jan" Scott is the *New York Times* and *USA Today* bestselling author of numerous contemporary and paranormal romances, including the Sinclairs novels and *Ensnared, Entangled, Enamored, Enchanted,* and *Endeared* in the Accidental Billionaires series. She's an avid reader of all types of books and literature, but romance has always been her genre of choice, so she writes what she loves to read: stories that are almost always steamy, generally feature an alpha male, and have a happily ever after—she just can't seem to write them any other way! Jan loves to connect with readers. Visit her website at www.authorjsscott.com.